MW00680691

Katie's Ladies

Andrew R. Nixon

Blue Sun Studio, Inc.

Katie's Ladies

by Andrew R. Nixon

On the Web at: http://andynixonwordsmith.com

Copyright © 2019 by Andrew R. Nixon

Cover & Interior design: Blue Sun Studio, Inc.

ISBN: 978-0-9991520-6-5

Dedication

This book is dedicated to immigrants who built America into an exceptional country, to the brave women and their supporters who fought for equality, and for those still fighting for human rights.

Acknowledgements

I would like to recognize the countless people who saw me through this venture, including the many readers that insisted a sequel to "Three Lives of Peter Novak" is in order. Kudos also go to those who provided support, talked things over, read, wrote, offered comments and observations, and assisted in the proofreading, editing and design.

In particular, I would like to personally thank the following people and organizations for their contributions to my inspirations and knowledge and other help in completing this book. First and foremost, my deepest appreciation goes to my favorite Reading Specialist and critic, my wife Pat, who not only offered suggestions, and support but made sure I was well fed. Also offering suggestions and encouragement: Betsy Luffy Lloyd, Howard Kazanjian, Richard L. Lattanzi, Vincent Ross, June Blaszkiewicz, Ruth Coleman, the SC Prime Early Supper Club, and the many current and past residents of Clairton, PA who provided historical and geographical information.

Readers and editors: Jamie Carpenter, Red Pen Girl, Lori Anderson, Kathy Tachior, The Thing at the Place, and the Southern California Chapter of the Historical Novel Society writers groups.

Publisher Deborah Dorchak of Blue Sun Studio, Inc. so graciously offered direction and advice in the process and mechanics of putting a novel together. Coaching and suggestions were invaluable.

Individuals and organizations that provided background and research information include the Grisnik family, Lincoln Highway News, Clairton Public Library, Jefferson Hills Public Library, Mifflin Township Historical Society, and Carnegie Library of McKeesport. Last but not least I beg forgiveness of all those who have been with me over the course of the years and whose names I've failed to mention.

Prologue

Tainted

"It is best not to exist at all." —H P Lovecraft

AUTUMN 1919. The usually nattily-dressed Albert stumbled numbly out of the stinking jailhouse into the crisp night atmosphere, leaving behind several friends still wallowing in the stinking, urine-splattered box that had been his hell for what seemed like forever. His once expertly-pressed, midnight blue suit hung on him, crumpled in disarray. Blood from his puffy lip caked on his face and clothing. Soft Argentine leather scuffed, untied shoes graced his feet. Laces had been removed by jailers, socks went missing. Friends from the underground community had put up his bail, but not before he was raped, sodomized, and beaten in the dank, overcrowded, holding cell.

Sunday night had begun with a promise of good times, another night of drinking, dancing, and fun, but in the blink of an eye, a heavy knock on the rustic mahogany front door turned Albert Lhormer's life upside down, his future inside out. In a heartbeat, that night became the death knell he always feared. Monday's Pittsburgh Daily Post newspaper would shout the scandalous breakup of a homosexual dating ring.

He sucked in the black, putrid Pittsburgh air until his lungs burned. His arms gesticulated to hail a Pullman taxi.

"Drive me to Clairton."

The middle-aged driver chewed for a moment, then spat a wad of tar-colored tobacco juice onto the brick street. Using the back of his hand, he wiped away a trickle of dark spittle that ran down his chin as he coaxed the filthy sedan's engine to life. "Gonna cost ya', Buster, ta' go way the hell out there. With all the rain this week, that River Road is a bitch, then I gotta come back wit' no fare."

The salty taste of tears dampened Albert's cheeks and touched his tongue as he slid onto the well-used upholstered rear seat of the Model-T Ford. Inside the hack the misty night air turned to a musty smell of a wet towel that had dried a large dog. He gagged, but managed to utter, "Don't worry about the fare, Sir, just get me to Clairton." The exhausted passenger did not want to return to his residence in Pittsburgh. He knew reporters would be waiting for him there, hungry to hear salacious details.

Albert shivered in the back seat of the unheated hack, contemplating his possibilities for the future. Pulling the overcoat tightly around his slight frame, he peered out the partially open window at the low-hanging clouds, knowing the fate awaiting him.

The blackness hovered, a silky mixture of soot, smoke, and rainclouds. Street lamps cast a thick, gray, gloomy bubble around the cab. A light drizzle gave the lamps an aura that might have seemed beautiful on any other evening, but this night would end badly. Of that Albert was certain.

Upon arrival at his destination Albert paid the cabbie the hefty fare, plus a generous tip. He did not look after the car as it made a U-turn in the middle of the empty street, splashed puddles, chugging away into blackness. The hack rumbled down the St. Clair Avenue grade toward State Street and the rutted River Road that led back to Pittsburgh.

Albert fished keys from the pocket of his overcoat, unlocked the door of the Clairton Savings and Loan, and trudged up to his office. Not bothering to light a fire for warmth, he instead lit the kerosene lamp on his desk, pulled out pen and paper and began to write his last confession. Had his eyes held any tears, they surely would have fallen to dampen the parchment, but he had nothing left to weep.

It took over an hour to compose the letter. Finally finished, he lifted his favorite book from the desk shelf. The Children of the Night, by Edgar Arlington Robinson, dog-eared and well-read, spoke to him. He felt a kinship with the subject of the poem. Tucking his own composition inside the book alongside his favorite verse, he silently recited the poem to himself:

Whenever Richard Corey went downtown,
We people on the pavement looked at him:
He was a gentleman from sole to crown,
Clean favored and imperially slim.

Without looking down, the beleaguered businessman retrieved a pistol from the top desk drawer.

And he was always quietly arrayed,
And he was always human when he talked,
But still he fluttered pulses when he said,
"Good Morning," and he glittered when he walked.

Placing a cartridge in each of the chambers of the gun, he smiled wryly, realizing he only needed one bullet to complete the task. With a single puff of breath, he snuffed the flame in the lamp, closed his eyes, and lifted the pistol.

And he was rich—yes, richer than a king,
And admirably schooled in every grace:
In fine we thought he had everything
To make us wish that we were in his place.

The steel revolver rose slowly until, clamped in his trembling hand, the icy cold barrel's tip imprinted against the warm flesh of his temple. All the courage needed to complete the task emanated from within as he summoned his index finger to complete the contract he'd made with himself.

So on we worked and waited for the light,
And went without the meat and cursed the bread;

And Richard Cory one calm summer night,
Went home and put a bullet in his head.

At precisely 3:30 that morning, his finger squeezed the trigger as his last words, "Forgive me, Katie," evaporated into a deafening roar that split the late-night stillness, followed by a ghastly silence.

1

The Urchin Cometh

"Death pays all debts." —William Shakespeare

KATIE DREAMED WITH LATE NIGHT FERVOR. A brightness flashed inside her mind. An awareness of a power within her spoke silently. She had heard from the power before in her dreams. Though unable to wrap her thoughts around its meaning, she had utter confidence the power bespoke a substantial change in her future. Visions of darkness and bruises mixed with anger and hostility scintillated at breakneck speed inside her subconscious state.

The power's vague perception of the future did not frighten Katie. This unseen mentor had earned her unconditional faith. This morning, however, the message arrived in both a vague and unsettling manner. The essence appeared to be dark. A bad omen, perhaps. In the dream, she saw the image of the tarot card of Death himself, portrayed as a skeleton riding a white horse, holding a black and white flag. He wore armor showing him to be both invincible and unconquerable.

"When will it happen?" she asked Death. "Who will you take?"

Death did not answer.

As she slept inside the master bedroom, box springs on the large double bed creaked under the weight of her body. The fabric canopy above waved as though in a gale as Katie continued to toss and turn while dreaming.

The wind-up clock on the nightstand ticked. Its longer hand jumped to strike half-past three. Katie, wrenched from her dream, sat up sharply. She'd heard something. What was it? She was certain she'd heard a crack, an ear-splitting, window rattling report.

Images on the flowery yellow wallpaper flickered, lit by the starlight. They seemed to form the outline of something in disarray in the heavy atmosphere of the master bedroom, but the woman could not make out what. She rolled over and tried to get comfortable in the bed but it was no use. Tossing the silver-blue goose feather down blanket aside, Katie climbed out of bed and trudged toward the oak dressing cabinet.

"What's the matter?" Pete asked, speaking to his wife in their native tongue. *"Are you okay? You're talking in your sleep again."*

"Don't know what, but something's wrong. Did you just hear a loud noise?"

"No."

"A raw feeling inside has been bothering me all week. Tonight, it's really bad. I feel like an object just pierced my heart. Something is wrong."

"We'd better check on the children."

"No, it doesn't have to do with them. Whatever it is, it didn't happen here. It's at the office. I don't know what's wrong, but I have to go."

Pete finally opened his eyes to the starlit night outside the picture window. He glanced at the clock. *"It's only three-thirty and I didn't hear anything. Can't you go back to sleep and at least wait until sunrise?"*

"No. I don't know what the problem is, but something is very wrong. I have to go now."

"Okay, let me make you some coffee."

Katie's husband climbed out of bed, long johns covering his slight frame. Yawning, he thought, This morning is going to be ancient before the sun rises. He pulled the sleeping clothes tight and tiptoed on the highly varnished cold wooden floor. Peeking into the next room to check on the children, he discovered both sleeping soundly. He returned to his bedroom, pulled on a pair of bib overalls and thick woolen socks, then traipsed down the carpeted stairs to the kitchen.

The black solid steel Franklin stove, a wedding gift from the bride's family, commanded a corner of the small kitchen. It sprang to life as flame from a single match touched the tinder inside, flickering at first, then licking the sides of the stovetop. A steel arc-shaped handle positioned the disc above the fire as he filled a kettle, full of water. The boiler slid easily over the wood stove onto the iron disc.

Flames began to lick the crinkled newspaper as wood cuttings crackled inside the pot belly stove announced it was beginning to heat. Pete scooped a double helping of ground coffee beans and poured the concoction into a waiting receptacle, sure to make a strong pot of black liquid. He'd learned the art of making Turkish coffee as a boy in Europe.

A basin half full of water sat on the marble-top nightstand next to the bed. Katie splashed the contents on her face to help pry the sleep from her eyes. She hastily pulled on her house clothes, an oversize pair of men's work pants and two loose-fitting sweaters, and hurried down to the kitchen.

In an effort to calm his anxious wife, Pete posited, *"I'm sure it's nothing too serious. You could probably wait until dawn, but if you feel that strongly about it, you better check it out. I see clouds just blocked out the starlight so it's now dark outside. You'd better take a lantern. I'll get one while you finish your coffee. And I'll fill a Dewar Flask with more hot coffee for you in case you have to stay a while."*

Without waiting for a response, Pete left the kitchen and walked to the cellar. Located two steps up, above and behind the living room, it served as a catchall for wine barrels, wash tubs, children's toys, and served as a general catch-all for odds and ends that had nowhere else to light. Since the house was built into a hillside, the cellar, usually located beneath a house, rose a dugout a few feet above the first floor in the Novak home. One advantage to the dugout cellar included a unique solution. Whenever more room was needed, a larger space was simply hollowed out.

He looked through the items, all neatly arranged, until finding the flask that he'd used for a dozen years while working in the steel mill. He returned to the kitchen, lantern and flask in hand.

Lifting a chipped cup in one hand as a salute, Katie toasted him, *"Old Man, you make the best coffee in the state,"* downing the hot Turkish coffee in one gulp, shuddering. *"Damn! That will wake a body on a chilly autumn morning, won't it? I feel the heat all the way down to my toenails."*

Tucking the flask under her arm, she reached across the table to a nail pounded halfway into the wallboard, removing the keys to the office. Pete lighted the lantern and handed it to her as she left the house.

Katie tread cautiously in the smoky dark night, grateful she remembered to wear flat walking shoes. Along the river, steel mills were alive, going full throttle, clanking, moaning, and belching black soot into the air. A lone Pullman taxi motored past, heading toward Pittsburgh along the River Road. She noticed a truck leaving the mill gate, lumbering along State Street and considered flagging it down to get to the office more quickly. But the driver was too far away, and between the clanking of the big truck's engine and the racket from the mills, the driver neither saw nor heard her. The idea of what the driver might have thought seeing a shabbily-dressed woman out in the middle of the night never crossed her mind.

Katie climbed the stairs to Waddell Avenue, the street above the house, and alternated between running and speed walking toward the deafening silence ahead. Her mind flickered between approach and avoidance. She wanted to clarify the message of the voice inside her, but she didn't want to face a traumatic scene. Nevertheless, the voice urged her onward.

Breathing heavily as she rounded the corner of Miller and St. Clair Avenues, the crisp night air bit her lungs. The office came into view. Ahead of her, she made out the form of a policeman holding a squirming urchin fast against the ground. She recognized the cop as an old family friend and Irish immigrant named Seamus Patrick Kelly.

Officer Kelly, nicknamed Jim, called out to Katie, "I got 'im, mum. Watched 'im break the side window 'n climb in, I did. I jist waited til 'e cum back out, 'n I grabbed 'im by the scruff o' the neck. Went through 'is pockets, I did, and found these here coppers and this brooch. Dirty little thugs like this 'un with their dirty clothes run rampant through our city streets, pinchin' food and stealin' anythin' o' value. But I caught this 'un red-handed."

It was difficult to hear the policeman above the screaming of the pinned ragamuffin, face streaked with coal dust, grime, and tears, and hands spotted red with fresh blood. Yammering incomprehensibly, the child wailed, "I didn't do it. I swear. I found a few coins in the desk and took the brooch from the drawer. Tripped over him. 'Twas so dark inside I couldn't see and I tripped over him, but I didn't do nothin' bad, I swear it."

Katie tuned out the noise between the policeman and the child and rushed to the office door. Placing the large key inside the lock, she turned it, releasing the deadbolt. With the lantern held high and ahead of her, she entered the large front room and grimaced, dropping the Dewar Flask as her eyes adapted and focused on the darkened office. The flask shattered. Shards of glass and droplets of coffee peppered the floor of the ghastly scene.

Her dear partner and mentor, Albert Lhormer, lay slumped in the chair. A trickle of dry blood had coalesced starting from his right temple, down the side of his face, cheek, and neck, staining the collar of his rumpled white shirt. His left arm sat neatly across his lap. His right arm dangled over the side of the chair. On the floor lay a pistol.

Seamus Patrick Kelly followed Katie into the office, still holding the gamin by the nape of the neck. The police officer's steel-blue eyes adjusted, then squinted, as he took in the grisly scene. "Oh, Katie. I'm so sorry. Will you be okay to stay here for a while? I gotta go back to the station to get a supervisor. I'll take the kid with me and hold him until we can figure out what, if anythin', he had to do with this. Don't touch anythin' in case the Department needs to do an investigation."

Katie was overwhelmed at the pique of the moment. She heard neither the child's moans and protests nor the words of the policeman.

The youngster quieted, but still squirmed against the solid grip of the officer. Kelly left Katie, taking long strides as the child beside him hopped as quickly as he was able, skittering, his toes barely touching the ground.

Albert's blood had stained the glossy wooden floors. His lips, pale blue, were nearly the color of his eyes. His gaze held a penetrating stare, though frozen, seemed to follow her every move. His mouth was partly open, as though prepared to utter the words he never had a chance to say to her.

Still in a trance, Katie slunk to her knees, wrapping her arms around Albert's limp body hunched over in the chair. She eased his still-warm frame to the floor and onto her lap, closing his eyes, ending the ghastly stare. As she cradled him in her arms, a book tumbled onto the floor. She recognized the well-worn tome that he read over and over during slow times at the office.

A cursory glance at the book revealed several handwritten pages of parchment tucked inside. She recognized Albert's perfectly printed penmanship. Gently releasing the body to the floor, but keeping his head in her lap, she removed the papers from the book. One arm embraced his lifeless body as she positioned his head in her ample thighs. She saw her name on the outside of the paper: To Katheryn Novak, my deepest admiration for my closest friend.

Doing her best to focus, but still bleary, words on the papers came to life in the dim glow of the lantern.

My Dearest Katie,

You must know that you are the brightest star in my life, and that I have loved you like a sister since the moment I first set eyes on you. You made our business blossom. All you touch turns to gold. You are truly my queen to King Midas.

Perhaps you wondered why I did not express my love or attempt to make our business relationship a personal one. Katie, my Dear, I have carried secrets with me, secrets that you would never have known, could never imagine. Heed me now as I make my last confession to you, my guiding light.

My preference for romance has always been toward those of my own biologi-

cal kind. I kept this proclivity hidden in my early years. But even as a boy I knew I was different from the others.

I lived in Augsburg, Germany throughout my fiscal and accounting apprenticeship, and rose steadily through the ranks of the banking industry. There my secret, lonely life continued. I'm sure my family suspected nothing different about me. I was quiet and devoted to my work. I never had a relationship with man or woman until one day a young Austrian bank intern confessed his love to me. He whispered it quietly in the bank's vault with nobody to witness. Such a beautiful boy, so gracious and kind. He became my first love, and I his, or so he said. We tried to be discreet in our relationship but became reckless and were found out and reported to the bank's president.

Our discovery resulted in a series of crushing blows to us both. To avoid involving the bank in a scandal, my young lover returned to his family in Vienna. We both signed papers agreeing to never see each other again under threat of prosecution by the authorities.

My family disowned and banished me. My father reminded me of the shame I'd brought to the family and told me I was dead to him. And those were the kindest words from my family. It was a brutal time and I must admit I considered ending my miserable life at the time. Instead I moved to Munich, a large city where I could become anonymous and start over. First order of business, I changed my surname from Lehmann to Lhormer, and began working at another bank, again working my way up.

After several years I had saved enough money to go out on my own. When the opportunity arose, I fled to America and settled here, living at first in a self-imposed celibacy.

Katie, do you have any idea how difficult it is to live without the touch of another human, or without love, even if fleeting and physical? I took an apartment in Pittsburgh that I'm sure you must have known, but what you do not know is that my apartment allowed me to have friends that have the same predilection as I do. A homosexual community of mostly well-to-do professional men meets regularly to dance, socialize, and occasionally find comfort with one *another. It is a very closed and secret group, of course, and our meetings are carefully planned. We use assumed names and take every precaution to avoid any contact with the straight community, and avoid legal entanglements at all costs. Still, no interaction between two human beings is one hundred percent safe. We are often preyed upon, robbed and beaten, and when such incidents occur we dare not go to the authorities.*

I've studied the laws related to sodomy. Did you know the penalty for a homosexual relationship is ten years at solitary hard labor and a fine of $ 1,000? And there is precious little sympathy for "our kind" outside our own group. I even feared revealing myself to you, my dearest, closest friend, until now. I pray you will not judge me too harshly.

Last night our party was disrupted by a heavy knock on the door. The room became as quiet as a fly lighting on a feather duster. The pounding continued, louder as cries of "Police! Open up," emanated from the other side.

No escape. No other entry existed besides the front door. We were doomed. Each man inside the apartment froze, as still as a graveyard at midnight, hoping in our minds' fantasy that the pounding would cease and whoever was on the other side of the door would disappear. But the fantasy evaporated as the police squad ripped the door from its hinges and spread as locusts coming to consume all in sight.

The police brought along photographers and newspaper reporters to document what in their mind is shameful behavior. I recognized one of the officers as a man who had attended several of our parties. He was notable as he had a droopy eyelid. He had spoken to me on many occasions. My mind would not process whether he had been a plant to discover our lair, or one of us who also served on the vice squad and lived a double life. No matter. He did not make eye contact with me.

The story, with sordid, often untrue details will run tomorrow in the Pittsburgh Daily Post, complete with names of all those arrested. I am ruined. I hope that by taking my life, the impact will lessen the hurt to you and the business. My last will and testament is in the company safe. Everything I own, all my belongings, including my share of the business is yours.

Once more I must say to you, I'm sorry, Katie. Sorry I could not trust you enough to tell you my secrets and sorry you did not know me for what I am.

Your loving servant,

Albert

Tears streamed down Katie's face. She sat on the hard, cold wooden office floor, rocking Albert's body as she read the confession. When finished, she hugged him tightly, as she would her children, and cried out, not in her native Slavic tongue, but in broken English, "Of course I knew, Albert. I knew from first day we met, silly goose." Sobbing profusely now, she added, "Oh, if I only turn back clock ... if only you tell me ..."

* * *

Clairton Savings and Loan's office occupied the entire ground level in a square, three-story, nondescript building located on the corner of the two main streets in Clairton — St. Clair and Miller Avenues. Apartments were located on the top two stories, one of which served as Albert's quarters: a small, tidy one-room studio, cold water flat, furnished with a Murphy bed. The hovel served as Albert's humble home during the week and some weekends. Other times he stayed away for a few days, but Katie had no idea where or with whom. She reflected on a recent conversation.

"Albert, how come you always here in office before me?" She teased. *"You hide girlfriends upstairs?"*

Her partner blushed and tried to deflect the subtle query. *"Katie, you know you're the only woman in my life. You and the Savings and Loan are all I care about."*

She hesitated before pushing the envelope a bit more. She felt certain he kept an apartment elsewhere but rarely spoke of it. Gazing around the office she teased, *"No girl here. Maybe you keep her lock up somewhere when you go 'way for weekend."*

Albert bit his lip but said nothing, though his face flushed.

With his discomfort growing, the conversation eased. "Okay, Partner. I not pick on you no more."

The business did not charge Albert for the small apartment. The Savings and Loan held the mortgage on the entire office building, including the apartment. It was one of the few perks Albert allowed himself. He took a meager salary that allowed the purchase of a natty wardrobe as his only luxury.

Thinking of him, his work ethic, his evasiveness, and the opportunity he gave her to join him in the business stemmed the flow of tears and brought Katie a staunch resolve. She spoke to him as though he sat at his desk that very moment.

"Albert, you make me very, very mad that you do this thing. I gonna miss you so much. But I forgive you. And this I swear to you, my dear one, I be proud to keep you name on front window of Savings and Loan, and keep business growing to best of my ability. I gonna use part of our proceeds to help oppressed people like you and others. I don't know how yet, but as God be my witness, I swear on my children that my life from this day on gonna be devoted to help those in need."

Startled by footsteps on the entry steps, Katie arose. Officer Kelly and his Sergeant, Ashton Brown, had returned with the urchin in tow. "Nobody else is on duty until six o'clock when Patrolman Don Lloyd comes on shift, mum. I didn't want ta leave the kid locked in a cell, so I brung 'im with me. He got away from me once but Sarge Brown grabbed 'im, bum leg and all."

For the second time that morning, the waif quickly spun out of the grip of Sergeant Brown and attempted to escape, darting across the office, avoiding both police officers. Leaping over a desk, and running smack into an overwrought Katie, he nearly knocked the portly woman flat on the floor.

A former baseball star, Sergeant Ashton Brown stood red-faced, apologized. "I'm sorry, Mrs. Novak. This bum knee ended my career with the Pirates. Seems to still cause me problems in the damp weather. I'll take the rascal off your hands and get him back to the jailhouse. This trick knee gives me fits sometimes, but I can still hobble."

"Damn humid weather make joints hurt like hell. Mine, too. Maybe someday somebody figure out how make new one and replace bad one."

"Ha! That'll be the day. Replace old joints with new ones. I wish!"

Sergeant Brown limped toward Katie and the boy, but she shook her head and wrapped her strong arms around the lad, holding him until he stopped flailing. The sergeant backed away as the youngster collapsed in a complete breakdown onto her ample chest.

Maternal instincts took over. Her voiced mellowed. She asked, "What you name, boy?"

The lad did not answer her question but blubbered, "I only seen one dead person before. I didn't do it. Just wanted to find a few pennies for to buy me some food. I ain't ate for a long time. I'm so hungry. I'm sorry for takin' the brooch but it's so pretty. I never seen nothin' so pretty. Please don't hurt me."

The police sergeant started to say something but Katie held up her hand and wagged a finger in a gesture to let her handle the child. "I can feel you ribs sticking out, little one. We gonna let policemen finish up work here and I take you home and get you fed, okay?"

The child nodded and quietly allowed himself to be taken into Katie's control.

"My old man ... uh, his name Pete. He's home with two young ones. He gonna get you cleaned up, fed, and then we get you back to your parents."

She turned to the two officers. "Leave boy with me. I know you have work do here. I no want press charges. I take him home, then get back here to help you do what need be done. Please call Finney and tell him pick up Albert. I know Albert gone, but I need you promise me you handle his body with most care and respect."

"Of course, Katie. Once the daylight shift comes in, we'll get going here. And if you decide you're sure you're not going to press charges against him, we'll leave the youngster in your custody."

Katie nodded in agreement and departed, the urchin beside her walking with a slight limp.

Ashton Brown grew up a farm boy in Wisconsin. He had little formal schooling, going straight from his parents' farm to playing professional baseball. The ace pitcher had a stellar record until he strained his knee during a crucial game. The manager refused to replace him, saying, "You are a better pitcher on one leg than any of my others are on two."

He won the game but hundreds of repetitions stretching off the pitching mound during inclement weather ruined his knee, ending a promising baseball career with the Pittsburgh Pirates.

Being a local sport celebrity, Ashton had little difficulty securing a job with the Clairton police department. He achieved an added level of fame, not over his gimpy knee, but his fractured spelling.

Early one morning Sergeant Brown took a call to investigate the death of a horse. A citizen discovered the carcass on Mendelssohn Avenue. The city had not yet erected street signs in that part of town, but of course, the sergeant knew every street in the community.

Arriving at the stated location, he examined the animal to be sure it had expired. It had. Taking out his pencil and notepad he began to write his report. *"Hors kilt Mson Av."* Knowing that he had misspelled the name of the street, and fearing the report location might become confused with other street names, he scratched out the message and tried again, *"Hrse kilt Manaslo Av."*

Still not satisfied, he scratched out the street listing and made several more attempts, but remained unable to find a spelling that would reflect the correct name of Mendelssohn Avenue.

Frustrated, he went to the trunk of his police wagon, retrieved a rope, and returned to the horse corpse. Tying one end of the rope around the dead horse's neck, he secured the other end to the back of his police wagon. He returned to the front seat, started the wagon and dragged the corpse several blocks to Fifth Street. There he wrote the following report: "Hors kilt 5 St."

Once again, on this day, the police sergeant demonstrated his creative penmanship and faulty spelling skills. Using a scrap of paper, he made a sign announcing, *"Clost. deth in fambly,"* and attached it to the front door of the Clairton Savings and Loan.

2

The Secret

"…one must be woman-manly or man-womanly." —Virginia Woolf

THE SUN HAD BEGUN TO CAST a brief look through the smoke and clouds by the time Katie took the boy gently by the torn elbow of his tattered coat and led him down the muddy street to her house. The clouds had parted and the rain stopped, allowing a peek of daylight to slip through black belching smoke spewing from the mill. It was a quiet walk. Katie noticed the slight limp and asked if he was injured. He shook his head. She asked the lad several more questions but he appeared to be in a trance and said nothing in response. Together they walked, sloshing through the unpaved, mud-caked streets and stepping over puddles, walking in silence except for Katie's unanswered questions. Soon they arrived at the house on Arch Street.

Pete greeted them, sitting on the swing under the grape arbor, a child on either side of him. *"Who is our guest?"* he asked Katie, speaking in his native Bosnian language.

She answered, also in her native tongue. *"This young man had a difficult morning. Can you make him a nice meal and give him a bath? And let's burn those stinking hand-me-down rags he's wearing. Do you think we can find something here to fit him?"*

"I don't think so. Not here. He's too big for our baby's clothes and too small for mine. We can ask Danica if she has something one of her kids has outgrown. If not, I'm certain the Glover family has something we can use. A couple of their kids look to be about his size. Does he speak our language? Where did he come from? Who does he belong to?"

"He doesn't seem to speak much at all, but I did hear him utter a few words in English. I'll tell him what's in store for him. Do your best but don't be surprised if he doesn't talk to you."

"What happened at the Savings and Loan? What was the problem? You look a mess."

"Oh Pete, it's terrible. The boy broke into the office looking for coins to buy food. He tripped over Albert's body."

"His body? What are you talking about? Did Albert have a heart attack? Is he going to be okay?"

Her voice wavered as she related the scene for the first time. *"Albert shot himself. He's dead! That had to be the bad feeling I had in bed. I can't give you the details right now. I need to clean up and hurry back to the office. Just take care of the boy for me. That would be a big help. I don't think he's eaten for quite a while, and from the looks and smell of him, soap or water hasn't touched his body for too long. Take care of him. Get him a good meal and a bath. I'll get back as soon as I can."*

The normally unflappable Pete stood dumbstruck, stunned into silence by the revelations. After a long pause he managed, *"Albert dead? By his own hand? And tell me again, how does the boy fit into the events?"*

Katie ignored his question for the moment, turned to the youth, and began in English to explain what was about to happen. "Dis my husban, Pete. He gonna' cook nice meal for you after you take bath."

The child showed little emotion or reaction.

The five of them; Pete, Katie, the boy, and the two small children moved from the porch into the house.

"I goin' get wash tub from cellar." Katie maneuvered around Pete's wine casks of fermenting liquid, sorting through the mess until reaching the tub. "Ah, here it is. I gotta keep this closer. Looks like Old Man hides it from me."

The wooden half-barrel doubled as a wading pool for the children during summer months, as well as a tub for bathing during cold or inclement weather. She grunted, dragging the half-cask as it thudded down the steps. She lugged it into the space that served as a living room and den, behind the kitchen. The room shared a common wall with the Franklin stove on the opposite side, thus making a warm area ideal for bathing.

Pete stoked the glowing embers in the stove and added wood to the fire to heat buckets of bathwater, and to fry a slab of bacon and three eggs for the lad. The two Novak children stared at the urchin as he sat, eyes downcast, hoping for a meal to stave off the hunger pangs that had become a constant companion in his dreary life.

Pete set the plate of bacon, eggs, a huge slice of bread slathered with butter, and a large glass of milk before the youngster. He didn't look like much of an eater but immediately began to devour the chow the instant it was placed before him, attacking it as though it were his last supper.

Ruža watched in awe as she ventured, "You like my Daddy's cooking?"

No response, only the crunching of food stuffed into his mouth.

Pete offered a mild admonishment to the child. "You take easy, boy. No want for tummy ache."

The lad ignored him and continued to ravage the meal.

Katie, meanwhile, dashed to a neighbor's house before changing clothes and returning to the office. Danica Suica was also an immigrant, brought to America as an arranged bride. Though several years separated them, the two had become best friends.

"Anybody home?" Katie called at the front door.

"Come in, Katie. Mrs. Glover and I were just chewing the rag."

The Glovers, an African American family, lived just up the street from the Suicas. Their children were about the same age and played together. Bessie Glover's husband, Rob, had worked with Pete in the mill.

Katie spoke in English for Bessie's benefit. "Hi, Bessie. I got question. Danica. You got clean clothes to borrow for boy 'bout thirteen, maybe fourteen year? I have visitor. Tell you more 'bout it later but Pete need get him wash, feed, and dress while I go back to office."

"Sure, Katie. I've got tons of stuff that my kids have outgrown. Let me find you something." She dashed into a bedroom, opened a closet, and sifted through piles of well-worn clothing, tossing several items aside. Returning with three pairs of overalls, two shirts, socks, and a jacket, she handed them to Katie. "These aren't new but they're clean and have plenty of wear left in them. How 'bout shoes? Any idea what size?"

"I don't see no shoes for the mud, and don't think he wore no socks, but let me take pair shoes and socks just in case."

Bessie added, "If you need more, I got plenty up my way."

"Tanks for you, Bessie. Today is crazy day. Lots happen already and mill whistle not even blow yet for shift change. I tell you more after but need get back to loan company."

The women sent Katie on her way with good wishes and offers to help with whatever is needed.

Back at the house, Katie reflected, knowing she had to be strong. She freshened up, changed clothes, kissed Pete, her two babies, and the interloper, then before setting off for the office, began thinking out loud.

"I'm going to close the office for the day, maybe longer. I don't think I'm up to cleaning it. I'll ask the baker, Frank Grisnik, who he uses for janitorial, and hire them. Be back as soon as I can get things settled. When I come home I'll give you all the details about Albert and we can figure out what to do about the boy."

She kissed Pete and the children again, then returned to the office.

* * *

The Novaks' guest finished his attack on the food as though he were a starving man, then let out a long, loud belch, causing the children to giggle. All three followed Pete into the room behind the kitchen, then sat as Pete pointed to the floor. Pete dashed out to the stove and hauled the two buckets of water that had been heating on the stove. The boy watched Pete empty the water bucket's steaming contents into the tub. He haltingly tried a little fractured English, but mostly used hand motions, pointing downward. "Put you clothes on floor. Here is new clothes for after clean you."

He handed the boy a bar of brown laundry soap, but first mimicked washing himself, then pointed to the hand-me-down outfit and gestured to dress in it once clean. The boy nodded but said nothing. Pete reached out to the two little ones and the three left the room. In an instant, the splash of flesh and bones entering a tub could be heard, followed by a yelp as the youngster's body slid into the hot water. "Daddy, who is he?" queried Little Ruža. She spoke in her father's native language but also spoke fluent English. Such is the advantage of growing up in a bilingual home.

"He is our guest, and you can see, a hungry guest. Soon he will be our clean guest with a full tummy."

Pete tidied up the kitchen, then played peek-a-boo with his children. Both Ruža and Little Petey roared with laughter at their father's antics while their visitor basked in the tub in the next room.

Nearly an hour passed before Pete heard the slosh of water as the boy began to exit the tub. Rushing to offer an extra towel, he stepped into the room, then froze in his tracks. Standing naked in the tub before him was not a boy, but a teenage girl! Her hair had been cropped short, and her figure was mostly skin and bones, but the facial features, slight figure, and swelling of small budding breasts that nobody seemed to have noticed did not lie. They were clearly the soft features of a female, not yet a woman, but certainly not a child, and definitely not male.

Both stood awkwardly, gaping at one another until Pete gathered his wits about him and handed the tub-girl a towel. He pointed at the clean clothes, snatched up the filthy rags that she'd discarded, and left the room, flustered.

As the mystery girl dressed, Pete told Ruža to watch her little brother while he ran to the neighbor Danica's house. She and Bessie Glover were still on the porch chatting. Pete ordinarily would have spoken in English as a courtesy to Bessie, but in his state of upset and disarray he spoke in his native tongue. *"Can you tend the children for a while? I have to get up to the office and see Katie."*

Danica answered, "Of course, Pete." She wiped her damp hands on her apron and followed him out of the house. "How did the boy like his clean clothes?"

"Oh Danica, this has been such a day! Once he got out of the tub ... I was taking him a towel and ... I mean taking HER a towel ... I mean, I didn't know. I thought he ... she was a boy, and just brought a towel and discovered it was not a him but a her. This is such a confusing day."

"A girl! That IS a surprise. How could you think a girl is a boy?"

"I don't know, Danica. I'm so confused."

"Never mind, Pete, let's get you back to your house. We'll get it all straightened out." Switching to English she spoke again. "Bessie, do you have time to come with me? Seems like the Novaks' young male guest turned out to be a girl."

Bessie shook her head. "I've got things to do before my man gets home from work, but be sure to tell me everything once you find out."

The two returned to the house to discover the girl, washed clean and in fresh hand-me-down boy's clothing, sitting at the table eating leftovers and tending Ruža and Little Petey. It seemed like a normal tranquil family scene. Though it may have been tranquil, it was anything but normal.

Pete spoke again to Danica. *"I need to check on Katie. She's had a shock this morning. She discovered Albert has taken his life. She thinks this girl is a boy, and I have no idea how he, uh, she, fits into the picture. See what you can find out from him, I mean her. I might be a while."*

"Jesus, Joseph, and Mary! Albert took his own life? How? When? How did she find out? No, wait a minute. Let me calm down. No problem my staying with the kids, Pete. I can get the details about Albert later. Please tell her I'm sorry for her loss and she has my deepest sympathy. You, too. I'll try to talk to the girl. Does she speak our language?"

"I don't think so. Katie said she seemed to understand English. I haven't heard her speak a word, so I'm not sure. Your English is much better than mine. Do what you can." He raced out the door, shaking his head and mumbling to himself, *"Boy is girl. Girl is boy. Albert is gone. How did this all happen?"*

* * *

Danica walked to the table, smiling, and asked first if the young girl spoke the Serbo-Croatian language, "Govorite li Hrvatski? Srbski?"

No response.

She tried again. "Italiano? Deutsche?"

The girl's eyes brightened a bit on her next try. "Eengleesh?"

The girl nodded but did not smile.

"Ah good. My Eengleesh not so good like youz, probably, but we can talk."

As Danica approached, the girl blanched and raised her hands in a defensive motion. "Please don' hit me. I din' do nothin' bad. I was so hungry, looking for food or money to buy some. I'm sorry. I didn' do nothin' bad." Tears streamed down the girl's cheeks. She collapsed into a river of sobs as Danica wrapped her large, motherly arms around the child.

"Oh, beba, you no be in no trouble. You safe in dis house. Deeze nice people. Dey feed you good, wash you, give you clean clothes. You okay now, honey. No be worry. You get 'nuf for eat?"

She nodded, but said nothing.

"What you name, little one?"

Exhaustion had caught up with the youngster. She sat, glassy-eyed, but in apparent comfort after Danica's calming words. For the first time in a long while, she felt safe in the husky arms of this woman who held her.

Danica rocked the girl like an infant, gently, back and forth until she fell asleep in the arms of the nurturing neighbor. Ruža and Petey sat wide-eyed at the table, watching the scene play out. Danica gently lifted the young damsel and carried her to the well-worn blue brocade couch in the living room. Ruža slid off her chair, helped Little Petey down, and led him by the hand, following the woman and child into the living room.

By this time the girl had fallen into a deep sleep.

"Who is she, Auntie Danica?" Ruža whispered to the neighbor. Danica was not related to the Novak family, but the title Auntie was used as one of respect among family friends in the ethnic communities surrounding Pittsburgh.

The auntie held one finger to her lips and spoke in a hushed tone using her native language with the Novak children. "This is a visitor to your home. Like all children, she is a gift from God. Let's play quietly in the other room so she can sleep."

Ruža's eyes widened. "Is it her naptime?"

"That's right. It's her naptime," the woman repeated, "we'll let her have her nap." Danica took the two small children back into the kitchen, cleaned the table, wiped the stove, and entertained them as she waited for their parents to return.

3

Reflections

"One of the saddest things in life, is the thing one remembers." —Agatha Christie

PETE HASTENED TO THE CLAIRTON SAVINGS AND LOAN where he discovered the handwritten sign on the entry door, composed and placed by Police Sergeant Ashton Brown, announcing, *Clost, deth in famly*. He rapped on the door until Katie answered. No words were spoken as they embraced and quietly sobbed for what seemed like only a few moments, but lasted a quarter hour.

Katie finally broke the silence. *"Oh Pete, I cared for him so deeply. He was my mentor and friend. I don't know if I can go on without his guidance."*

"Of course you can, my dearest. You are strong, smart, and have learned much from Albert. You will find a person to train just as he taught you about the business. I wish I could help you but I'm afraid business is not what I do best."

"You're right there," she smiled. *"You are a man of the earth and a wonderful father. We have a lawyer and an accountant for the business issues and I look over their shoulders to track what they do. You're right again; I can do it. I'll need to hire some additional help, and with your support I can keep the business afloat. And you are so good with the children ...*

She was suddenly jolted from daydream land to reality. *"Wait! The children! Where are the children? You didn't leave them alone, for sure. Is Danica watching them? And what about the boy I brought to the house? Where is he? What is he doing? Did you get him fed and bathed?"*

"You mean, the GIRL."

"Girl? No, Silly. The boy I brought home with me. The one who broke into the business last night. What girl?"

That's what I'm trying to tell you; she's a GIRL!"

"What? Who's a girl? Pete, what is the matter with you? What are you talking about? Are you out of your head? I'm asking you about the boy. The boy I brought home! And you're telling me about some girl?"

Pete took a deep breath, trying to calm himself. *"Okay, let me start over. I got so caught up in the emotion of it all, I forgot the reason I came here to find you. Things are very, very confused."*

Katie stood stone still, not moving or speaking until Pete was prepared to tell her of the morning's events, to help her sort things out in her own mind, unsure whether she could handle another shock this day.

She also took a deep breath and began. *"Albert's death was a terrible shock, Pete. Our world has been turned upside down. And then there's the little thief who broke into the office last night. I'm asking about him. How is he?"*

"That's what I've been trying to tell you. HE is a SHE!"

"WHAT? What are you saying, Old Man? Have you lost your mind? A he can't just turn into a she. I'm really confused. He seemed all boy to me."

Pete calmed himself with another deep breath. *"No, that's why I came looking for you. I don't know what to do. After his, uh, I mean her bath finished, I took in another towel and the urchin that stood up in the tub was a girl. She looked like a boy when you brought her home, with hair cut short and dressed in baggy boy's clothes, but she is a tall, skinny girl."*

"Did she say anything? Where she came from? Who she is?" Katie paused and startled herself as the next thought struck her. *"You left her alone with the children??"*

"Danica is tending all three of them. She brought some old boys clothes for her but that's when I thought she was a boy. I don't know what to do."

By this time, Katie had gathered her wits. *"Bessie Glover has grown girls. I'm sure we can get some hand-me-down clothes for the child from her."*

Katie sat and pondered for several minutes, sifting the events through her mind, and with the savvy of the highly-organized businesswoman that made her so successful, prioritized the tasks ahead of her. Taking a pad from the desk, she picked up a pencil and began, *"Let me make notes first. Then we can talk."*

Pete nodded.

Touching the pencil tip to her tongue, on the first line of the pad she wrote: "Albert takes his life. Must make arrangements." Next line, "Need to close office for this week." Next, "Must hire more help." Then, "Office broken into. Fix window."

She continued organizing, writing furiously and occasionally retouching the lead pencil tip to her tongue, until she had listed on the pad every detail that needed to be accomplished. Taking a deep breath, she began to speak. *"Now we come to the girl. Do you know anything about her background, where she came from or where she belongs?"*

"No, Katie. She has not spoken to me. Maybe Danica has been able to get some information from her."

She tore a page from her notebook. *"Here are the things I need you to do. We can set up a cot in the children's room until we get things sorted out with her. I don't want to send her to the authorities. They'd likely place her in an orphanage and I don't want that to happen. We'll just have to find where she came from and get her back to her parents. It can't be that hard. How many lost girls could there be? Go ahead back to the house and let Danica get home. Find out what you can about the girl. The cleaners are due to arrive any minute."*

Glancing at her notes, she continued, *"I'll finish up what I can do here, then take Albert's Last Will and Testament to the attorney. I'll get home when I can."*

Pete gave her a peck on the cheek and another hug, and left to complete the tasks she'd asked him to do.

While waiting for the janitorial service to arrive, Katie reflected on how she herself had gone from recalcitrant teen to a sole business owner. Had she and Branko been caught stealing cigarettes as a teen, her life might well have been different ...

As if in a trance, Katie's mind reflected upon her own childhood and her arranged marriage at age fifteen to Pete. He was twenty-five at the time. At first, she refused to marry him but her mother coerced her with an ultimatum of marriage or a seat on the railroad tracks to await a train that would surely end her life. Katie chose the tracks and sat for hours awaiting her fate — certain death — until she finally cried herself out and agreed to the marriage. What the child did not know at the time that the mother knew; no trains were scheduled to pass that day.

The shaky beginning of their marriage seemed so long ago. In reality, just a few years had passed since Katie and Peter had taken their wedding vows, but it felt like a lifetime. Pete had purchased a large plot of land that overlooked the Monongahela River. Together they built their dream house, the pride of Katie's parents and envy of their neighbors.

In the early days of the marriage, Pete worked as a laborer in the dangerous, filthy steel mill. Ten-hour shifts were followed with daily work on the building of their home. Besides overseeing the house, Katie, a natural entrepreneur, kept chickens, hosted gambling nights, ran a boarding house, took in laundry, and sold moonshine to keep the family's finances above water. She also found time to give birth to two children.

A unique parental role reversal in the Novak household came about suddenly and unexpectedly.

A contentious steelworker strike at the Clairton's Crucible Steel Plant found Peter Novak out of work and facing a dilemma. He was prevailed upon by the boss who hired him to continue working during the strike, but was threatened by union leadership if he crossed the picket line. Pete's solution did not include either option, but rather, to escape the walkout by a sojourn, moving temporarily to live with Katie's relatives in Johnstown, some seventy miles away. There he sat out the work stoppage while Katie tended the home front. He knew the Johnstown location would be safe from the violence and intimidation of the strike in Clairton.

Once the strike finally settled, and despite his efforts to avoid confrontation, the union banned Pete from working in any union steel mill. A co-worker falsely accused and identified him as a scab who had crossed the picket line during the strike.

Pete's banishment became a blessing to the Novak family. Factory work did not suit him. Filthy, hot, dangerous tasks, long hours, poor working conditions, and job instability faced workers daily. Despite support and concessions to unions, many workers lost their jobs or faced pay cuts after the long, grueling, brutal strike ended. After ten years in the mill, Pete was no more a steelworker than he'd been the first day on the job.

In his heart and by trade, Pete had always been a farmer and a nurturer. As a small child, he helped his father plant, weed, and reap the fields, and helped his mother with the younger children. At age eight he began a ten-year period of indentured servitude to a horse breeder in Germany, tending horses and honing skills as a farmer.

Once Pete settled in, operating his own small farm on the land he'd purchased, Katie, ever the entrepreneur, dreamed of owning several rental properties. Smiling to herself she remembered her first introduction to Albert. The fledgling Clairton Savings and Loan company also served as a real estate office, opened in the commercial district of the community.

Katie Novak, the family's life savings in her tote bag, waltzed into the office and in her very limited version of the English language said, "Want buy place rent." Dropping a purse full of cash on the desk she added, "How mush?"

Albert asked, "Madam, do you wish to place your cash against a loan? Or purchase a property outright?"

"Want buy place rent." Emptying the rest of the contents of the purse onto the counter, she again asked, "How mush?"

"Do you plan to occupy the residence?"

Unable to understand the nature of his question, she gritted her teeth. Her face reddened with frustration. Raising her voice, "I haf money, want buy."

Albert Lhormer, proprietor of Clairton Savings and Loan had the reputation as a patient man. The Jewish-German immigrant spoke fairly good English as well as several other European languages, including his native German. He did not, however, speak the Balto-Slavic languages. Katie spoke only Croatian, with little grasp of English. Unable to make herself understood or understanding the owner of the business, she scooped up her money and stomped out of the office spewing a string of epithets that made reference to Albert Lhormer's parentage, his sexual prowess, and other allusions to his family in general, America, and money lenders in particular. She returned home frustrated, continuing to spackle the air with curse words, the only component of the English language she spoke fluently.

The following day Katie returned with Pete at her side. The two men conversed in German, spoken flawlessly by Pete from his years being tutored in the language while indentured on the German horse farm.

"My name is Albert Lhormer," began the proprietor. *"I served as a banker for twenty years in Germany before relocating to this community."*

"Peter Novak." He extended his hand to meet the realtor's. Without mentioning that he had been little more than an indentured servant at the time, he offered, *"As an employee in Germany I studied the language."*

"You speak our language eloquently, Herr Novak. An educated man to be sure. I apologize deeply for any offense or misunderstanding I might have caused your wife. I tried to explain to her that many banks are reluctant to lend money to immigrants. Further, even if she were to acquire the funds to purchase a house, or two, the rental home business is fraught with problems. I suggest she consider taking your savings and loan the money to other immigrants for home purchases. The risk is lower and profit far better."

Pete translated the broker's words to Katie, who responded in her native tongue. The husband gave her words back to Albert. *"Sir, with due respect, she asks if the business is so good as you describe, why do you not loan your own funds?"*

"A fair question. This industry is highly regulated. I have applied for licenses to do that very thing. My papers should already be approved and I'm expecting to receive them any day now."

Katie spoke again. Pete translated, *"Would you consider a partnership?"* Pete then added, *"I have no interest in the business but my wife is open to the possibility."*

Albert paused at the suggestion, gave it thought, and answered, *"I would be willing to hire Mrs. Novak as an employee for six months to see how the profession fits her and to give her the opportunity to improve her English skills, to be able to work with English-speaking customers. At the end of the trial period, we can make a decision."*

Pete translated and Katie held up three fingers and responded in Croatian. *"Tell him I'll be ready in three months, not six,"* then also added, *"I'll leave you two to talk. You see if he seems to be on the level."*

Albert Lhormer, the transplanted German banker, listened as Pete translated Katie's comments. Katie turned on her heel and left the small office.

"Your wife is something special. I see in her a charm, wit, drive, and work ethic that could make the ideal business partner. If she were to join me in the loan business, we would both make money. She needs to polish her English skills. I'm willing to hire her to work in the office. Once she masters filing and improves her conversational English language, we can discuss a further business relationship."

Pete, still dressed in his fine wedding and funeral suit, dodged the puddles and animal excrement, hastening to return home. He recounted his conversation with Albert. Katie was excited at the opportunity. *"Old Man, you just watch me. I'll master this language and be the best loan agent in the office. Do you think I can do it?"*

Pete smiled. *"My dear, I've seen you be successful at everything you touch, from doing a foreman's job on our house, to running gambling nights, to selling whiskey and keeping the sheriff at bay. I would never bet against you. But this is a big step, even for you. I know how hard it is to learn another language. Though if it can be done, you'll do it. I'm sure of that."*

As he lit a hand-rolled cigarette he continued, *"I'll do what I can to help by tending the children, keeping the house in good order, and having dinner ready when you get home, just like you used to do for me."*

It took Katie just a little over two months to improve her English to the point that she conversed in English well enough to join Albert as an employee. Her golden touch was exactly what the business needed. Within three months the partnership solidified.

For her first big coup, she secured an open letter of credit from steel magnate Henry Clay Frick. With a nearly unlimited source of credit from the wealthy steel magnate, and ethnic customers who mistrusted Anglo-favoring institutions but trusted Katie, transactions at the Clairton Savings and Loan Company flowed like an untamed current.

Word spread and as the community's population boomed, so did the business. A natural businesswoman, Katie soon gained the confidence of immigrants and English speakers alike. Unlike the more traditional stodgy banks of the era, Albert and Katie's Clairton Savings and Loan company took chances on the newest Americans. The bets paid off in spades that dug the earth for countless new homes.

* * *

A sharp rap on the locked door of the Savings and Loan brought Katie back to the present day. Her stiff body rose from the chair. She unlatched the door and greeted the janitorial service crew.

"You clean up office and fix da broken window. I need run few errands. I probably be back before you finished. If you get done before I get back, lock door and leave keys with baker man Grisnik."

The janitors nodded and brought their equipment into the office to begin the task of removing red stains from the wall, floor, and desk, and repairing the broken window.

Katie's first order of business upon leaving the Saving and Loan office to the expertise of the cleanup crew included walking to the nearby funeral home operated by the tall, perfectly attired undertaker, Mr. Finney. Nobody seemed to know his first name, nor did they ask. Everybody in town simply called him Mr. Finney.

Earlier in the day a police officer stopped by the funeral parlor and per Katie's orders, directed Mr. Finney to have an employee retrieve Albert's body, take it to the mortuary, and hold it there until she came by with further instructions.

Mr. Finney answered the knock on the door with a smile of condolence. "Hello, Mrs. Novak. I'm so sorry for the loss of your business partner, Mr. Lhormer. What a fine man, loved and respected by all who knew him. How can I help to ease the pain in your heart?"

"Thank you, Mr. Finney. You always be gentleman. When I tell Kelly bring him here I forget Albert is of Hebrew race. I now on my way to see holy man for his religion. I don' know they traditions, but I not want you to do nothing that don' be proper or against religion beliefs of his people."

"I understand, Madam, and it is very gracious of you to consider Mr. Lhormer's creed. I have dealt with the Jewish community in the past and it is my belief that they will wish to handle the arrangements themselves. Do you know how to reach the town's rabbi?"

"I think so. Our company be finance building of new synagogue on Reed Street. I go there on my way home. If clergyman not there, I sure somebody tell me where find him."

"Fine. I'll wait to hear from you or a member of the synagogue."

"Thank you, Mr. Finney. Please send me bill for your services."

"There is no bill for you, Mrs. Novak. You and Mr. Lohrmer have given so much to this community. Give my best to your husband."

The rabbi took charge of Albert's body. According to his faith's tradition, a Shemira (guard) retrieved the body and stayed with it until burial. Members of a holy society cleaned him and dressed his body in a shroud, then placed him in a casket. Albert Lhormer was buried in a nearby cemetery the same day he died.

4

The Mystery Child

"…for at that moment Quasimodo was really beautiful. He was handsome — this orphan, this foundling, this outcast." —Victor Hugo

THE GIRL WAS STILL ASLEEP when Katie arrived. Pete had sent Danica home with great thanks and a loaf of his famous pogača: Slavic bread baked in the ashes of the fireplace.

Katie hugged and kissed both her children, then asked Pete, *"Did you talk to the girl?"*

"No, she's been sleeping since I got home. Danica said the child did not speak much of anything, other than fear she would be beaten."

"I guess she is still worried about breaking into the office. Let me go in and wake her."

Katie walked to the couch and smoothed the child's short golden hair, pasted against her forehead with perspiration. *"Wake up, little one."*

The child stretched and blinked her still-glassy eyes, but said nothing.

"What is your name, little one?"

The child stared blankly. Realizing she had spoken in Croatian, Katie repeated in English, "What you name, honey?"

The girl looked at Katie, then beyond to Pete and the children, but said nothing.

Katie spoke again, "Can you hear me?"

The girl nodded but did not speak.

"You understand me?"

She nodded again.

Several moments passed as the girl surveyed the room, the same room in which she had enjoyed a warm bath. The half-barrel tub sat across the room, having been emptied of the filthy, jet black bathwater.

Katie asked calmly, "What you name?"

All eyes were fixed on the interloper who again looked around the room and finally uttered flatly, "I don't know."

"Where you live?"

She gritted her teeth and closed her eyes tightly, trying to draw the information from her memory.

"I can't remember." Then incredulously she added, "I don't know who I am."

The child seemed sincere in her answers.

An air of anticipation hung over the room. Little Rûza spoke first. "If you don't have a name, I'll share mine with you. My name is Ruža, but if you're American, you can call me Rosie."

Katie reached around her daughter offering a one-arm hug, took a deep breath and gently asked, "What you do remember?"

The girl stared off into the distance for several moments, then spoke slowly. "I remember being hungry. Very hungry and cold. I wanted to find some money to buy something to eat. I broke a window. Went inside and found some coins in a desk. Then I tripped over ..."

She stopped speaking for a few moments and began to shudder. Her inflection and grammar changed as a blank stare crossed her face, then continued as though in another voice, "I tripped over it. I ain't never seen no dead body before ..."

Katie waved her hand to catch Pete's eye and commented, *"It's like two different people talking."*

The girl reacted to Katie's raised hand, becoming frightened. She placed her arms in a defensive motion, pleading, "Don' hit me no more. I jus' wanted ta' get somethin' ta eat."

Katie spoke deliberately and calmly, "Is okay, Honey. Nobody going hit you or hurt you. You safe here. You can tell me you name."

The girl shivered and closed her eyes tightly, trying as best she could to reach into her past for a name, then shook her head. "I don't remember. I'm sorry."

"How you no remember you name? Everybody knows name."

The girl again squeezed her eyes tightly and tried to recall. Tears rolled down her cheeks Her voice wavered. Clenching her teeth, she tried again but nothing came. "I can't remember. I don't know who I am."

Katie remained calm and spoke to the girl in nonthreatening tones. "You think real hard, honey. Tell me what you 'member. Anyting."

The girl began to reflect. "I remember walking along railroad tracks. Not sure where or for how long I walked the tracks. Days for sure. I remember that. I found some food in a trash bin behind a café near a train depot and ate it. The food made me sick to my stomach and came back up so I mostly ate berries after that. Lots of them grow along the track down to the river. Drank from springs running into the river but not much food besides berries.

"A train stood ready to leave at a depot and I climbed aboard when nobody was looking, and hid in the lavatory. But once the train started to move, I came out too soon and the conductor caught me and threw me off when the train stopped at the next station. I was so hungry. Walked along the tracks looking for some scraps or berries or anything to eat.

"I came upon some boys who were cooking something they had trapped. It might have been a rat but I didn't care because it smelled so good. I asked for some but they laughed and said something in another language. They thought I was a boy. I pointed to my mouth and asked again. One of the boys got up, motioned me over, then punched me in the face. The others threw rocks at me so I ran away back toward the train depot and hid under the steps that lead to the platform until after sunset.

"I think I fell asleep and waited until long after dark, then walked up the hill to town where the shops are. That is when I thought there might be some food or coins in an office. Maybe I could find something that I might use to buy or trade for some food. I saw a small window on the side of an office building and broke it to climb in. Found some coins in the desk and took them to use to buy food. Then I saw the brooch. I knew it was a sin to steal it and didn't mean to at first, but it looked so pretty. I'm sorry."

"That's good you start to remember. Try again think you name."

She concentrated as hard as she could but came up empty. "I just can't remember. Wait! I remember something else. A boy on the tracks. His name, he said … Zach was his name. He was nice to me. Told me if I wanted to survive on the tracks I better quit talking so prissy and learn to jaw rough, like other guys along the tracks."

"Okay, good. Do you remember anything else?"

"No, just in my head I keep hearing somebody screaming. Can't see who it is but somebody. A man keeps hitting and punching me. Trying to protect somebody but can't see who. It hurts when the man hits me and he throws me against a wall, but I don't cry. Another person is getting beaten worse than me. Begging for help. But who is it? I can't tell. I can't see their face."

"That good start for now. You say he throw you at wall. Was wall in house or outside?"

The girl thought for a minute. "Inside. All the beatings took place inside a house."

"You no be worry, child. We gon' help you. Give you place to sleep and food. Tomorrow we go see doctor. He gon' fine out why you no can remember name. For now, we all go eat supper. My old man, Pete, he fix up place for you sleep in kids' room."

The girl began to cry.

"Why you cry? Everything goin' be okay."

"Because you are being so nice to me."

The family had dinner together, complete with the newest member.

Once the two children and the girl were asleep, Pete and Katie repaired to the kitchen. Peter had been quiet during Katie's questioning and through dinner. Once alone, he asked, *"Well, Katie, what did she have to say, and what do you think?"*

Katie related what the girl had told her. *"She is a mystery, for sure, Old Man. I've never heard of anybody who didn't know their own name. Do you think it is possible?"*

Pete took a pinch of tobacco from his Cutty Pipe pouch, placed it onto a thin, white Zig-Zag paper, licked the edge, and twisted each end. The routine gave him time to reflect and let the silence stimulate thought. He lit the cigarette and took a deep drag, exhaling a series of perfectly formed rings.

"When I worked in Germany, Herr Richter hired a professor, Dr. Klaus Braun, to tutor me in the German language. You already know that. To improve my vocabulary, the professor often related studies to me that he'd read and written about, then asked me to repeat what he had just said. One study I remember told of a man who went to a large city on a business trip. While there a group of thugs attacked, beat, and robbed him."

"That's terrible. But what does the story have to do with the girl? Do you think a gang of thugs beat her? She obviously had nothing of value to steal."

He took another long drag on the cigarette then exhaled. *"I'm getting to that. The man was beaten senseless. He lay unconscious and near death in an alleyway for hours before being discovered and taken to a hospital for treatment. When he awoke, he couldn't remember anything about his life, including his name or his hometown or even his family."*

"Oh, my goodness. What happened to him?"

"The authorities searched while the man recovered from his injuries in a sanitarium. Eventually they discovered a missing persons bulletin that his wife

had filed. From that authorities were able to determine where he worked and reunited him with his family."

"Oh, thank heavens. So, then he remembered everything, right?"

"No, his wife and children remained strangers to him. Doctors examined him and determined the man to be in a state that in German is called amnesie. Professor Braun told me that sometimes memories can return, and in other cases they will not. There is no way of knowing."

"And you think that is what is wrong with the girl?"

"Possibly. When you take her to Dr. Rascati tomorrow ask if he thinks she needs a doctor who is a ... I don't know how to say it in English, but in German it is a 'psychologe'."

* * *

The following day Katie had a busy schedule. She did not think the mystery girl needed Dr. Rascati or any other regular physician. Aside from being a little malnourished, the girl appeared to be physically fit.

Her first order of business took place over the telephone. Katie phoned a client of the Clairton Savings and Loan, Dr. Roland Kunz. Originally from Europe, Dr. Kunz had financed his family home through her company.

He took the call immediately. "How can I help you Mrs. Novak. Is my note overdue?"

"No, Dr. Kunz. I have serious question 'bout girl just come into our life." Katie explained her dilemma and described the girl's symptoms.

"Most interesting. Let me make a phone call to a colleague and I'll get back to you directly."

Within an hour, Dr. Kunz called her back. "I contacted an old friend and former colleague, Dr. Fritz Gleirscher, a psychologist who now practices in Pittsburgh. We attended medical school together in Europe. When I described the symptoms to him he said he would be willing to evaluate the patient. His office is near the Penn Station on Liberty Avenue." Dr. Kunz gave Katie the address.

"When he can see us? Did you make appointment for us?"

"He'll work you in whenever you arrive. Today is a good day for him if you can make it."

"Thank you, Doctor. I take girl to him this afternoon and let you know what he say."

"You are most welcome, Mrs. Novak. I'll phone Dr. Gleirscher and let him know you'll see him after lunch today. One more thing. I heard about your partner, Mr. Lhormer. You have my deepest sympathy. Please let me know if there is anything I can do."

"You very nice for offer, Dr. Kunz. Thank you. Savings and Loan office gonna be close until we get everyting put back together. I let you know if we need anything but for now we okay. Thank you for ask."

She replaced the phone and gathered up her newest family member. The mystery girl cleaned up nicely but she still looked more like a boy than a girl, especially in Danica's sons hand-me-down clothes.

Before boarding the train for Pittsburgh, found Katie and the girl in Skapik's clothing store, preparing to outfit the young lady with female undergarments and a few changes of clothes. Katie took pleasure in helping appoint her new charge, striving to dress the child in the same fashion that her late partner, Albert Lhormer, had dressed her.

The salesgirl, Mary Louise, knew Katie well. The two of them, similar in age, occasionally spent Saturday mornings looking through catalogues to find the latest fashions. Katie seemed to have a knack of finding just the right outfit that would flatter her but not be overwhelming. Albert taught her well.

Chic women's fashion designs of the first World War era reflected a military look that included military style tunic jackets, belts, and even epaulets. Gender-dictated clothing relaxed. Skirts became shorter and colors muted. By the time the war ended, skirts grew narrow again and hemlines dropped below the calf. Katie and Mary Louise kept up on all the latest fashions.

Mary Louise approached and greeted Katie. "Good morning, Mrs. Novak. I'm so sorry to hear of Albert's passing. You have our sympathy. How can we help you today?"

"Thank you for you kind thought. We need couple outfits for this young lady. She is guest in my house. What you have for her?"

She turned to the girl. "Oh, come this way, miss. We will get you dressed in the latest styles."

"I want you dress her nice, like Albert dress me. Let her wear one complete outfit today, from underwear to fancy coat before we leave. I want her look nice for Pittsburgh trip today. I would like for you deliver other clothes to my house when they ready. Take clothes she have on and send to my neighbor Danica with thank-you card and voucher for ten dollar store credit."

She picked up a piece of jewelry and added, "When you deliver, please include this, and make nice note for thank her for let us borrow them clothings."

Mary Louise noted Katie's requests and nodded her assent.

Turning to the girl, Katie added, "we gon' haf good time today."

Without further introduction, she motioned toward the girl. "I like get her two, maybe three outfit. One for travel, one for dress up, and one for every day."

Mary Louise eyed the mystery girl for several moments, then began. "Waistlines are dropping. It's the latest trend from Paris and New York. I can show you a full hip-length tunic over a narrow, draped skirt. No more wide at the hips and narrow at the ankles. 'Hobble skirts,' as we call them in the business, are out. That style made long strides impossible. The trend today is for loose and softly defined waistlines, dropping to the natural waistline, calf length. Women can now walk with a sense of purpose."

The girl stood quietly, listening to the interchange between Katie and Mary Louise.

Katie smiled, "You sound just like Albert when you talk 'bout fashion. What else you got?"

"Well, let's see. We'll tailor her a suit, matching skirt and jacket for travel. How about a hat?"

"Hat good with suit. How 'bout for scarf, too?"

"Mrs. Novak, you'd better not go into the fashion clothing business. You'd be too keen a competitor. Drive me out of business. A scarf would fit the ensemble perfectly."

Katie chuckled and winked. "No be worry 'bout me get in you fashion business. I got plenty keep me busy. You safe for now."

Mary Louise spoke to the girl, "Your short hair makes a fashion statement as well. You can wear it as you have it, or if you prefer a fuller look on top, I can have a postiche made up for you. That's a small, individual wig. We can add curls or even buns if you like. You see, styles are changing quickly. The new fashions are considered very practical and patriotic."

Speaking for the first time since entering the store, the girl addressed Mary Louise. "Gosh, you know a lot about clothes. I didn't know styles changed so much."

"Oh yes, as the War took young men from the work force, more women assumed jobs, demanding clothing better suited for their added roles. Dark colors and simple cuts became the fashion. Cumbersome underskirts disappeared and dress hemlines were shortened to mid-calf. We women are making fashion statements. I believe we will one day even have the right to vote. But listen to me prattle on." Mary Louise took a deep breath. "Now, what shall we do about footwear?"

Turning again to the girl, Mary Louise asked, "How about a pair with criss-crossing straps? Very in. Also, for everyday you'll need a good pair of sensible laced shoes with rounded toes, like the ones I'm wearing."

She lifted her skirt to mid-calf to show the shoes, then led the two women to the shoe display. Picking up a pair she pointed to the shoe's construction. "See the lower wedge heels? Very comfortable."

An hour later the two women sat in in comfortable, first class cabin aboard the local train headed for Pittsburgh. The girl wore a striking new outfit, looking every bit the proper young lady.

Upon arriving at the psychologist's office, a receptionist greeted them.

Katie spoke first. "We here to see the doctor. Dr. Gleirscher. We referred by Dr. Roland Kunz of Clairton."

The receptionist smiled as she pushed a button on a device at the corner of her mahogany desk. "Won't you please be seated. The doctor will be with you momentarily."

She barely finished the sentence when a tall, slender man wearing a monocle over his right eye opened the door to the waiting area. He was followed by another man, formally dressed in a three-piece seersucker suit. The first man spoke with a European accent.

"Good morning. I am Dr. Fritz Gleirscher, the psychologist referred by our mutual friend Dr. Kunz. I have invited my colleague Dr. Vitori to join us for the examination."

Dr. Fritz Gleirscher had been educated in Germany and Austria, studying under some of the finest and most notable physicians and psychologists in the world. He stood over six-and-a-half feet tall, had a receding hairline of short, closely cropped red hair, A twisted handlebar moustache below his nose pointed in opposite directions. He wore a fine tailored worsted wool suit with subtle blue thread that hinted at a square design.

The second doctor nodded and Gleirscher continued, "Dr. Kunz briefed me on the situation. I have asked Dr. Vitori to do a separate evaluation. He is a professor of linguistics at the University of Pittsburgh. Dr. Vitori has done extensive studies of dialects, accents, and manners of speech of area residents. My own expertise will include the examination of the patient's body and mind. Dr. Vitori will make note of the manner of speech and suggest possible geographical locations of origin. We will perform a series of tests on the subject, then analyze the results to determine whether the data will give you some of the answers you seek."

Katie nodded. The girl sat quietly.

"Please step into the examination room so we may begin."

Katie and the girl followed the two men into the inner offices.

For the next few hours, the girl, or as the doctor referred to her, the subject, underwent a series of thorough physical and psychological examinations. When the exploration was completed, he directed Katie and her charge to the waiting room for refreshments as the two men pored over the results.

Within an hour the analysis had been completed. Dr. Gleirscher invited Katie and the girl into his study. Thick pile carpet covered a highly-polished dark wood floor. Books filled shelves on three of the four walls. The fourth wall was mostly taken up by a huge picture window that overlooked the three-river confluence of Pittsburgh.

The two females sat on high-back plush leather chairs and the psychologist took a seat behind his desk. Dr. Vitori remained standing.

The girl studied the view outside the window, then spoke. "I see the Monongahela. That must be the Allegheny River meeting it to form the Ohio."

Speaking with an Austrian accent Dr. Gleirscher took the lead. "I see you are a student of our local geography. Have you seen the three-river confluence before?"

She shook her head. "I'm sorry to interrupt you, Sir."

"Not to worry, my dear. Let me give you a little medical history. Some thirty years ago a German physicist, Wilhelm Rontgen, discovered a machine that allows us to look inside the body. This machine, uses what Rontgen calls 'X-rays,' and allows us to see organs and bones. It has been a boon to medical science. I have one such machine and used it in my examination for this case."

He paused, inhaling a breath from the pipe bowl he held tightly, then continued. "In my professional opinion, the subject, Caucasian female, is between thirteen and fifteen years of age. The X-ray machine revealed several broken ribs and a broken arm that had not been properly set, but healed on their own. Also, a fractured hip that has since healed, hence she walks with a slight limp. Those mended breaks and fractures likely did not occur from untreated falls or other natural child behavior. Rather, I am led to conclude the subject has been physically abused."

The girl sat stoically during the analysis, but Katie blanched at the thought of the maltreatment she must have endured

The doctor continued. "As far as the psychological examination results are concerned, I find her to be of well-above average intelligence, highly astute, in fact, honest and forthright, and severely amnesiac, most likely caused by a traumatic event or series of events.

"Her memory may or may not return. At this point it is impossible to predict. The slang language that you described when she first came into your life, as well as the short-cropped hair, boy's clothing and mannerisms were likely defense mechanisms, a persona that she created to survive in a hostile environment.

During my conversation with her I found her to have a vocabulary commensurate with a well- educated adult." He turned to his colleague. "Dr. Vitori will now provide further analysis."

The professor took center stage and began as though he were giving a classroom lecture. "My area of expertise has to do with mannerisms and speech pathology. Speech patterns have local and regional nuances. From your manner of speaking, for example, Mrs. Novak, I would posit that you grew up in Eastern Europe in the vicinity of the City of Karlovac and the area along the Kupa River."

He paused. Katie nodded and sat without speaking as the professor continued. "I further would extrapolate from your speech that you currently live along the Monongahela River and that languages come easy to you."

This time Katie was quick to respond. "You correct, Sir. I be surprise you know that just from how I talk."

Dr. Vitori continued, "I wanted to lay the groundwork to lend credence to my analysis of the young lady's origins. From carefully listening to her manner of speech, colloquial terms used, and general lilt of her verbiage, my conclusion is that she established her speech patterns in southwestern Pennsylvania near northern West Virginia. Her manner of speaking suggests a home in which both formal language, meaning that of a moderately well-educated parent, was spoken as well as more recent introduction of a less formal household resident, perhaps a cousin or uncle who came to live in the household. As noted earlier, her most recent expressions suggest an adapted language to suit her environment. From what she reported, she can remember assuming the role of a ragamuffin boy in order to survive in the rough and tumble environment of homelessness. That self-reporting is consistent with her speech patterns."

Once the professor took a seat next to the desk, Katie spoke. "So what you think, Doctor? Will girl remember who is she or where family lives?"

Dr. Gleirscher responded, directly to the girl. "The mind is the most fascinating of all human components. It has been studied in depth for many years but we are still able to predict little of its behavioral outcomes. My best prescription is to build your life as though it started today. That would begin by giving you a name and a purpose in life."

Turning his eye contact to Katie, the psychologist asked, "What would you like to name her?"

Katie smiled at the doctor, then at the girl, and said, "If she is smart like you say, and harmed in past, it not be up to me up for name her."

Turning to the child, Katie declared, "Is you life, my dear. You choose you own name. What you like for be call?"

The girl, who had been silent throughout the analysis of her condition, sat pensively for several minutes, then finally spoke. "Mrs. Novak, you and your family have given me so much in such a short period of time. If I ever remember my past, we can deal with that at the time it happens. But for now, I would like my name to be Hope, for that's what you and your wonderful family have given me. And if you have no objection, I would be honored to use your last name as well. Hope Novak. My life began when you rescued me. You told me on the train ride today that you lost somebody very dear to you when I came into your life. Perhaps a small glimmer of his soul might have been transferred to me."

It was Dr. Gleirscher's turn to sit stoically. Despite his formal demeanor and professional behavior, his eyes became glassy at the scene before him. "I think that is a wonderful idea, Hope Novak. Let me be the first to call you by your new name. But I must also caution you that the possibility remains that all or part of your memory may return. Should that occur, I want you to contact me immediately and we will have you return to work on the next phase of your development. Otherwise, come to see me in three months and we will do a review and see what changes have come into your new life."

Katie and Hope stood and spoke in unison. "Thank you, Dr. Gleirscher and Dr. Vitori."

Katie added, "Please send me bill. You have address of my office on card."

The two women hugged, and as they left the office the psychologist whispered to Katie, "You will not receive a bill for today's session. This has been one of the most meaningful experiences I have had in my professional career."

The ride home was jubilant. The two of them, both child prodigies, each with a challenging past, made up a game. Katie started it. "What name machine in doctor's office?"

"Oh, that's easy. An X-ray machine. Who invented it?"

Katie thought a minute before answering. "Wilhelm Rontgen. How 'bout you tell me where I grow up."

"In a village on the Kupa River near Karlovac."

And so it went for the duration of the hour-long train ride. A woman and a girl, both with photographic memories, each trying unsuccessfully to stump the other.

5

Katie's Gift

"Dreams are the touchstone of our character." —Henry David Thoreau

IN SLEEP IT SPOKE TO HER, in dreams it came. It hovered deep inside her head, and always spoke her name. It was a power that she was powerless to explain.

The last thing she remembered before waking that morning, the recurring scene in the recurring dream: Katie Novak, adult businesswoman became the schoolchild, Katarina Radić.

* * *

The guile of the teacher-nun reached its limit that spring morning. She'd overslept in her small slanted cell, furnished with a few pieces of bland mismatched furniture, well-worn to its tan and chestnut brown roots. Startled, she leapt from the bed with a start, knocking the repainted bookstand onto her legs, grimacing at the pink brush-burn abrasion left on her calf, and hurriedly slipping into her clean but well-used habit.

The nun skipped morning vespers, risking the wrath of the principal, who most likely already considered her an infidel. Racing into the recently completed but still shabby coffee lounge, the novice grabbed a steaming cup of coffee that awaited one of the other sisters. One huge gulp of lava-hot liquid snapped her to reality as it burned her lips and seared her throat.

A muffled scream erupted. The vestal spat the seething libation, spewing it onto the wall of the tiny room and splattering dribbles over the front of the dusty grey, faded garb she had laundered the previous night.

A protruding nail from the unfinished coffee room table snagged and ripped a triangular hole in the garment as she rushed to her classroom. "Damn it!" she mouthed silently in spite of herself.

Ahead of her, sounds of unruly students hushed when the glowering principal stepped into the unmanned teaching space. By the time the teacher arrived, a somber class awaited her, under the piercing glare of an even more somber headmistress.

The school's director, heavy cross dangling from a chain around her neck, assumed a leaning, angry stance, shooting a look that served as a reprimand toward the tardy instructor. Piercing eyes drained what little fortitude remained in the gut of the hapless teacher. At least she escaped total humiliation of the principal's pointing a bony finger, as she would have done to a recalcitrant child. Instead, the dignity of the teacher-nun was temporarily spared an upbraiding in front of her students. Surely that would come in the office after the school day ended.

Without a word, the director turned on her heel and strode out of the quiet classroom. An air of superiority followed her turbulent wake.

The coffee stains on the teacher's dull, discolored habit permeated the v-shaped rip from the nail, but the stain no longer smelled of the aroma of mountain grown coffee. Instead it reeked with the stench of humiliation, anger, and frustration. This Sister was in no mood to be trifled with that morning.

All but one child in the strict classroom quaked in fear, first of the principal, and now of the disconcerted teacher. On her best days, the teacher-nun found little Katarina Radić to be a challenge. On this day, she had zero patience. Storm clouds brewed on her emotional horizon.

Katarina Radić saw through the teacher's emotional storm clouds. Always upbeat and ready with a quip or explanation to assigned school problems, the child did not perceive the teacher's reactions to her out-bursts as a series of unfortunate events, but as a chance to exercise her ever-inquisitive mind. The combination brilliance and creativity that made her different from other children were assets at home but potential liabilities in the strict Catholic school. She simply did not fit the mold of an ideal, obedient, quiet, pious little schoolgirl. Her curiosity made a habit of stumping classmates and often the teacher; a trait not lost on the nun who punished the youngster almost daily. Despite her diminutive size, the girl in the dream stood tall, refusing to kowtow to the adult.

The instructor tried various techniques to curb the enthusiasm of the child. Some days the seven-year-old's mouth was taped shut. Other times her feet and legs were tied to the legs of the desk to keep her from standing to get the teacher's attention. The moppet responded to the punishment with aplomb, pretending it did not bother her. But it did. On this day, in this dream, an unstoppable force would clash with an immovable object in a storm not witnessed before in the history of the parochial schoolhouse.

Once the teacher calmed herself from her series of morning traumas, she asked, in an unsteady voice, "Who can answer today's problem?"

Pressing a wooden pointer against the black slate board, she scoured the room for any child except Katarina to offer an answer. Nearly every student stared blankly away from the teacher's glare, or buried their heads in a book, an age-old practice of hiding to avoid eye contact, hoping not to be called upon.

Every student quaked under the duress. Every student except one. Katarina bounced in her seat, waving her hand in the air, shouting, "I know! I know!

The exasperated teacher attempted to ignore the child but the sum total of this morning's frustrations had reached its limit. Katarina's exuberance became the tipping point and the teacher-nun's patience and self-control became undone. Taking three or four giant steps toward the imp, she strode to the back of the room where the child sat and brought her hickory pointer down hard across Katarina's back, again, and again, and again.

The small classroom became a two-person war zone.

With each flog of the stick she grunted at the pupil, "Can't you just shut up for once? I'm sick! And tired! Of you! Always trying! To outshine! Me and the other children! Little miss know-it-all!"

The rant continued. "You are a millstone around my neck! My curse from the devil for something one of my ancestors must have done in another life! Do you have any idea how much better this classroom would be without you?"

With each sentence segment the nun's voice became louder as she repeatedly struck Katarina across the shoulders and back until the wooden pointer broke in two. One half flew across the room, the other half still grasped tightly in the teacher's trembling hand.

Katarina's back and shoulders stung from the sharp cracks of the pointer. Strident red marks and welts appeared under her neatly-pressed blue school uniform, but she would not give the teacher the satisfaction of knowing how much the weapon had hurt her. Katarina, too iron-willed, steadfastly refused to give in to the teacher's bullying, however harsh and vicious.

After what seemed like hours to Katarina, the pummeling stopped. The exhausted, quaking nun stood over the child, her voice wavering, "Are you ready to be still now?"

Katarina somehow gathered herself. Choking back tears, the schoolgirl mumbled loudly enough that in the frozen quiet of the classroom both teacher and children clearly heard. "You old cow. Why don't you stick that pointer up your habit?"

Moist eyes stared up at her torturer. Teeth clenched, awaiting the next barrage of punishment, the iron-willed child refused to give the nun the satisfaction of surrender.

A collective gasp, the only sound to be heard, rippled through the classroom. Not a single child moved. Not one breath of air rustled the paper on any desk, nor a pleat in the children's school uniforms, nor the nun's torn habit.

The stillness of the moment broke with the nun's total loss of composure. Screaming loudly enough to wake the dead in the school's churchyard cemetery, the pointer, broken half of the stick in her hand aimed toward the classroom door.

"Out! Out! You child of the devil! Get out of this room and do not ever return! I don't want to see you and I don't want to see your guardian ever again! Go! Be gone!" The teacher panted heavily. Her screeching voice resonated throughout the hallways of the small schoolhouse.

Katarina slowly stood at her desk, feeling blood oozing from stinging welts on her body. Turning away from the quivering nun, she picked up her lunch pail, walked ten paces toward the door, then, still hiding her tears from the other children, she bent at the waist, wiggled her derriere at the nun, and ran from the building.

The screaming and screeching brought other teachers and the principal racing to the classroom, but by the time they arrived Katarina had disappeared. The teacher stood next to the unoccupied student desk in a semi-trance, a babbling bundle of nerves.

The principal spoke quietly, wrapping a steady arm around the teacher's waist. "Come with me, Sister." She nodded to one of the several postulants gathered there. "Sister Mary Catherine will cover your class."

The principal escorted the traumatized teacher out of the classroom, down the dank cloister to her quarters. "Lie down, Sister. I'll get you a cool towel."

The teacher-nun remained in bed the rest of the day, eyes closed and blathering to herself, a cool compress draped across her forehead.

* * *

The dream ended abruptly. Katie woke with a start, still in that netherworld between asleep and awake, eyes clenched shut and confused to whether she was conscious or reposing. The nightmare came from long ago. Beads of sweat oozed from the pores of Katie's forehead. Unable to fully awaken, she dropped back into a state of slumber, allowing the dream to continue.

Tossing and turning as she slept, wrapping blankets around herself, the pace of the dream quickened. Like flashes from modern moving pictures at the local movie house, scenes rapidly changed.

A hastily-conceived venture to America. Arranged marriage to a stranger ten years her senior. The building of a house with bare, calloused hands. Neighbors helping. Husband banned from working in the mill. A thriving business for her ...

The dream again ended abruptly. This time bright rays fell across her face. The burst of sunlight burned her eyelids shut. As the sun moved higher in the sky, more radiance joined the dayglow, sneaking through the huge plate glass picture window at the foot of her bed, and onto her face, dazzling the sleeping beauty. Harsh insolation revealed the milky-white complexion of a woman whose skin tone suffered from too much time spent indoors.

She squeezed her flimsy clamshell shutters together, trying to keep the harsh reality of daylight at bay. Still drowsy, her mind formed the first words of the morning. *"If eyes are windows to the soul, I want my soul locked tightly inside, behind a drawn shade. Morning is not my favorite time of day."*

Somewhere in a distant corner of dreamland came a jarring voice, howling her name in a soft whisper. *"Katie, Monday morning. Another day at the office waits for you."*

She pulled a pillow over her head but to no avail. More sunbeams intruded. She wanted to continue the portending dream but like it or not, the rhythm of her circadian clock rang in the first day of a new work week. She would reopen the business after a week of mourning Albert's death.

"Vat time, Old Man?" she mumbled groggily to the shadowy figure that had been standing in the doorway. In reply she heard only gentle thumping of feet on stairs as Pete returned to his morning routine.

Katie sat erect, stretched, and again pried open her lids, spreading them with her thumb and forefinger. Squinting the orbs several times, she allowed the brightness of the birth of a new day to penetrate in small doses.

Wiping away the fog of sleep like a child, with balled-up fists, she stretched again, then lazily abdicated the coziness of the fluffy eiderdown wrap that ensconced her body.

Eventually Katie stood and arranged her twisted nightgown as the silky teal-blue comforter slid from the bed, wrapping itself around her thick ankles. Kicking the bedclothes aside, she strode to the dresser. Water from the half-filled basin atop the chest of drawers cooled her face and slowly removed its mask of slumber.

"Why mornings no come in afternoon? Be better for me, but not for business."

Slowly turning from the bureau, she studied her reflection in the mahogany wood-framed full-length mirror. The looking glass cast back a plump Rubenesque figure, considered attractively ample in the early twentieth century. Her image revealed an alluring woman, pretty without the waif-like body and athletic build she'd brought from Croatia. Had Katie Novak lived in the seventeenth century instead of the twentieth, she certainly would have graced a canvas as one of artist Peter Paul Ruben's fleshy models. But she knew nothing of such things. She knew only of her business, her husband, and her children, and now of her recently-adopted charge, Hope Novak.

Dipping a washcloth in the basin, she sponge-bathed using long, lazy strokes.

"Things be look up for me," mused Katie Novak, speaking in her singular broken language to the mirror's image, "I miss Albert for sure, but when I come this country, I be little girl with big dreams. Now big girl with big business, two baby, old man for take care, new girl, and house. I got nice life. Worst ting is get dressed in fine lady's clothes for work. Need help for dat."

Dropping the damp cloth back into the basin, she reached for the clothing Pete had hung for her before setting out to do his morning chores. Smoothing invisible wrinkles from her freshly ironed attire, she struggled to pull the full skirt over her portly hips before raising her voice, "Hey Old Man, come lace me up."

Pete, patiently enjoying breakfast with their two children and adopted teen, reached across the table to wipe egg drippings from the little ones' gooey chins and oatmeal from the table with a dish cloth. "Keep eating your breakfast. You too, Hope. Papa be come right back."

Little Ruža, age three, and eighteen-month-old Petey smiled as they watched their father's every move. Hope smiled, too. Still unable to recall anything before her arrival to Clairton, she felt that she'd been given a fresh and new lease on life.

Hope also began to understand Pete's short phrases spoken in a foreign language, and Pete attempted to integrate some English into his vocabulary. He had difficulty pronouncing her name. Hard as he tried, "Hope" came out of his mouth as "Oop."

"Oop, you wach leetle ones for minute. I be come right back."

Hanging the soiled dish cloth over the back of his chair, Pete hiked up his Blue Buckle Overalls and once again took the steps two at a time. He loved this time of day, family all together and early morning chores completed. He had already milked the cow, fed the chickens, gathered eggs, and cooked breakfast for the children. Now he hurried to help his lovely Katie dress for work.

Katie, finally fully awake, listened as thumps on the stairs grew louder until Pete reached the top, turned into the master bedroom and called out, giving thought to his good fortune. "I'm the luckiest man in America!"

During his youth as an indentured servant, and even his early days in America, Peter Novak could not have imagined owning his own home and small farm, having three wonderful children, two by birth and one adopted, and a lovely, successful businesswoman as a wife.

He strode into the bedroom, picked up the discarded comforter and tossed it onto the four-poster bed that he would make after Katie left for work. *"Okay, my beautiful bride, we will get you ready for your customers."*

"Clients, Old Man, dey clients, no customer."

"Clients, customers, same thing."

"Cow, horse, same ting, too?"

He chuckled. *"Okay, you win. We'll get you ready for your clients."*

Conversation from the family home regularly rang out in a discordance of Bosnian, Serbian, and Croatian languages, all Balto-Slavic, and similar enough that a speaker of one comprehends the others. Most immigrants to the area spoke a pidgin conglomeration that was understood by all. Katie struggled to add the English language needed to operate her business to her repertoire. She'd mastered the message if not the syntax.

"You men so lucky. Pair pants. Shirt. Work boots. Take you two shakes of lamb's tail for get dress. I haf take all morning. One day womens gon' haf easy job dress. Like man."

The husband spoke practically no English, choosing instead to converse in his native Bosnian language, or in a pinch, German. Whenever Katie prodded him to speak in English Pete responded, *"I speak two languages. That is all that fits in my brain. I'm too old to learn another. Besides, I'm a farmer. My plants understand me. My animals understand me. My family understands me. Anybody else with a question can ask you in English."*

"You crazy, Old Man. Help me finish dress. I no want be late for open office."

Beams of light spilling throughout the room and onto the unmade poster bed beckoned the couple to the large window of the second story master bedroom. An expanse of beauty stood before them. Steel mills belched filthy black smoke that meant prosperity for their community. Behind the bustling mills ran the mighty Monongahela River, its forward surge making a mad dash downstream toward Pittsburgh. Beyond the river, a sandy bank against a hillside of green grass, shaded by large trees of a yet-unnamed hollow. The stunning view, clearly one of the best in the bottom land of Clairton, Pennsylvania, had become their exclusive panorama.

Katie peered through the large window, across the river, and along the rolling hills, gazing lazily as a breeze created a whirlwind that scooped up piles of leaves scattered among the massive oak trees. She kept an eye on the leaves, watching them dance as she held in her stomach, twisted and contorted her body to help her husband with his task of dressing a lady in her early nineteenth century attire. She moved in time with the blowing leaves that hinted of fall colors to come; yellow, orange, red, and brown waiting to replace the green of late summer.

"I give you credit, Old Man. You pick nice spot for build house."

Pete responded with a manly grunt. As Katie tucked several locks of errant hair into her tightly-wound chignon, Pete pulled and strained, wrenching the long skirt over her head. The stubborn garment fell into place beneath her white starched bodice. The dressing dance ended. He helped cinch, tie, tug, hook, clasp, and otherwise served as an expert clothier for his young spouse, then kissed her on the cheek and returned downstairs to finish feeding the children.

Pete cooked a second breakfast of bacon and eggs while Katie finished dressing in a conservative black suit over a plain white blouse. Many days she dressed smartly to the nines, but this day she planned to do some office cleaning and rearranging so she wore less formal attire.

She arrived in the kitchen, kissed the little ones, and enjoyed the morning repast.

"Okay, Old Man, I got be go work now," Katie announced as she kissed the children again. "You baby be good for Papa. Hope, you help do what Pete show you. But start Wednesday, I gon' bring you to office to learn trade. You need be able take care you self. Never know what be happen in life."

"Yes, Ma'am."

Pete spoke to Katie, *"We'll have a good time in the garden. My two helpers pull weeds better than I do, even if they grab a healthy vegetable every once in a while. My training in Germany has not been needed here before young Hope came to us. But now I've become the teacher and I'll show Hope how to keep a proper house, set a proper table, and maybe teach her a bit of the German language to boot."*

An avid farmer and devout homebody, Pete thoroughly enjoyed tending to the home, his garden, and children while his wife grew the booming business in the small office on the hill. Both spouses did exactly what suited them best.

As Katie left the house she called back, "Old Man, check top step. Feels loose to me."

"No be worry. She be good like new when you come home."

Setting a strong pace, the brisk walk up the hill several blocks to her office refreshed her.

6

Homer Hammer, Freelance Writer

"Journalism is the first rough draft of history." —Oscar Wilde.

HOMER HAMMER AND MEI LAMISON spent many days and evenings together during their Northern Virginia high school years. Fellow classmates teased them, calling them an old married couple. Their relationship, though intense, focused not on romance of each other, but writing for the school newspaper. A platonic, rather than romantic, alliance tied the two together as co-editors of their school newspaper, *The Virginian*. And their senior yearbook, Precious Moments, yielded top-notch results and won both them and their school many awards and accolades.

Homer, clearly the more adventuresome of the two, saw himself not only as co-editor of the newspaper, but as an investigative reporter, rooting through documents like a pig searching for truffles. His results often led nowhere, but occasionally unearthed deeply buried secrets for stories. He discovered a secret White Feather group in the community.

The story began, *A white feather has traditionally been as symbol of cowardice to shame men, targeting those who had not enlisted in the military, especially during wartime. The movement began in England in the eighteenth century, and is so named after cockfighting roosters. The belief is that poultry that sported white feathers would not fight.*

Despite the custom being one mostly occurring in Britain and its territories, similar groups showed up on American soil. Homer and Mei authored and published an essay under a dual byline. Their essay, *Cowardice on Campus*, won a statewide award. The recognition and accompanying award earned both Mei and Homer college scholarship offers.

The morning after Mei received her scholarship offer in the mail she rushed to school to share the news with her best friend. "Homer, I'm dancing on air. I'm so proud I can't stand it! Look at this letter. A college offered me a full scholarship to study in their journalism department. I want to be just like Peggy Hull."

"Who?"

"Peggy Hull. Her real name is Henrietta Eleanor Goodnough. What a woman! She was embedded with the troops that chased Pancho Villa across Mexico, plus she is one of the most accomplished writers in America."

"Oh, I remember. You did a story on her. I'm sure you'll be every bit as successful as Miss Hull. The offer is fantastic, Mei. You deserve it. One day you'll be more famous a writer than your idol, Peggy Hull, and I can tell all my friends that we wrote together in high school."

Mei blushed. "Come on, Homer. You know you did most of the research. You chase a story like a bulldog. What will you do after graduation? Have you picked out a college?"

"Not sure about college, Mei. My grades aren't spectacular and my test scores stink. I got one nibble from a small college in Alabama. Not too exciting."

"But you — you're the one who did all the work on *Cowardice*. Your writing is fantastic. I wish I had your talent. I just touched it up. If you don't get the school you want, why not go straight into the world of work? I know you'll get a byline."

Homer smiled. "From your lips to God's ears. I'd like to do just that, Mei. I've sent resumes to newspapers up and down the Eastern Seaboard. Nobody seems to be hiring."

"Well, if a career in newspaper is what you want, become a stringer. Write stories on sports and politics, two high-interest topics with never enough coverage. Submit them on spec. Once they see your style, the papers will be clamoring to hire you."

Homer laughed. "Thanks, Mei. If I ever go into politics, you'll be my campaign manager, for sure."

Mei graduated as class valedictorian and took advantage of her scholarship to attend college. Homer, with considerably humbler scholastic achievements, earned the accolade, "Boy Most Likely to Succeed."

Homer eschewed his lone partial scholarship offer and stayed home. He believed he had newsprint in his blood and had dreams of becoming a newspaper writer and editor. He peppered news editors with dozens of unsolicited freelance articles, sending them to local newspapers in Northern Virginia and as far away as New York and Boston, but his name on a byline remained unseen for the longest time.

The result of fate, chance, or Kismet, events usually happen unexpectedly. What would become his first big break came as the result of a broken leg — not his.

The aspiring newsman Homer Hammer lived in a small loft upstairs of his parents' house in Alexandria, Virginia. Engrossed in his latest freelance story about the country's abuse of Civil War veterans, he pounded the keys of an ancient second-hand typewriter on this particular day. So focused was he that he did not realize his mother had entered the room.

"Homer, stop that racket for a minute. We received a telegram from your Aunt Margaret. You know Dad's brother, Uncle Bert, passed away last year and she's been living alone ever since. Well, she took a fall down the cellar stairs in her home and fractured a leg. She needs somebody to tend her for a few weeks until she's able to manage on her own. I volunteered you. Are you up for a few weeks' vacation in Pennsylvania?"

Homer stopped pounding and looked up. "What did you say, Mother?"

His mother was more direct this time. "Would you mind going to tend your Aunt Margaret while she recuperates from a broken leg?"

He pondered his mother's request for several moments. Her tone suggested less of a request and more of an order. The lad responded. "A fractured leg. A broken ankle, arm, collarbone, displaced knee. Could a single catastrophe lead to a writer's success? Did Van Gogh sacrifice an ear?"

"Oh, Homer, you do talk in riddles at times."

Homer had written voraciously and sent stories almost daily to area newspapers on topics ranging from sports and politics to meetings of the local Women's Book Club, but received no nibbles. He begged the editor of the Chesapeake Ledger for a job as a copy boy or an assistant researcher to any of the byline writers, but the editor told him to get some experience first. He repeated his mantra to himself, *How the hell can a person get experience if nobody will hire him without it?*

Pondering his mother's request/command briefly, he answered, "I guess so. I've tried every slant I could think of in this hamlet. Maybe I need some fresh faces. Or perhaps I should say 'dirty faces,' of the coal miners and steel workers. Doesn't she still live in that dirty old steel mill and coal mining town outside Pittsburgh? We used to visit them when I was small. I still remember gagging on the smoke."

"That's right. She lives in the small village of Clairton. It's not Alexandria for sure, but you will find a different perspective and that might help with fresh ideas for your writing. You can take the train to Pittsburgh, then transfer onto a local hop to Clairton. I told her you'd do it for love of family, but you know Margaret. She'll insist on paying you something."

He thought for a minute, then offered her a quoted reaction, "Go West, young man, go West and grow up with the country ..."

"What?"

"That's a quote from the famous newspaper editor, Horace Greely. He's one of my idols. I'll be following his advice."

"I think he was talking about the wild west, with cowboys and Indians. Pittsburgh isn't exactly that, but it isn't Washington or Alexandria either."

With a combination of chagrin and wanderlust, he retorted, "Greely also said, 'Washington is not a place to live in. The rents are high, the food is bad, the dust is disgusting, and the morals are deplorable.'"

"Oh Homer, you have the most interesting way of putting things. Aunt Margaret will love your little quips."

"Let me get my things together. I can leave tomorrow."

"Wonderful! I'll wire her that you're coming. Be sure to take her address."

* * *

Homer looked a sight as he headed for the railway station. Bushy red hair piled high on his head and flopping over his eyes, a well-worn bowler hat, and a trunk that weighed nearly as much as his own slender body. The combination presented a curious spectacle. Dragging his luggage to the train, he was trailed by a trunk strapped to a two-wheel dolly. The crate contained just two changes of clothing and underwear. The rest of the space inside the chest took the form of his trusty typewriter, numerous pads of paper, a cache of pencils, two pairs of sturdy walking shoes, and a second beat-up bowler hat with a square paper that read, PRESS, carefully placed inside the band.

"Check the bag for you, Sir?" asked the porter as Homer heaved the contraption onto the loading dock.

"No, thank you. I'll just take this inside with me. I don't want it to get lost or misplaced."

The Redcap, a husky black man well over six feet tall, huge shoulders tapering to a smaller, but still substantial waist, spoke patiently. "I'm afraid that trunk won't fit in the passenger section of the train. Even if it could, the equipment you have it attached to is not permitted in your car. It must ride in the baggage car."

Homer was stymied for a moment. "That locker contains everything that I need for my work. I can't take the chance of it getting lost or damaged."

"May I see your ticket, Sir? I might have a solution."

The redheaded teen fished the ticket from his pocket and handed the crumpled document to the porter.

"Ah, good. You're going to Pittsburgh and on to Clairton."

Homer nodded, "I'm going to visit my aunt. I'm a newspaper writer."

"My, that is impressive, Sir. A newspaper reporter. Impressive indeed."

The lad looked around to assure no interloper overheard their conversation. He lowered his voice, "Well, I'm not exactly a reporter yet. But I will be. Everything I need to write my stories is in that trunk."

"Hmmm. Well, how about this? As it happens, this is my regular run, Alexandria to Pittsburgh, then on to Cleveland, overnight and back again. I usually take an empty seat in a quiet passenger car but sometimes, when the train is full of passengers I ride in the baggage car. That way I can catch up on the sleep I missed. How about if I make the run in the baggage car today and personally watch over your possessions? I give you my word they will arrive in good order."

Hesitating, he muttered, "Well, if you're sure."

"You have my word, young Mr. Writer. See me at the loading platform at Pittsburgh's Penn Station and I'll have your possessions waiting for you. Your train to Clairton is a local that will likely be nearly empty so you can take your trunk on board with you."

A sigh of relief passed through Homer's nostrils. He noticed the grey hair under the cap of the man and thought him to be about his father's age. "Thank you. I'll see you in Pittsburgh. What is your name?"

"Arnold Everson. I have relatives in Clairton. Go there often to visit. Station Master will take good care of you and your contraption."

Train travel had become refined during Homer's young life. By the time he made the trip to his aunt's home, hundreds of thousands of miles of track lay in service across the United States. From his home near Washington, D.C., he could have traveled in comfort south all the way to Key West, or he might have continued west to Los Angeles. Passenger trains of this era achieved levels of comfort, dependability, and speed that set the standard for the half century that followed. But glamorous destinations were not on Homer's mind for this trip. Rather, the excitement and anticipation of the three-hundred-mile trip to Clairton, Pennsylvania and new opportunities occupied his thoughts.

As he boarded Homer gawked at the train's amenities that included a lounge car, dining car, and carpeting throughout. He peeked into one unoccupied rest room and discovered it offered running water to accommodate passengers, chuckling at a sign above the toilet that read, "Please do not flush toilet while train is standing at the station."

With a renewed confidence, bolstered by Mr. Everson, he walked through the rail cars, then took the seat his ticket dictated on a second-class bench. Once settled he ruminated, *I sure hope that porter takes good care of my belongings.*

The several hours' ride from Alexandria to Pittsburgh found Homer running every possible story angle he could think of through his mind. Dirty and dangerous work conditions, low pay and long hours, black lung disease, fatherless children from on-the-job accidents ... there seemed to be a myriad of fresh topics available to him, but in the end, the story he chose to write was not about trials and tribulations of the miners or steelworkers, but of a feisty immigrant woman, owner of one of the most successful businesses in the area.

Upon arrival at the waterfront depot in Pittsburgh Homer hastened to the baggage car to find Arnold Everson guarding his gear that arrived in good order. "Thank you, my good man," he said as he slipped the baggage handler a generous tip; an amount that could have upgraded him to a first-class ticket. But he didn't care about riding the pines instead of relaxing in plush overstuffed chairs. He was grateful to have the tools of his trade safely in his possession.

Dragging the wheeled trunk behind him in the huge Pittsburgh station, Homer and his cargo easily transferred to the smaller local train heading for Clairton. In less than an hour's time the train's brakes screeched metal-on-metal as the engine, coal car, and single passenger car came to a halt. A jerk of the rail car and whoosh of steam acted as an invisible conductor to announce the train's arrival at Clairton, just a few minutes behind schedule.

Passengers milling around the train depot, mostly steelworkers and miners, jabbered in foreign tongues, a common sight at the small station. Immigrants walked to the terminal to meet the train and hopefully find newly-arriving relatives. Homer found the cacophony of chatter fascinating as he listened to the funny-looking people, many in colorful travel attire, speaking odd-sounding languages.

Dusk crept upon the scene. Perhaps the phenomenon resulted from a setting sun, or from smoke and particulates hurled into the late afternoon sky, but whatever the cause he wanted to get to his destination before nightfall.

Homer hailed a railroad employee, a wild-haired country boy with buck teeth. "How do I get to ..." looking at the paper in his hand ... "313 Miller Avenue?"

"Easy to find, mister. See that trolley?"

The young man nodded.

"That there is the St. Clair Avenue trolley. Cost ya' a nickel to ride it. Get off in four blocks, top o' the hill. That'll be Miller Avenue. Three blocks up Miller and you'll see yer address. You could'a walked it if ya' wasn't luggin' that case. Watcha' got innair anyhow? Gold? You'd a thunk so way yer holdin onto it."

"Well, Sir, it is as valuable as gold to me but trash to anybody else. The tools of my trade are inside this box. Thank you for the direction."

"Well, ya' better quit yer jawin' and hie over to the trolley. That driver an' his horse don' wait fer no one."

"Thank you, Sir. I'm on my way," he cried, walking with a hasty gait, dragging the wheeled luggage behind him.

"Let me help you with that, young man." The trolley driver reached down to help load the burden. "Going far?"

"Just to the top of the hill, I guess. Miller Avenue. My aunt lives at 313."

The driver thought about the address for a moment. "You mean you're going to see Mrs. Margaret Hammer?"

Homer nodded. "Yes, how did you know that? She's my aunt. I'll be staying with her for a while."

"Small town. Everybody knows everybody else, and their business. 'Sides, she's one of my regulars. Or was at least 'fore she took that fall. We go to the same church, First Presbyterian. Me, Margaret, and Bertrand, God rest his soul. I used to pick them up every Sunday morning and ride them to church."

The trolley driver continued. "First Presbyterian Church is moving, you know. Sold the building to a group of Serbians. They're planning to move the whole kit and caboodle clean over from where she stands on Park Avenue over to Reed Street. Gonna call it St. Something-or-other. It'll seem strange to see that building with another religion attending. They paid cash money for the building, though." He sighed. "But I guess that's progress."

"Moving a church across town. The church changing religions? That sounds like a story I can use. Why did they sell the church? Dwindling membership?"

"Oh no, just the opposite. Place is bursting at the seams. Needed a bigger place of worship. Church. Elders appealed to the Presbytery and they approved the sale and loan to build another one higher up, corner of Mitchell and Fifth Street. I'll tell ya, the new one is gonna be grand. It'll serve us for a hundred years. I seen the plans. Nave and chancel have a meeting room with folding doors on either side. Forms the shape of a cross when they're opened. Big stained-glass window facing south to catch the sun. It's gonna be grand.

The driver continued. "Sorry for the loss of your Uncle Bertrand. He was a good man, taken too soon. Somebody from the congregation checks on your aunt regularly since Bertrand passed. Makes sure she is eating okay. Feisty woman, Mrs. Margaret. Really feisty. Then she took that trip down the cellar stairs. Bad luck. Damn shame. She got around pretty good before that, after Bertrand's death. You must be her nephew from Maryland. She told me you were coming to help out."

"Virginia," Homer corrected him, but the driver continued to talk nonstop.

"Yup, mighty nice of you to come all this way. You tell her Jay Huffman sends her his best." He pulled up on the reins as he called to the horse, "Whoa now, Augustus. Let's let this nice young man off the trolley."

It seemed to Homer that he'd just boarded the tram. He didn't even realize they'd left the terminus. The driver's conversation made the trip go by in a heartbeat.

After climbing down and retrieving his trunk, Homer watched the trolley continue up St. Clair Avenue, then he turned and lugged the crate three blocks up Miller Avenue. Fortunately for him the only two hard-surfaced streets in the small mill town were Miller and St. Clair Avenues, so he did not have to drag his onus through the mud.

Arriving at her doorway, he rapped on the door and called her name, "Auntie ... Aunt Margaret."

From inside came a strong voice, "Door's open."

"Auntie? It's me, Homer from Alexandria. May I come in?"

"Of course, silly boy. I'm just having a snack. I've been waiting for you. How was your trip ... and come in here where I can see you so I don't have to shout."

Homer set his trunk down with a thud and approached his Aunt Margaret.

She used one of her crutches as an aid to boost herself upright in the chair while Homer bent to hug her. "You're such a good boy to come here to help your old, clumsy, invalid aunt."

"Aww, go on. You're neither old nor an invalid. But I'm here to help until you can get up and around. As for me, remember, I'm a journalist, not a sous chef, but I can find my way around the kitchen, and when I boil water it usually doesn't stick to the pan."

They both chuckled.

Margaret added, "Oh fiddlesticks. I can hop around and cook for my-self in a pinch, but I just need somebody nearby to make sure the house operates in good order. Since your Uncle Bert passed on, God rest his soul, the rain gutters haven't been cleaned, the cellar steps need to be repaired — especially the loose one I tripped over. A squirt of oil here and a slap of the hammer there, and as quick as a wink this old house and its owner will be ready for our next challenge."

"Aunt Margaret, how long do you expect to be laid up? I'm at your service as long as you need me, but I'd like to get a sense of the time I have to organize, arrange, and write stories."

"The doctor said it will take another three to five weeks until I'm able to put my full weight on it. I can't believe I tripped on that stair. I must have navigated it a thousand times, but it only takes one slip, I guess. If you're in the middle of a project when I'm ready to take over my own nursing duties, you're welcome to stay here as long as you wish. We are proud to have a famous newspaper reporter staying with us."

"Thanks, Auntie. And thank you for the compliment, though I'm any-thing but a famous newspaper reporter. I don't even have a real job yet. All I do is produce freelance stories and send them out, hoping a paper will pick one up and print it. I've run several ideas through my mind searching for an original slant. The tram driver gave me a lead."

"So you met Jay Huffman? Wonderful man. Looks after me like a mother hen since your Uncle Bert passed on."

"Yes, Mr. Huffman. He sends his best. Told me about the church being sold and a new one to be built. That will be my first story while I'm here. Any ideas on what's hot in the world of steel and coal? Uncle Bert must have talked to you about issues that could be fodder for a story or even a series."

She thought for several moments, then offered a possibility. "Well, I don't know if this will pique your interest or not. When your Uncle Bert got into a chatty mood, he used to tell me about a fiery immigrant woman who lives down the hill near the mill entry gate. As the story goes, her husband got himself fired and blackballed from the mill for crossing a picket line during a strike. With two adults and a pair of little mouths to feed and no income, she looked for work, took in laundry, ran a gambling game for workers, sold vegetables, illicit liquor, and who knows what else, to keep body and soul together. Nothing is a secret in this town. Well, I remember when …"

Homer interrupted his aunt's tale to bring her back to point. "She sounds like quite a lady. Or maybe a fish story."

A clearly miffed Margaret continued. "Well, I heard much of the account from our church choir director, Miss Morgan, so you can take it for what it is worth."

Homer pulled out a pad and pencil, touched the pencil to his tongue, and began taking notes, then asked a pointed question. "So how much of the yarn do you believe?"

She continued smugly, "I'm not finished yet. As the story goes, the woman and her husband had some savings that the husband brought with him, from Europe - Germany, I think. She took the money to our local real estate agent in hopes of making an investment. She wanted to buy rental properties, so the story is told."

Homer took notes furiously as his aunt spoke. "Umm-hmm. This is getting interesting. Did she find a suitable investment?"

"That's just it. Another German man from Europe owned the local real estate company. Jewish fellow. She didn't buy houses, but instead she joined the real estate company as an employee. The German immigrant man hired her just as the business received paperwork to operate as a Savings and Loan company. It turns out she happened to be a whiz at business and the savings and loan has prospered, in large part due to her efforts."

Homer thought a moment, then asked, "I don't mean to be indelicate, Auntie, but do you think the owner brought her on board for a little hanky-panky?"

"I don't think so. Her partner seemed to be a little light on his feet, if you get my drift. Besides, I met the lady one afternoon standing in line at the bakery. We chatted for several minutes. She has the vocabulary that would singe a sailor's ears, but she showed such honesty and had a natural way about her. I'm told that every customer who walks through the doors of her business falls in love with her. Bertrand and I have not done business with her, though. We went through the First National Bank for this house."

"Hmmm, it sounds like a good story but missing the juicy parts. Perhaps I'll interview her and if it turns out to be a dud I'll try another angle. What do you think, Auntie?"

"But wait, there's one more tragic part to the story. Turns out the man who started the business didn't like women romantically. You know he was … well, liked I said, a man who liked other men. He got caught up in a scandal over it and took his own life. Right here in Clairton. Inside their office! The story ran just a few weeks ago in the Pittsburgh paper. That's when it all happened."

"Can you give me details about his affairs?"

"Just never you mind. You don't need to be associated with writing that kind of trashy yellow journalism sleaze. I hope your story is a human interest one about a strong woman who came to this country with few opportunities and had many obstacles facing her. Our minister, Reverend Crilly, often uses her story in his sermons, telling how she overcame setbacks with faith and hard work. You don't need to feed the trashy side of public interest with salacious details of what might have happened."

Homer smiled a sly grin. "Auntie! It sounds like you might be the one to write about her."

"Oh no. You are the journalist in the family. But I'll tell you this much … if girls were encouraged to go to school and into professions when I was your age, I might have pursued your noble occupation myself. In my day, the worth of a young woman was measured by how well she married. By those standards, I did pretty well. Truth is, though, as a woman I can't even vote for the president of the United States of America. But the world is changing. By the time you marry, and if you have a daughter, she will have opportunities young women of my generation only dream about. I so admire Katie Novak. I live vicariously through her successes. Why, not only are so many walks of life closed to women, we don't even have the right to change our lot. So you interview that woman and get the story out."

"Wow, Aunt Margaret, I had no idea you were such a radical thinker."

"Humph. I can get wound up and spin a narrative at times and go on about issues. That is true. Perhaps it's a family trait that you inherited, but you do your story-telling on paper."

Homer thought for a moment. "Auntie, since I'm descended from Uncle Bert's side, I couldn't have inherited my genetic proclivity for the written or spoken word from your side of the family ..."

Smiling, though a bit nonplussed, she had a ready rejoinder. "Oh phoo. Now let me finish this snack before it gets stale."

Homer spoke as his aunt nibbled. "I just wanted to be accurate as every journalist should be. This lady sounds like somebody I'm going to have to interview. Auntie, in case I haven't told you lately, I love you. What is the name of this fascinating woman and where can I find her?"

Margaret took a large swallow of the ebony liquid on her tray, sighed, then answered, "Name is Katie. Katie, uh, Katheryn Novak. You will most likely find her at Clairton Savings and Loan office just down the street on the corner of Miller and St. Clair Avenues. You would have passed the place on your way here. As the result of her partner's death, she is now the sole owner of the business."

* * *

The next morning, Homer rose early and made a hearty breakfast of bacon, eggs, and steaming coffee. He carried a tray to Margaret's room, set it on a table outside the door and knocked. "Auntie, may I come in?"

"Please do, dear boy. Something smells delicious."

Lacking the skill of an experienced butler, he lifted the tray from the dainty table, then discovered the door latched. Rather than setting the tray back on the small buffet, he clumsily tried to unlatch and open the door. Balancing the tray and its contents on his arm as steadily as he could, and trying unsuccessfully not to spill anything, he awkwardly used his elbow to unlatch the door handle. The door was finally pried open and he carried the breakfast to the nightstand on his aunt's bedside.

"Sorry about the coffee splashing. It's soaking the napkin. Let me get you another one."

Sitting up in bed, Margaret teased, "Well, I hope you're a better writer than you are a chamberlain."

His face reddened. "I'm sorry, Auntie, I just didn't want to set the tray down to unlatch the door, and ..."

"Oh dear boy, I'm just teasing you. The food smells delicious and this is the most pampering I've had since your Uncle Bert and I were newlyweds."

"I'm glad you're awake early. I wanted to get up and out before the Savings and Loan office opens. I want to be the first one there in hopes she will give me an interview before things get busy."

"Oh, you have to get up pretty early to beat me. I'm an early riser. Have you eaten?"

"Yes, I had breakfast before bringing up yours."

"Well, you get freshened up and ready for your day. I'll finish this lovely repast and read a while. Don't worry about tidying up in here. I can do that with some effort. I might be a little gimpy on this leg, but I'm certainly no invalid."

"Okay, Auntie. Thank you. I have time to clean up the kitchen, redd-up the living room, and get dressed. But I'd like to ask you a few more questions to prepare for my interview."

"You go right ahead if you don't mind my chewing around your questions."

"Okay. How well do you know ... what's her name?"

She paused to swallow before answering. "Katie Novak. I don't know her well. Just in passing. But she seems to be a pleasant woman. Remember, since her business partner recently passed away she might still be a bit off her game, so don't go in there like a house afire."

He waited for her to clean the breakfast plate, then continued. "Tell me about the scandal."

"Well, you know, it is terrible the way people who are different are treated by society. The very idea that this country was settled by people seeking freedom from their bonds is admirable. But you see every day that we've not yet matured to accept and help those who are afflicted in many ways. I can remember as a child seeing Civil War veterans who had been wounded, begging for food and help. Even today, those who are infirmed are often maltreated; those with illnesses of the mind are treated even more poorly than others. Your uncle visited and treated some in institutions and told me some horror stories about them."

Homer held up one finger, then pulled a second pencil pad from his tunic nodded, and encouraged his aunt to continue.

"The man who started the Savings and Loan business was an immigrant who had an illness of the mind, according to many doctors. It is something the police believe should be treated by locking up, or even worse, beating and abusing those so afflicted. The gentleman tried his best to keep his predilection to himself while conducting business, but when discovered, and he knew he would become an object of your fourth estate, he could not bear the thought of it."

Homer scribbled relentlessly. "We are of the same mind on this issue, Auntie. Don't worry, I have no intention of excoriating this man or others of his persuasion in my piece. My interest is to write a story about a person who rose from a poor, illiterate, immigrant housewife to become a successful, well-to-do businesswoman. As far as the gentleman is concerned, I appreciate the fact that not only are those afflicted with certain conditions often abused, but as you say, we are still growing as a country. Blacks who are descended from African slaves are still mistreated in many ways, despite the Emancipation Proclamation. And the very fact that you are a woman ... our country was robbed of your pursuit of journalism and so many other opportunities. Heck, simply because of our plumbing, you can't even vote, and I can! How unjust is that?"

Margaret smiled and blushed in spite of herself. "Well, my astute young nephew, perhaps you can beat the drum with your writing to help change some of these inequities. Now, get on with you. Go to your interview and let me be the first to read your story."

"Thank you, Auntie. I'm on my way. I'll be back to cook you another spread and we can talk more over dinner. Oh, and to let you know that times are changing, my best friend from high school, a girl, attends a private college as a journalism major. Look for the byline of Mei Lamison one day." Pad of paper in hand, bowler hat hiding most of his red hair, and with square of paper reading 'PRESS' tucked diagonally into the band, Homer Hammer, ever the optimist, set out for what he hoped would be his first big story.

7

Unintended Consequences

"You can't blame gravity for falling in love." —Albert Einstein

HOMER STOOD ALONE, waiting impatiently at the door of the unopened business as two women approached: one portly, walking with an air of confidence, the other smaller, appearing to be younger and more reserved in her manner of walking. The younger woman seemed to walk with a slight limp.

The humid trek, trudging up the hill from her home, left beads of perspiration on Katie's forehead and caused several ringlets to pop loose from her hairdo. She ignored them, inhaling deeply. Dirty air proclaimed prosperity to her city. The late summer day promised to be sunny and cloudless in the Clairton community, despite the congested air.

Hope walked with her. Not actually alongside, but half a step or so behind. Katie huffed, Hope paced her, as though a long-distance Olympic runner readying for the final lap sprint; not a bead of perspiration nor a single lock of very short curly blonde hair flopped out of place on the forehead of the younger girl.

The trolley Homer had taken the day before ran the seven-block length of St. Clair Avenue, beginning its route on State Street, less than two blocks from the Novak house, proceeding to Seventh Street, but Katie preferred to walk and Hope offered no objection.

The sooty morning air was crisp. Katie sucked it deep into her lungs, smog and all, then exhaled, watching the fine mist escape from her nose and mouth. Trees bearing leaves of nearly every color of the rainbow in full bloom graced the area. It was a beautiful morning for a walk. The rapid pace would have taken them first to a bakery, in under ten minutes, then to the office. But this morning they espied a person waiting at the Clairton Savings and Loan building so they walked directly toward the office.

The pair approached the door as the older of the two women spoke. "You early bird, Mister. Maybe you be looking for catch worms?"

Barely twenty-years-old, Katie had the mien of an older, more sophisticated woman. Hope, just a few years younger, appeared to be at least a decade her junior.

Homer smiled at the humorous remark, catching her meaning of the John Ray "early bird catches the worm" idiom. "Good morning, Madam. My name is Homer Hammer and I wish ..."

Katie cut him off in midsentence, holding up her hand in a halting gesture. "No yet, Mister. No work allowed be discussed in my business before morning rolls and coffee — or tea if you like, unless this is emergency."

Her disarming smile and manner caught him off guard. "No Madam, no emergency. I can wait, and the sweet offerings sound like a perfect day to start the way, uh, day. Perfect way to start the day." His remarks were spoken almost reflexively, for he stood mesmerized, unable to concentrate on his words, watching the younger lady who accompanied the business owner.

Turning to her associate, the proprietor said, "Hope, you go bakery for pick up morning sweet rolls. I start hot water inside." The owner held out her hand to him in a friendly gesture, "My name Katie Novak, business owner. Please come in and have seat while I get hot water get started. My associate she gonna brings morning pastries. First we chew, then we chat."

Katie prepared coffee and tea as her mind wandered to her business partner, her mentor, and friend. No matter how early Katie arrived at the office, it seemed, Albert had already busily prepared for the day, one step ahead of her. She wondered if he didn't stay awake the entire night. He had no wife or children, and no local family. His entire life had been devoted to the business. She did not know much about his personal history prior to his death, aside from the fact that Albert had been a banker in Munich, Germany and like so many others, migrated to the new world to begin a new life. He spoke English very well, but with a thick German accent.

Katie's English tended to be more raw and colorful than that of her partner. Her syntax often led to laughter and good-natured kidding by clients. Her manner of speaking, however, and easy way with people brought in and kept many patrons.

The expression "chew before chat," began each day at the office as one of Albert's many popular phrases. He did not have many vices that she knew of, but he definitely had a sweet tooth for early morning snacks. How she missed Albert. It had been just weeks since his death and his spirit permeated every nook and cranny in the building. To honor his memory, she established a daily routine beginning each workday with fresh baked food from one of two local bakeries and tea service presented on Albert's silver tray and tea set.

One of the bakeries, owned by Frank Grisnik, established a little after Albert had arrived in Clairton from Europe in the fifth year of the twentieth century, shortly after Katie's parents began a boarding house. Frank became one of her parents' first tenants. For the next decade and beyond, thousands of immigrants arrived in the area to work the steel mills and coal mines. Many spent their entire working career in the mill. But not Frank. A few weeks on the job in the heat and filth of the steel mill convinced the Grisnik family scion to eschew labor of the steel industry in favor of the trade he'd learned in his home country. His became the first, as well as most popular, bakery in the area.

Hope made the short trek to the bake shop, cupped her hands around her eyes, and peered through the foggy water droplets that covered the pastry store window. Condensation formed in a giant half-moon shape on the glass. She shifted her weight from one foot to the other in an anxious stance while rapping on the front window of the yet-unopened sweet shop.

After several solid raps, a figure emerged from the kitchen. His hair and face obscured with flour created a ghostlike appearance. He shook himself and a white cloud settled onto the floor before unlocking the door. The bell attached to the door jamb tinkled its announcement of the day's first customer.

Once inside, outstretched arms of warmth from the ovens encircled Hope. A blended aroma of yeast, flour, cinnamon, and frying fat settled on her shoulders. The sun, higher now, slanted through the front window reflecting off display cases that held the beginnings of that day's bounty. In the glass case, granulated sugar sparkled like snow on the jelly doughnuts. Cinnamon twists gleamed inside their translucent glaze. Brown bread in big round loaves put forth an aroma of wholesome goodness. A barrel stood in the corner revealing fresh, slim stick bread that reached for the ceiling, comfortably resting next to loaves of French bread and pumpernickel rye, each wrapped in its own crinkly, brown paper scarf.

Frank Grisnik addressed his first customer of the day. "Good morning, Miss Novak, how's business? Are you ready to take over the Savings and Loan yet?"

She laughed at his teasing. "Every day I learn more and new customers keep coming. Katie says there is more business than we can handle. She's training me to fill-in for now and plans to interview more help this week. Albert's passing left a huge void, plus all the new business keeps her running ragged. If you know of anybody with good skills, send them over. We surely could use them."

"Ha! If I could find half a dozen good workers I'd hire them myself! We're growing so fast and there is so much work in the mills that good help, or any help for that matter, is hard to find."

"That's exactly what Katie says, but she realizes that's also a good thing because both our businesses are doing well."

"I've sent for two cousins from our bakery back home. At least I know they can begin working on day one. And I could really use somebody up front to sell and tend the cash register." He paused, then asked, "What'll you have today, Miss Novak?"

"Please call me Hope."

"Only if you call me Frank."

"Deal, Frank." Pointing to the display case, "I'll take that cinnamon coffee cake and some nut horns. Half a dozen."

"I've got lady locks in the back that I just finished filling and powdering."

"Okay, I'll take a half dozen. Not for me, of course. For the customers," she winked. "And a loaf of pumpernickel rye."

Hope paid the baker and left, arms loaded with freshly-baked goods. Sweet aromas wafted through the morning air, challenging the acrid smell of the industry that ran along the river. Mill scale residue spread by the city as a street cover, crackled beneath her feet as she scurried to the office.

Homer caught sight of her through the large front window as she traipsed up the street with an armload of goodies. He sprang forward, racing past Katie to hold the door open for her. "Please allow me," he uttered to a harried Katie. Quickly unlatching the door, he reached out to offer a hand and ease her burden of baked goods. Smitten and star struck over the sight of her, and stumbling over his words he began, "If I promise not to squeeze you, can I ..."

Hope retorted, "WHAT?"

Turning crimson, his face now the color of his hair, he stuttered, "Not you! I mean the bread! I meant not to squeeze ... oh shucks. I'm sorry. The last thing in the world I want is to offend you."

Hope chuckled and nodded coyly, deciding to let the embarrassed young man off the hook. "No harm done. Apology accepted. And yes, I can use some help with this armload."

Homer helped arrange the baked goods on a silver platter she had set out, while Katie heated water for tea and prepared coffee in the office's small kitchen.

The sight of the damsel bewitched the young journalist. Unable to stop staring at the beauty, he made a futile effort to cast his eyes downward. The girl's close-cropped hair, growing back after having been shorn to help her pass as a boy, hinted at its pure honey-blonde color. Blazing fiery China-blue eyes complemented her face, though her emotions were not easily hidden. He could see the pain in every crease of her brow and pale pink cheeks. Her lips, full but not pouty, refused to smile, hinted at pain as she took great care to arrange the baked goods.

Again, the eyes. Perfectly shaped, glistening azure eyes, regarded as pools reflecting her soul. Homer studied them closely enough to see they cast back a hidden pain, but also a beauty and passion that he could only fantasize might one day open to his yearning. Intertwined with this new-found passion, he pledged to fight and defeat whatever foes might have caused her hurt and pain. He had to quietly pinch himself to return him to the purpose of his mission this day.

Katie and Hope disappeared into the office and returned to set up a table of baked goods in one corner. Homer had regained his comportment from his earlier faux pas.

"May I help you with these morsels, Madam?" Homer inhaled deeply. "Ah, fresh warm baked goods. A man's desire."

"Woman's desire, too, Mister," Katie scolded. "Not forget women. Some this for us but for ladies come interview for job, too."

Homer's embarrassment returned as he thought, *Don't blow this, dummy. Take a deep breath and act like the professional journalist you wish to become.*

Once the pastries and other baked goods had been placed, Homer's good fortune continued in that no customers arrived during the first hour of the business day. Hope sat at the reception desk, filing, while Katie and Homer moved into the smaller office area.

"Mrs. Novak, I would like to do a story on you. It will include as much of your life as you would like to share."

He touched a nerve. "Wish paper for you write? Some of them write lies and bad things about my business partner when he die. If you work for any them, I no be interest."

"Well, Madam, let me be begin by being perfectly honest and up front with you. First, I do not write for any particular paper. I'm what is called a stringer or freelancer. I cover events and submit my stories unsolicited to various regional and national newspapers in hopes one or more of them buy my stories. When I do sell a story, it appears with no name attached to it, just a random story. For example, I usually cover the Washington, D.C. beat. If something happens in politics, I usually write about it.

"Second, let me tell you that I do not believe in 'yellow journalism,' scandal, sensationalism, and unnamed sources. If I wrote that way no doubt I would sell more stories and make more money, but I'd rather put out quality news articles and earn a reputation as a legitimate reporter with my own byline. I hope my story about you earns me a byline, but if it does, it will be because the story accurately represents the subject, namely you."

Katie interrupted his comments. "What is byline?"

"A byline is the name, and sometimes even accompanied by a picture of the person writing the item. That is what every newspaper writer strives to have associated with his work. It brands him as a legitimate reporter.

"To continue, third, to prove that I am honest in what I say I will allow you to read the piece before I submit it. If you discover any errors or misrepresentations I'll make changes, but the final content is my decision."

"If you not have you byline in paper, why you care what it say?"

"The goal of a stringer or freelancer is to have his name associated with the stories he writes and have his byline recognized by readers. I have not had my byline printed yet but I firmly believe that if I maintain profes-sionalism in my submissions, that when I do achieve my goal I'll do so with honesty."

She seated Homer in the chair next to her desk.

8

Will it Play in Pittsburgh?

"Schools have two great functions: to confer, and to conceal valuable knowledge." —*Mark Twain*

THE INTERVIEW BEGAN. "Okay, Mr. Homer Hammer, what you want know 'bout Katie Novak?"

"Start from the beginning. Let the words, 'Who, What, When, Where, Why, and How' be your guide. Who are you? What is your life like now and before you came to America? When did you arrive? Where did you come from? What motivated you to emigrate? How did you get into this business? Why have you been so successful? Just talk."

"I only have one hour today before my interview start for hire. Business growing and I need more help so I set interviews today."

"No problem. Let's talk as long as you have time today. I can come back tomorrow or whenever you have the time, interview you at home, or meet wherever you like."

Homer had a knack for putting people at ease. Katie sat back in her chair and began to tell her story as Homer, pencil in hand, scribbling frantically, took copious notes.

"I won't tell you whole story 'bout when I was child in Croatia, but I still dream it every night. For now, I just tell you I stop go school when seven-year-old. That was day I remember. In Croatia they call me Kata, nickname for Katarina. In America is Katheryn or Katie."

"It rain night before my last day for school. Where I walk, dusty hard clay path is village main street. But that day it be lots mud. I no care. I skip over puddles and how you say? Hopscotch like dancer so I no step on shit from ox, horse, donkey, and other animal what use street. Not clean streets like here.

"I spend day walk alone in village to edge of Kupa River. That river close to my house. Kupa River no big like Monongahela, but big 'nough. While I walk, birds sing to me. Smell of trees wave in breeze. Then I smell sandwich meat in lunch pail. My grandmother, her name Baka Mara, she make me lunch every day. I live with her 'cause my parents, they in America."

Katie paused to gather her thoughts and Homer took the moment to ask, "Are your parents still in America?"

She nodded, "They own boarding house over on tracks. Millworkers, most from Croatia and Balkan countries live dere. Baker Frank Grisnik, he live dere and work in mill before he quit mill and open bakery."

"Tell me more about your time in Croatia near the river. Can you spell it for me?"

"Kupa River. K-U-P-A. Easy spell. No like Monongahela."

Both chuckled as Katie continued.

"Autumn leaves crackle under feet. Dey make noise when I kick them. I see piles of red, orange, and yellow leafs. Dis still my favorite time of year. I decide when walk, I know 'zactly how and where I gonna spend dat late summer morning.

"I think I never returning that school. I remember so much be beat by nuns and feel she don' like me. When I was in classroom I feel like I have be all tie up with invisible chain. Jus' den I know I not gonna suffer no more. I tell myself I not go back to school and pain I have every day. My future be for freedom. Freedom if I want, could wander, swim, and don' have face torture in school."

Homer transcribed her words, changing her disjointed syntax into more proper spoken words as he went along. At first, he had to slow her down, but as the conversation continued, the pace of his writing quickened and he translated as she spoke, changing first person to third for all except direct quotes. He continued writing what would be the first draft of his story. Taking very little editorial license, he wrote just as she spoke. The first installment continued as he wrote:

"Out of breath from the brisk walk and exciting thoughts of not returning to the school, she plucked a berry from a large bramble bush that hid her from prying eyes. Popping the morsel into her mouth, she chewed slowly, taking time to let the bright purple juices dribble down the sides of her mouth and trickle down her throat. The berry had the flavor of freedom; a wild taste of growing wherever it chose. Smiling to herself she remembered earning a sharp rebuke from her teacher when she answered a question about berries announcing, 'Blackberries are red when they're green,' then laughing at the joke she made. Her classmates didn't get the joke. The teacher looked puzzled, glared, then moved on with a boring talk about the area's flora and fauna.

"Rich dirt along the riverbank, nearly the color of chocolate, smelling of rich loam, had spawned her freedom berry. Squeezing the lush soil with her toes, she allowed it to ooze between them."

In a single motion, Homer dropped one completed pad to his side, took another and continued to write vigorously as she spoke.

"Climbing into a thicket among trees and overgrowth, she found just the right spot, hidden from view above the edge of the deserted beach. A bright sun peeked through the overgrowth above the cloudless sky. Surrounded by brambles and briars, a cove offered a private changing room. She undid her shoes, removed her socks, slipped out of the jumper, the school uniform required of all girls at the school, then piled the clothing neatly in a corner of her hidden change room.

"Once she'd stripped off her underwear, folded it neatly, and placed it atop the pile of clothing, she left the solitude of the thicket, marching confidently toward the river's edge and into the water.

"Freedom of spirit flew above as she eased into the cool water. Stinging welts of clotted blood from the beating of the instructor's hickory stick were soothed by the balm of cool river water.

"Kata had discovered this secret refuge some time ago. It served as a place where she could think her most intimate thoughts. A place where no teacher could punish her, no classmate could mock her, no invisible chains could bind her. Her sanctuary, a hideaway about which nobody but Kata knew. No danger lived in or nearby her secret thicket.

"Grandmother Baka Mara and other old ladies told tales of wolves near the river carrying off babies and attacking children who wandered too near the shore. Ha! With the overconfidence of a child, she dared any wolf to challenge her as she waded into the cool water.

"The baptismal immersion felt cool against the remnants of the lash marks, ahead of full submersion. A cleansing salve that erased the residual traces of sting from her body. Too young to understand baptism's religious meaning, she knew only that repeated immersion into the water meant a cleansing from being mocked and teased by classmates, the death of teacher's demeaning rituals, burial of her past scholastic trauma, and resurrection onto a life of freedom.

"Stepping farther into the stream her bare feet touched the cool smooth river bottom. With one deep breath, she eased herself into the pristine liquid, ducking her head beneath the surface. Shivers lasted but a few moments until her body became acclimated to the water's temperature. Then she sprang dolphin-like above the surface in a grateful arc and slipped back into the flowing abundance, fully submerged.

"Beneath the water's outer bounds, with eyes wide, she watched a school of fish swim by. Holding her breath until her lungs burned, she breached the water's surface again and exhaled as the wind prickled her face and shoulders.

"She swam with schools of fish instead of schoolchildren, wallowing in the chilly, refreshing, relaxing stream. Without a word, she considered asking the fish for permission to be accepted into their school. They surely would agree and accept her into their academy.

"She silently spoke to them. *Your school is always open,* words forming in her mind, *you are always in class. But no teacher fish scolds or browbeats your class members just for being the best swimmer or the smartest fish in the class.*

"Thinking further she added, *Your entire school of fish must be smart. The dumb ones get caught on a fisherman's hook and are served up for dinner!*

"Kata was certain the fish smiled at her. She smiled back at the analogy, bubbles escaping from her mouth. At that moment, she decided to become more like her fish classmates and less like those from the Catholic school she'd left behind.

"Her body again broke the surface. She exhaled stale air from her lungs. Drawing several deep gulps of clean, fresh respiration deep into her chest, she dived again, silently speaking to the fishes. *Can I enroll in your school?*

"Certain they'd agreed, it became clear to her that instead of returning to her old school to face more ridicule and punishment, a change of faculties drifted through the air, or more precisely, the water. She decided to enroll in a new academy, *The Kupa River School of Kata and the Fishes,* in her secret school place. Every day she would join her fellow fish scholars to learn about the world of the underwater.

"Kata climbed onto the riverbank and garnished bramble bush berries over the sandwich Baka Mara had prepared for her lunch, enjoying the gustatory sensations.

"She knew that once the school summoned Baka Mara and made her aware of what had happened, the old woman would try to get her to return to that horrid place. Kata would vehemently refuse, knowing that the school officials would make no attempt to find her or get her to return. Indeed, Sister found relief to be rid of the hellion who challenged nearly everything for which the school stood.

"Kata returned to the water and bliss. The Kupa River became the child's classroom, her pathway to freedom and a venue to release her from chains that had bound her to that hideous school. Adults and classmates had judged her. The cascade of water and her newfound friends did not. The old school served as a prison, the river her refuge. Fish never teased, mocked, or made fun of her just because she knew the answers. This is the place she was meant to be.

"Floating on her back, tracing the cloud shapes in her mind, she made out fish, animals, and even (ugh) an outline of the old school. In a moment, a shape that she was unable to perceive began to take form. She studied it and wondered what it could be. She examined it intensely but could not make it out. She focused on the shapeless cloud until she heard a voice. Not a voice exactly, more of a feeling. Did it come from the cloud in the sky or the water below?

"Something whispered her name. *Katarina.*

"The wind? She listened more closely. The triad of the cloud, water and a zephyr seemed to flow together to become more of a feeling or impulse than an actual voice. As she concentrated on the feeling, the perception became stronger. Words from the impulse seemed to flow inside her.

"Katarina, you are in grave danger. You must leave this place now.

"Certain of this being the same voice and feeling she'd heard such a warning once before, she focused all her energy on it. The message became clearer. She was in danger, but from what or whom? No time to ponder.

"She did not argue with or question the feeling inside her, but swam quickly to the shore, dried herself as best she could with her school uniform before slipping into her undergarments. Gathering her jumper, shoes and socks, without bothering to pick up her lunch pail, she scampered up the bank just ahead of rushing floodwaters.

"Storms over the past several days had drenched the hilly area upstream, saturating the dirt and compromising a small earthen dam. The dam burst, flooding the Kupa River and sending torrents of water along the banks. Roofs and other parts of homes, uprooted trees, and debris hurtled down the river where Kata had been swimming just moments earlier. Had it not been for the feeling-voice warning, the child surely would have been consumed by the deluge. That marked the first time Kata realized the power of the gift inside her."

Hope rapped lightly on the door, breaking the spell of the story. "Excuse me, Mrs. Novak. The first applicant is here for her interview."

"Thank you, Hope. Please offer cakes and coffee. I come get her in moment."

Homer rose as Katie stood. She walked him to the office door. "I sorry I talk so much 'bout my childhood. Maybe you find something to write in what I tell you."

"Katie, you are quite the lady. What we did today just scratched the surface. I'd like to continue our interviews. It might seem like you've had a lot to say today but the writing of a quality article requires hours of interviews. I hope you'll be amenable to additional questions."

She thought a moment. "What happen if you get too much talk?"

"If I have that much material I'll write a series."

"You tease on me."

"If you think I'm joking about a series, you're half right. Let's continue the interrogatories and see how it all shakes out. When can we meet again?"

I be here in morning early, before open. If we no finish then, you come to house."

"Perfect. I'll see you in the morning." He thought for a split second, then venturing a question, added, "Uh, will Miss Hope be here?" His longing to see Hope again burned in his gut as much as the desire to continue the interview with Katie. His heart fluttered at the thought of seeing the girl again.

Katie interrupted his mental self-flagellation. "Hope be here, too. I need somebody watch office while you ask me question."

As he bid Katie adieu, Homer's mind raced. *I must focus on the interview. I must be professional. I shouldn't have even asked that question about Hope. How foolish of me.* "Great. See you tomorrow. But before I leave, may I take a few photographs of you and the building?"

Katie demurred. "Why you want old married woman in picture. Take of Hope and office."

Thinking quickly, Homer replied matter-of-factly, "Of course I'll take a photo of your trusted assistant and the place of business, but if the story is to be about you, I need you to be in the photograph."

Kati reluctantly agreed and Homer took as many candid shots as he was able without becoming intrusive. His subject in most the candid shots were of the young blonde assistant.

Once he left, the morning became a busy one at Clairton Savings and Loan. Three scheduled applicants, meetings, and Homer's impromptu interview took most of the morning and released Katie's mind from more pressing issues for a time. During Katie's conversations with Homer, or when otherwise or encumbered, Hope handled the office duties with aplomb, fast becoming the office Girl Friday.

9

The Hopeful Newsman

"I became a journalist to come as close as possible to the heart of the world." —Henry Luce

OVER THE NEXT FEW WEEKS Homer returned regularly to interview Katie, both in the office and at the Novak home. Each time he approached a session his pulse quickened and his heart thumped rhythmically, not for anticipation of the upcoming session, but at the possibility of seeing Hope. When she met his gaze, he felt drawn in by her beauty, certain that the thunder of the vessel throbbing inside his chest could be seen through his clothing.

During the time that followed his meetings, Homer developed photos he'd taken, using an impromptu photography laboratory set up in his aunt's basement. When not in the photo lab, he pounded out his stories on the old Remington typewriter he'd toted from Virginia.

Most of his time at Aunt Margaret's house found Homer secreted, coming out of his room only to tend to his aunt's needs and take an occasional light meal of his own. The desk that held the aged Remington also held a photo that he had taken and developed himself. The subject, a beautiful, young blond girl with piercing expressive eyes, golden sun-goddess hair, and a shy smile.

He spent the rest of his time in Clairton writing, rewriting, and polishing the story until it became, he believed, as perfect as he could possibly make it. Walking gingerly down the stairs from his room, he called out to his aunt.

"On my way to the post office, Aunt Margaret."

"My, that is an armload of packages you have there. Tell me again the destinations."

Setting the large envelope packages on the dining room table, he reviewed the landing place of each. "Well, packages go to different targets. They're headed for newspapers in Boston, New York, Washington, Maryland, Virginia, and St. Louis. This is the first round. Keeping my fingers crossed but if I come up empty ... If I don't sell the story this first round, I'll try other venues. It is a great human interest story. I hope I've done it justice enough that it will catch the eye of an editor."

Within weeks he received his first response.

Aunt Margaret's leg healed nicely, thanks in large part to her nephew's pampering. Though she felt well enough to manage on her own, she appreciated the fact that Homer chose to stay longer than planned while his submission about Katie Novak floated through various publishers' offices.

The *Boston Traveller,* a daily newspaper with weekly and semi-weekly editions circulated throughout New England, the Northeast and Canada, was the first to respond. Homer quickly signed an agreement for the story to run exclusively in the evening *Traveller,* but with the option for other publications to reprint it after the exclusive had run. He added a line on the contract that required the *Boston Traveller* and any other paper that picked up the story to include the byline *Homer J. Hammer.* He was confident other papers would find the piece worthy of publication, printing it complete with his byline.

His self-confidence was rewarded as the narrative ran in several large dailies and reprinted in others. Homer J. Hammer had achieved the status of news writer with a byline. He had pondered over the exact phraseology of the byline. His parents had innocently named him Homer, after his father, with the middle name, John, a family surname name taken from his mother's side. He took plenty of teasing during his school years, not only for the alliteration of his first and last name, but also nicknamed Jack Hammer, combining the informal middle name with his surname. He'd heard it all: Jack Hammer, Sledge Hammer, Ball Peen Hammer, Claw Hammer, etc. But all that schoolboy teasing remained behind him as Homer J. Hammer became the first student from his high school class to achieve such success and live up to his title, "Boy most likely to succeed."

* * *

As the two Hammers enjoyed lunch, Aunt Margaret boasted with pride to her nephew. "Well, Homer, you certainly did accomplish quite a bit from our little town. You came to me a boy and are leaving a man, and a famous writer at that." Tears welled up in her eyes as she added, "I so wish Uncle Bert could have been here to witness the transformation."

To avoid becoming emotional Homer tossed about a bit of humor. "Well, Auntie, thanks to your gracious and constant haranguing I have become a certified nurse and sous chef as well as a bit of a newsman."

She dabbed her eyes with a napkin. "Oh, you silly boy. It has certainly been a pleasure having you. And I really am proud that you earned your ... what do you call it? Write line?"

"Byline, Auntie. From now on, whenever you see an article in the paper that I've written, my name will appear below the headline but above the story."

"Well, that's just fine. You ..." Her comment was cut short by the door-bell ringing. "My goodness, I wonder who that could be? You just sit there, Homer, while I answer the door."

Margret, wearing a slight smile, crossed the parlor and opened the oaken front door. A delivery man stood in the doorway. "Yes? How can I help you?"

"Delivery, Ma'am, for Homer J. Hammer. Need him to sign for this."

"Oh my, I wonder what that could be. Bring it right in and I'll summon him. Oh Homer! Come here, please. The gentleman needs a signature from you."

"Is it a telegram? I'm hoping to hear about a permanent job."

She could barely contain her full grin as she called, "Well, it looks a bit large for a telegram."

The deliveryman set the box on the table. Homer signed the paper and handed the man a tip.

"What in the world could this be?" Margaret pondered aloud.

Homer ripped apart the packaging to discover, first a card that read, *To my dear nephew, Homer, J. Hammer, the family's first newsman. Congratulations. I'm sure this gift will get plenty of use. Love, Aunt Margaret.*

Inside the box, a sparkling new 1918 Corona 3 Personal Writing Machine with an enclosed ad that boasted, *Fold it up, take it with you. Typewrite anywhere.*

The ad showed a drawing of a uniformed soldier in a battlefield encampment, sitting on a tree stump. Before him sat a small table that held a 1918 Corona 3, America's first portable typewriter.

"Oh, Aunt Margaret, it's beautiful. How can I ever thank you for this gift and your generous hospitality?"

"It is I who am indebted to you. You took such good care of me during my recovery. Lucky is the young woman for whom you will cook in wedlock. Any ideas who that might be?"

The young man blushed. "Marriage is not on the top of to-do my list at the moment. Rather, I must find a steady position that includes writing. Starting a family is the furthest thing from my mind."

"Well, then, I guess that little blond girl who stays at the Novak home isn't on your mind either?"

His face now fully flushed, Homer stammered, "What? Who? Uh, I, uh …"

"Sorry, my dear, I didn't mean to embarrass you but I couldn't help but notice the number of times you've alluded to her in our conversations."

"Oh, Aunt Margaret, I confess to you, she has stolen my heart. I've never felt this way about anybody before. Maybe someday I'll gather the courage to court her, but first I need to establish a career that will keep me and a future family, much like you and Uncle Bert."

"That is a responsible thing to do, my boy. But don't wait too long. I'm sure you're not the only young man whose fancy she's captured. Now let's get you packed up and on your way. I'm sure your mother is missing you as much as I'll be once you're gone."

With his work complete for the time being, and his Aunt Margaret's leg fully healed, Homer left Clairton and returned to Alexandria, Virginia, with mixed feelings. The editor of the Chesapeake Ledger had offered him as job as staff writer. He accepted, but pined for his first love, Hope Novak.

10

The Crooked Path

"In Chaos, there is fertility." —Anaïs Nin

KATIE, MEANWHILE, BUSIED HERSELF putting the business in order, still trying to replace the massive void left by Albert's death. He had taught her so much and her devotion to him and his memory made her even more determined to keep the Clairton Savings and Loan not only alive, but thriving and more successful than it had ever been. She felt destined to devote her life to the business of finance, providing low-interest loans to those unable to be served by more traditional banks. She also had in mind a mission to improve mankind, but she did not yet know what that mission would be.

Within the first weeks after reopening the Savings and Loan, several other orders of business awaited her. In addition to a soon-to-be adopted daughter, newly renamed Hope Novak, Katie hired three staff members: two women, both of whom had secretarial experience, and a man from a bank across the Monongahela river in the manufacturing town of Elizabeth.

Robert White, an honest, forthright gentleman had worked at the First Elizabeth Bank for over twenty years. Honesty, punctuality, and devotion to his place of business made him indispensable. He had risen in responsibility and title from teller to assistant manager to assistant to the president of the institution. Robert took part in few outside interests. The bank served as his family, his work, and his life.

When the president of First Elizabeth Bank died unexpectedly in an auto crash, Robert White, as did his fellows workers, presumed he would become the bank's next president. "Congratulations, Sir. I look forward to your holding the top position, 'Mr. President.'"

"Not so fast, my friend."

Employees continued to offhandedly congratulate him, though he smiled. "We must not be hasty. The bank is a highly-structured institution and protocol must be followed. We cannot get ahead of ourselves."

Best wishes and congratulations continued to follow him. Even at the former president's funeral, Robert expressed his sympathy to the former bank president's wife. "Ann, I'm sure I speak on behalf of myself as well as all the employees. You have our deepest sympathies. He was a good man, an outstanding banker, and a leader of men."

She whispered through her tears, "Thank you Robert. I take solace and comfort in the belief that you will ably carry on his work."

"Of course."

Robert's coworkers and customers expressed their grief to the family of the departed president. All were certain Robert would soon occupy the vacant position. But that did not happen. Instead, in an emergency meeting, the bank's Board of Directors, a four-to-three vote, named an outsider to the position.

As manager at the only bank in Clairton, J. W. Walters knew how to schmooze his superiors. A tyrant to his fellow workers, he had risen to the station of bank manager through the spreading of fear and intimidation. His clothing, smart and impeccable, made him the stereotypical vision of a bank official. Though he looked the part, his old-school methods of lending allowed the First National Bank in Clairton to serve only certain segments of the community. He refused to loan money to immigrants and took sadistic pleasure in hastily foreclosing on customers unable to meet their financial obligations. Years earlier Katie's parents sought a loan from the bank, wishing to purchase rental property. Walters insulted, demeaned, and humiliated the couple before tossing them out of his bank.

On the day the death of the Elizabeth bank's president was announced, J. W. Walters called his manager into the office. "Livingston, I'll be leaving early today. I have an important meeting with some Board members. You're in charge. Try not to give away the building or screw up the works. Remember, you can always be replaced by somebody who is actually capable of being a bank manager."

"Yes, Sir."

Orville Livingston had worked at the bank for as long as his boss had. The insults and threats no longer bothered him. He knew that if he ever lost this job, a man his age would have a difficult time finding another, so he bit his tongue and took the abuse.

Once free of the bank J.W. Walters took the train into Pittsburgh to his club, Walters reflected on the sponsorship. Membership in the club would not normally be available to one of Walter's social status. He had no direct association with the City's Captains of Industry. From their vantage point Walters was a pipsqueak president of a pipsqueak bank with minimal assets. But fortune smiled on him the day a teller knocked on his office door.

"What is it, Murphy?"

"Sir, may I come in? I have a matter to discuss that is extremely delicate."

The president rolled his eyes in disgust. "Alright. Close the door and make it fast."

The teller entered and stood as he spilled his agony. "Sir, this is embarrassing, but my sister is married to a Slovenian fellow who works in the mill."

"I said, make it fast."

"Yes, Sir. Their daughter, a single girl, works as a charwoman in downtown Pittsburgh. She works for a wealthy family and it seems, uh, ah, seems that she is with child."

Sensing a scandal Walters asked, "Who's the father?"

"He is a member of the Mahoney family."

"Eustis Mahoney?"

"I think that's his name. But I don't know what to do. The girl hid her problem until now and is too far along to terminate. They asked me for counsel. I don't know what to tell them to do."

A sinister smile crossed the banker's face. "Let me see what I can do, Murphy. Get back to work and I'll keep you updated."

The banker made a few phone calls and discovered that the industrial scion had a weakness for young girls and spent a small fortune to keep the results of his dalliances quiet. The following morning, Walters took the train to Pittsburgh and found the mansion that was home to steel magnate Eustis Mahoney. A butler answered the door and soon J. W. Walters sat in the parlor of the stately home, drink in hand.

"What can I do for you, Mr. Walters, is it?"

"Yes. I'm J. W. Walters, president of the First National Bank of Clairton, Pennsylvania."

"Never heard of it and never heard of you, so briefly tell me what you want."

"What I want, Sir, is for you to sponsor my membership into the Pittsburgh Club."

The wealthy man chuckled. "You have fifteen seconds to tell me why I shouldn't ring to have my butler toss you out of my house on your ear."

"Because I have a friend at the *Pittsburgh Post* who would love to do a story on you and the poor immigrant charwomen you seduced, and the child you are about to father with that sixteen-year-old Slovenian girl.

Mahoney did not change his expression, but answered curtly. "You can have your club membership because it costs me nothing. You may leave now, but rest assured that if you ever try to blackmail me again, or if any word of this gets out by any means, I will ruin you and your piss-ant bank."

From that day forward, Walters made regular visits to his club, gathering bits of gossip from loose-lipped members and the club's butlers. He spent the Clairton bank's money freely to get information he wanted and soon had a dossier on nearly every member of the Pittsburgh Club. He was scorned but tolerated by most other members out of fear that Walters might be privy to their own sordid indiscretions. Thus, Mr. J. W. Walters hobnobbed with the elite, including owners, board members, and shareholders of most of the regional banks.

The day he heard news of the death of the president of the First Elizabeth Bank, Walters left his own financial institution heading for his club just after lunch. First Elizabeth was considered a jewel among Monongahela Valley banks in towns and villages along the river south of Pittsburgh. He lobbied his fellow club members and Board members of the bank for the position, with subtle hints at the power he had over them. The following morning a formal announcement ran in a trade paper that J. W. Walters would be the new president of the First Elizabeth Bank.

At first Robert White continued as his trusted assistant, but it soon became clear that he posed a threat to Walters, who did not have the skills required of an effective bank president. The new president made arbitrary decisions and blamed underlings, particularly White, when his own decisions went askance.

Out of loyalty to the institution he had served so well for over two decades, Robert White continued as a loyal employee doing his best to exercise power behind the Walters throne to keep the bank's business running smoothly and in compliance with banking law.

When an error committed by Walters suggested chicanery in the bank's procedures, the owners and stockholders called the president, J. W. Walters, on the carpet and asked that he explain the discrepancy. Walters immediately accused his assistant, Robert White, a loyal employee with an unblemished record, of embezzlement. An outside auditor discovered that no embezzlement had taken place. Instead, the error, an oversight made by Walters himself, caused the discrepancy. The innocent error was quickly rectified, but the accusation wounded Robert deeply. Feeling his reputation had been besmirched, Robert White resigned.

When Katie heard through the grapevine of the events happening at the Elizabeth bank, she invited Robert for an interview. His having been falsely accused sounded strikingly similar to her husband's experience with the union. After having the story validated from his own lips, Katie hired him on the spot. Robert might not have had all the skills of her former partner, Albert, but she came to see him as loyal, hard-working, and the glue to help her hold the Clairton Savings and Loan business together. His acumen also allowed Katie a new luxury, time to herself. She considered taking a vacation, but had not yet gotten around to planning one.

Besides the hiring of Robert White and two additional staff members, Katie added Hope as her personal assistant. Before long the office hummed with nearly the same efficiency as it had before Albert's death.

Katie returned to the upstairs office she had shared with Albert. A wooden swivel chair served both Katie's desk and, when turned, faced Albert's unoccupied desk in the small room. One side of Albert's desk abutted the wall, providing an L-shaped extension and a surface for a type-writer. Behind the desk sat a small metal table with a dictionary. State and federal law books were stacked beneath the dictionary. Along the far wall, filing cabinets contained carefully filed client records.

The north wall housed a door that opened onto two steps leading down from Katie's office to the main area of business. A window allowed oc-cupants of Katie's office to see into the rest of the downstairs area, but when closed, it assured privacy. The glass that separated her office from the rest of the workspace downstairs also gave her a view of Hope, daily placing fresh baked goods and flowers on the table next to the windows, and generally tidying up the main part of the office. The view provided her the ability to monitor the other employees as well as clients entering the business.

Katie found complexities of certain aspects of the law books difficult to read and understand, of course, as the books were written in her second language. "Robert, how you like learn more 'bout law and compliance in Savings and Loan business?" The word *compliance,* one of the first she learned while working for Albert, rolled smoothly off her tongue.

"I'm willing to stay late and study the books. My coursework at Pitt touched on many aspects of law and compliance, so I'm not totally ignorant of the regulations."

"Good. You willing to do that. I willing to give you extra compensation." The four-syllable word was also spoken with clarity. With little fanfare, Robert left from the downstairs area for the upstairs office and took his position at Albert's desk. The change was cathartic for Katie, as it helped her move forward after the loss of her dear mentor.

Once he agreed to the additional assignment, Robert frequently stayed after work to peruse the law books as well as periodicals containing the latest statutes and trends in the field, and books that Albert had found crucial to staying in legal compliance with regulating agencies. Though his career to this point had been in bank management, Robert took to the compliance component of his new job like a Philadelphia lawyer.

Soon after his hiring, Katie spoke to Robert in their office. "I want change words on front window. Keep Albert's name there somehow and want people know he still part of business. How you think best way do that?"

"Let me give this some thought, Mrs. Novak. I'm sure we can arrange the wording to properly reflect the new status, yet preserve the integrity of Mr. Lhormer's contributions."

"Good. This now you project. I send sign painters to you and you tell them how change writing in window. Okay?"

"Consider it done. Do you want to see my recommendations before the signage is changed?"

"No. You boss for this one. I trust you."

The exterior of the front windows of the office soon showed off the changes made. Large gold letters on a black background proudly announced, "Clairton Savings and Loan." Smaller, gold letters edged in black announced, "Albert Lhormer, Founder," and beneath his name, "Katheryn Novak, Proprietor."

Katie was satisfied. Robert's presentation paid homage to Albert as the firm's founder. She felt he would have approved.

11

Curious Stranger

"When we do the best we can, we never know what miracle is wrought in our life, or in the life of another." —Helen Keller

LUCY BURNS PACED IMPATIENTLY, waiting for the early morning commuter train to arrive. Late again. This time by nearly thirty minutes. Standing among the throng on the crowded platform, a rumble shook fellow commuters announcing the arrival of the iron horse. The backdraft from the approaching railcars moved her full-length woolen coat, pressing it flat against her. A flick of the wrist discarded the lipstick-stained empty candy wrapper into the trash bin before boarding. Rogue wrappers, cigarette butts, and other debris swirled in the wind created by the transport. Metal on metal shrieking screamed the arrival of the tardy train. Monotone announcements over the loudspeaker told her what she already knew, that her train was boarding on track number three.

Her routine had begun at five o'clock that morning. No prompting required as the energetic early riser began her day at such an ungodly hour. Discarding her night clothes, she selected an outfit chosen by her venduese during a recent trip to Paris. Her thin figure allowed for skipping a corset under a smart blouse and gored skirt, enabling easy movement under the wool jacket and winter coat. Her reward for the early morning departure?

A nearly empty commuter train from Boston to New York City, complete with a private cabin and window view.

Once aboard, angry hissing of the steam engine preceded the chug, chug, chug of iron wheels toiling to get the monstrosity underway.

As the commuter rumbled along the tracks, a slight smell of burning coal teased her nostrils. She made the run so often she didn't pay attention to the blending view of industrial and commercial buildings and factories into rural farmlands. The back-and-forth motion often lulled Lucy Burns and many of her fellow passengers to sleep during the commute, allowing for a bit of extra pre-work shuteye. But on this morning Lucy was unable to drop into dreamland. She fidgeted anxiously, blankly gazing out the window. Looking but not seeing. Hearing but not listening. Bored and out of synch. Her activist efforts had not yielded the results for which she'd hoped. At least not yet.

Glancing down she espied a copy of a several day-old Boston Traveller newspaper, apparently left by the previous occupant of the seat next to hers and missed by the cleaning crew. She reached for it in hopes of reading some drivel or other to help pass the time and ease her anxiety. Smiling, she recalled the adage of thrift often spoken by her tightwad father. "A twice-read newspaper saves half-a penny."

Page one shouted a graphic description of the atrocities of war: "Precisely what artillery could do to human flesh and bones described by Jack Dorgan, a sergeant in the Northumberland Fusiliers, when his position took a direct hit from a German shell. He was unhurt, but two of his comrades were flung out of the trench by the blast ..."

She scanned an editorial that defended President Woodrow Wilson for sending American troops to fight "Europe's war."

Skimming several additional bits of news and gossip, she came upon another article that irked her. After scanning it she ruminated, *Once again this idiot president boasts that he refuses to support women's suffrage.* She slammed the paper down onto her lap in anger, but not before catching a glimpse of the photo of a woman next to the headline, *Woman Defies Society. Refuses Traditional Role. Runs Successful Business,"* by Homer J. Hammer.

Lucy spoke aloud to herself in the nearly-empty coach cabin. "Well, what is this? A woman who refuses to bend to male tradition? Must be another wealthy debutant."

A quick glance at the first paragraph proved her wrong and had her hooked. Reading the story aloud, not caring whether or not fellow passengers were in listening distance — they were not — she spoke loudly over the rumbling noises of the railcar. She smiled to herself as she read aloud. *"Katie Novak is no ordinary woman, to be sure. Born into the era of poverty and famine in Europe, expelled from a private school at age seven for knowing too many answers, and brought to America to participate in an arranged marriage. Instead of falling into line with other women of similar backgrounds, Mrs. Novak bucked tradition in a big way. With a partner, willing to train her in finance, an open letter of credit from industrialist Henry Clay Frick, and a work ethic that reached so far it caught the eye of the federal government, Katie Novak has become the most powerful businessperson in her community, man or woman."*

Lucy continued the story, opening the paper fully, and posited as she read further. "I've got to meet this woman and bring her into our cause."

Fully engrossed, Lucy continued reading and rereading the article until the train slowed and shuddered to a halt as it arrived in New York's Grand Central Station. Tucking the paper under her arm, she gathered her purse and umbrella and left her first-class cabin.

Exiting the coach, Lucy took little notice of her surroundings in the grand station. Twelve constellations painted in gold leaf overhead, 2,500 stars shone on the massive ceiling. The zodiac, purposely painted backwards according to Cornelius Vanderbilt, founder and benefactor of the garish building, was intended to be viewed from a divine perspective. But instead of giving thought to the depot's grandeur, Lucy observed the station to be more crowded than the one she left in Boston.

Little more than a vast cavity, the terminal was made to look grander by all the art and geld. Instead it seemed smaller by the hordes of all types of mankind: businessmen in clean pressed suits, families toting children by the hand, mysterious-looking Middle Eastern women with faces obscured by veils, and ever-present police walking their beats. Beggars under the watchful eye of the constabulary tried not to be noticed except by a possible mark.

Aromas of freshly baked pretzels and pastries filled the air, but Lucy ignored it all. She paid little mind to the gigantic opal clock, the crown jewel of the Main Concourse, nor to the acoustical phenomenon that allows one's whisper to be heard in the opposite corner of the edifice. Instead she rushed out of the building and hailed a taxi.

Exiting the Forty-Second Street and Park Avenue egress, yet another famous Tiffany clock passed unnoticed, adorned with a statuary of the Greek gods — Mercury, Hercules, and Minerva — representing virtues of the railroad, speed, strength, and intellect. She'd passed through these wonders of architecture so often they had become passé to her. Instead of viewing the scenes in awe, as so many new Americans must have done upon their arrival, Lucy simply glanced up to note the time, then waved down a taxi that took her to the garage to retrieve her stored car.

She'd wired ahead so the proprietor of the garage had the car brought forward, highly polished, filled with gasoline, and ready for whatever adventure its owner chose.

The proprietor asked, "Off on a lark, Mizz Lucy, or driving into the City?"

Neither, Geno, I have work to do in Pittsburgh, then Washington."

"I got your destinations from your wire. Most of the travel from here to Pittsburgh will be on the new Lincoln Highway, just opened a couple years ago. I ain't drove it yet but my customers tell me some stretches don't have gas so I strapped a couple extra gas cans on for ya."

"Thanks, Geno. Anything else I need to be wary of? Bears? Bandits? Bushwhackers?"

"Naw, it's pretty civilized. Just be sure to top off your tanks whenever you can. If you have to cross a stream, stop and wade in it to check the depth before trying to drive through. I fixed you up with chains, shovel, axe, jack, two extra tires and inner tubes, and a few other tools just in case. Oh, and don't wear your best shoes."

"You are a dear, Geno. What would I do without you?"

The garage man continued, "And to celebrate the journey, I attached a pair of Lincoln Highway pennants to the fenders. You'll be the cat's meow, no question 'bout that."

"Well then, it looks like I'm all set for the journey. Anything else?"

"Well, Ma'am, if you were anybody else I'd suggest you take a companion, but since it's you, I fear for the safety of any bear, bully, or brigand that stands in your way."

He provided maps and directions to the Lincoln Highway and onward to Pittsburgh.

"May I use your phone, Geno?"

"Of course."

Within sixty minutes of her arrival in New York, Lucy called her office from the garage and spoke to her director of research. "Estella, I want you to do a full background history on Katie Novak, N-O-V-A-K, of ..." glancing at the newspaper in her hand she continued, "Clairton, Pennsylvania. Use the Astor and Lenox libraries, as well as New York Public. Check arrival records from Europe. I want to know everything there is to know about this woman."

"Got it, Boss," shouted the voice on the other end of the phone. "What else?"

Lucy continued. "Book a room for me at the William Penn Hotel in Pittsburgh. Telegraph everything you can find on her to me at the hotel. Put all my other business on hold for the moment. I'm about to begin a long, bumpy motor trip, and I'm determined to meet and recruit a special lady. I want to convince her to join the cause of women's suffrage."

"Will do, Boss."

"Good. I'll call you from Pittsburgh."

Lucy hung up the phone and left the gritty office. Geno had the car running and waiting for her. "Thank you, my friend. Bill me for your services. Be sure to add the fee for the phone call."

He nodded and waved, watching the Model T grind into gear and chug out the garage and down the path toward the highway. Wiping his hands on a greasy rag, the garage man shook his head in awe. "There goes one amazing woman. She and that Alice woman are out to change the world. I have no doubt they'll do it."

Lucy Burns and colleague Alice Paul had organized the National Women's Party five years earlier. The group sought social change for women using tactics they'd learned from similar ventures in England. Strategies included participation in hunger strikes, picketing the White House — a first for the president's residence — and other means of civil disobedience designed to publicize the cause of women's suffrage.

* * *

Within several weeks after Homer completed his story on Katie and returned to Washington, a routine once again fell into place at the Savings and Loan.

Hope was deep in thought as she reviewed loans and other transactions scheduled for the week and did not pay attention to the noise outside her workspace, nor did she notice the black convertible Ford motorcar parking in front of the office building.

The car's lone occupant, a tall, thin, stately woman, exited the vehicle and strode into the Savings and Loan office. Assuming this person to be another applicant for the secretarial position, Hope rose from her desk, removed her spectacles, nodded, and greeted the woman.

"Good morning, Madam," she smiled, "how may we be of service to you? Are you seeking a loan or employment?"

Hope immediately noticed the woman's chic clothing. She loved fashion, discussing it with the buyer at Skapik's, and studying current fashion magazine trends at every opportunity. Hope eyed the woman closely, noting the tall, statuesque figure, impeccable ramrod straight posture and attire; waistline dropped toward her natural waist, calf-length dress over an ankle-length underskirt. She studied the v-neckline and guessed she wore a corset rather than the more restrictive girdle. Dark colors. Simple cuts. A Newboy cap sat easily above her loose chignon hair style. *This woman is a fashion plate, she thought. Her taste and style are right out of a fashion magazine and suggests she is upper class and does not live in Clairton. I'll bet she's a potential client, not an applicant.*

The stranger's sparkling deep set brown, almost black eyes, the color of the Clairton sky during a work day, complemented her olive skin. Her fresh complexion accented perfectly the clothing she wore. *Even Pittsburgh isn't up to her style. No, this fashion plate of a woman must be from New York City.*

The stranger announced, "I would like to speak to the proprietor."

"Perhaps I can get things started, Madam. Can our manager, Mr. White, or I help you?"

"No, my business is with the real proprietor, Katheryn Novak."

Her comment caught Hope off guard. Many new customers and visitors assumed she could help them. Robert White, the lone male in the office appeared to be the owner. Few asked who owned the business, despite the newly repainted window. Many assumed Katie, with her relaxed style, to be an employee. None were as direct, nor as intimidating, as the woman who now stood before them.

Hope cleared her throat, a bit nonplussed, but not miffed. "Certainly, Ma'am. I will gather her directly. May I tell her the nature of your business?"

"No."

Katie heard the exchange from her open office window. The proprietor also dressed smartly by local standards. Albert had seen to that. He had selected the wardrobe she wore today; ankle-length black dress puffed at the shoulders and buttoned up the bodice, accentuated by a classical feminine saltwater pearl necklace, delicately shaped oyster shell earrings to match, and flattering pin of pastel and monochrome palettes positioned above her left breast.

Sliding her wooden swivel chair across the polished office floor, Katie stood and promptly descended the stairs. Hope, facing Katie so the client could not see, rolled her eyes. No words were exchanged. The gesture tipped her off to proceed with caution.

Though Katie's syntax remained far from that of the King's English, she had come a long way with her use of the language and was comfortable speaking English. "I am owner, Katie Novak. How I can help you?"

The stately woman extended her hand, "Lucy Burns. Is there a place where we can speak?"

"You want go cross street to café or up my office?"

"The office will be fine, thank you."

Hope spoke, "Can I brew some tea, Ma'am?"

"Yes, thank you." Lucy nodded affirmatively and walked into the office ahead of her hostess.

"Mr. White, would you excuse us for a few moments?"

"Of course. I was about to brew some tea. May I bring some for the two of you?"

"Hope say she prepare us tea. Maybe you watch and give her few tips. You make best tea in city."

Robert bowed and left the room as Lucy seated herself and smoothed her skirt. Katie took the opposite chair.

Lucy began, "Mrs. Novak. May I call you Katie?" Her warm smile, revealing a dimple in each cheek, disarmed Katie's initial caution.

Katie nodded. Lucy continued, "Katie, are you familiar with the women's suffrage movement taking place in this country?"

"I know plenty women suffer, but not for movement. What means that?"

"Suffrage is a term meaning the right to vote in political elections. I'm sure you know that with few exceptions, women across America do not have that right at present."

The visitor to Katie's office had a unique way of speaking. Her elocution did not have the same ring of people in the area, not even speakers native to the region. Nor was it the accent of a foreign-born American. Katie heard many of those during any given day at the office, and her ear was acute enough to identify whether the speaker was a local American, or if not, from which country their first language came. Often, she narrowed an accent to the speaker's region of the country. But Lucy's speaking was different. Her words were articulated in a clear, crisp manner. Katie had never before heard a formally educated New Yorker speak.

Katie began with a mild boast, "Me and my old man, Pete, we both Amedigan citizen, but only he 'lowed for vote."

"Exactly. A movement is afoot to provide all American citizens that right regardless of gender."

Katie listened intently. Although she didn't understand some of Lucy's words, such as gender, the message was clear and righteous. *But why did this lady come to tell me this?* she wondered. *What is her game?*

At age thirty-eight, nearly twice Katie's age, Lucy Burns, the consummate activist feminist, still exuded the same level of beauty and energy that she had decades earlier while fighting vigorously for women's rights in both Britain and America.

"You are a highly successful businesswoman. Your money and position allow you many perquisites in society. I have examined the public records of your Savings and Loan company and can see that you and the gentleman…"

"Albert," Katie interrupted, still needing to honor her mentor's contributions. "My partner name Albert. Albert Lhormer. His name on window. He is founder. That mean be start business before we come partner. He mentor me and is reason business do so well. He pass 'way, but this business not be here if don' be for him."

"Yes, I know he passed recently, and I'm so sorry for your loss. You have my deepest sympathy."

"Thank you. That very kind of you. But now you tell me why you here and what can I do for you. You not look like need finance."

Lucy smiled at the astute manner hidden under her syntax. "No, Katie, we don't need your financial support as much as we need you."

At that moment, Hope stood awkwardly outside the door, knocking cautiously with one hand and balancing the tea service in the other. This would be her first opportunity to show off the serving skills Pete had taught her. Despite the lack of fine china in the Novak household and language differences between Hope and himself, Pete managed to teach her basic dining and serving techniques using a combination of broken English and his second language, German.

Katie again interrupted Lucy for a moment. "Come in, Hope."

Hope entered the office, holding a perfectly set silver platter that included a doily, teapot covered with a tea cozy, milk, nut horns, ladylocks, and two delicate china cups. She deposited the perfectly set platter between the two women.

Hope bowed to the women, showing off the German Pete taught her. "Hier ist Ihr Tee und Kekse, Tee ist heiß. Kekse sind süß."

Lucy smiled and said, "Danke schön, Fräulein."

Hope responded, "Bitte." Then added in English, "You speak German?"

"Yes. I studied at the university in Berlin."

"I don't really speak German. Mr. Novak does, though. Today is the first time I had an opportunity to show what I learned."

Lucy smiled at the girl. "You did fine, Fräulein. I can see you had an able instructor and he had an excellent student."

Blushing, Hope added, "May I pour?"

Katie looked directly at her charge. "No tank you. That be all, Hope. Thank you for fix nice tray."

Remembering Pete's instructions, she bowed to both women, took two steps back in formal European fashion, then turned and left the office.

Lucy smiled. "She is a gem."

"Long story, but we plan adopt her."

The two women ignored the tea and pastries for the moment. Lucy refocused and continued, "I have been an activist ever since I can remember. Really caught the fever while in England, helping organize events that supported the cause of women's rights there. My mission is to work toward placing our sisters on an even keel with men. Fellow activist Susan Anthony has written legislation. Congress has proposed her amendment to the Constitution that would give American women the right to vote. President Wilson opposes it.

"Two days ago I was on a commuter train traveling from Boston to my office in New York. By chance I glanced at a newspaper that had been left in the car. After reading your story, I had to meet you and convince you to join our cause. If that article depicts you accurately, there exists a fire in your belly that makes you perfect to join our sisters and our cause. You will be helping the women of America."

Pausing to let her words sink in, Lucy smiled and added, "May I?" Katie nodded as Lucy gracefully removed the tea cozy, lifted the teapot and poured the steeped tea for the two of them. "Milk?"

Katie shook her head. She'd never heard of milk being added to tea, but changed her mind and accepted once she saw Lucy add milk to her own cup.

The tea had simmered; now it was time for Katie to simmer over the suggestion.

Lucy placed her index finger inside of the cup loop up to her knuckle, placing the thumb on the handle to secure the cup. The bottom of the handle rested on her third finger, her fourth and fifth fingers curling back toward her wrist with perfect ease, demonstrating her early debutant training. She studied the younger woman's face as she sipped. Lucy knew she had Katie's full attention.

"I will not mislead you. Our plan includes picketing the White House, something that has never been done before, so we are not certain what the repercussions might be. You may be cursed at, spat upon, handled roughly by police, or worse. This is not a dainty tea party for wealthy women to play. It is a cause to which you must be totally committed. Those brave women who join our cause are not faint of heart. But our victory, *and we WILL claim victory*, will loosen the bonds that keep our sisters in chains."

As she further studied Katie's face she could see the wheels of her mind turning.

The taking of tea by the two women resembled a formal dance. Katie, deep in thought, watched the proper woman through the corner of her eye and mimicked the moves with her own cup. She followed Lucy, adding milk and gently swishing the spoon back and forth, until the color of the tea changed to a light brown. Not letting the spoon clink against the sides of the cup, she mirrored Lucy's every move. One after the other, both women removed the spoons, placed them on saucers, behind the cups, and to the right of the handles. Neither touched the neatly arranged baked goods on the tray.

The tea lesson and perfection of Katie's following her lead was not lost on Lucy.

"Tell me more 'bout women suffrage, good and bad. I want know every ting before I make decision."

Lucy Burns spent the next two hours educating her tutee on the history of the movement for women's rights in both America and Great Britain. Katie listened intently. It was a pleasant change to have a teacher whose lecture filled her head with new information. Her mind raced as she absorbed Lucy's every word. Had Lucy Burns been her mentor in the old country, Katie's schooling and life would have been much different.

Lucy took one of the nut horns from the silver tray and repeated, "Our next move is to picket the White House. As I said, this is something that has never been done before. The President is adamantly against our mission and we are bound and determined to change his mind and the minds of the men in Congress. The movement has already begun. When I leave you, I'm on my way to Washington. I'd like you to join us."

"My Old Man, he get medal from president."

The comment confounded Lucy. Her research team's thorough dossier on Katie's history did not reveal a relationship between Woodrow Wilson and Peter Novak, nor any indication that Katie's husband had done anything to earn a medal. As far as she knew, Peter had never even served in the military. She dismissed the statement, thinking Katie must have misspoken, but filed the incident away in the back of her mind.

Katie walked Lucy to the door and watched her climb into a bright red 1917 Model T. The Ford, an All-American automobile, cost $360.00. She studied the vehicle, a black enamel radiator with rounded corners boasted a script lettered FORD logo stamped across the front. Highly-polished brass adorned the radiator filler and hub caps. Katie giggled when Lucy pushed the button on the steering column and tooted "aoooogah." The horn, a new feature on the 1917 Model T, brought polite laughter from the office.

As she returned to the building, Hope followed her into the office where Robert had already removed the tea service and half-empty cookie tray.

Robert ventured, "Well, Mrs. Novak, that was quite the way to start the day. An interesting lady to be sure. I couldn't help but wonder what the two of you talked about for two hours."

"Her name Lucy Burns."

Robert thought for a moment then snapped to attention. "Oh, my goodness. That was Lucy Burns? From New York City? Of course! It all fits. The car. Dressed in the latest fashions ... I've read about her. Do you realize a celebrity just graced our business? Surely she didn't come asking for a loan."

"She want me help with suffer for women so we able vote."

Robert gushed. "Oh my goodness, oh my goodness. Lucy Burns in our little money store. I spoke to a celebrity. I can't believe it. I can't imagine this ever happening in the Elizabeth bank."

He rarely spoke of the bank in Elizabeth, but in such an exciting moment as this he forgot himself.

Katie remained calm, not unimpressed, but not as manic as Robert. "What you tink if I leave business for couple weeks? She want me go Washington picket on President Wilson. He no want give women's for vote. You tink you can handle business if I gone, Robert?"

Still dazed, Robert tried to make sense of what must have happened during the past two hours. "She asked you to join her movement? I hope I'm not brash if I ask how she knew who you are and where to find you?"

Katie shrugged. "She say she know all 'bout me. Remember young man who interview me? He say he gon' write my story in newspaper. Lucy see story on train and find me for cause I be immigrant woman success with business."

"The article must have been picked up in one of the New York dailies. That freelance reporter who interviewed you. You told me his name. Harvey? Harold? Hector? Hugo!"

Hope blushed and chimed into the conversation. "I'm not sure but I think his name is Homer, Mrs. Novak."

"You right. My old man say last name like hit on head."

Robert, showing the most emotion since his arrival at the savings and loan cried out, "Hammer! That's it. Homer Hammer. We never gave it much thought but he must have sold the story to one of the East Coast newspapers. How about that? I'm working with a famous businesswoman and didn't even know it."

"So, you tink if I go march with Lucy and other womens without hurt business?"

"Well, let's give this some thought. I'm confident that with Hope and the two secretaries we can hold down the day-to-day operations for a while. We've grown so much so quickly, but you've kept the files highly organized and many of my responsibilities from the bank transfer easily to the Savings and Loan. Yes, we can handle it until you return. You say what, a couple weeks? Yes, it will be hectic, but we can do it."

Hope had been quiet as Katie and Robert spoke, but she took her swing at responsibility. "You won't have to worry about the house with Mr. Novak and the children. I can help there. I'll come to work daily, but it would be nice if we had a telephone to reach you in an emergency."

Robert nodded in agreement.

"Good idea, Hope. Maybe I have one put in house, too. Pete, he no need you round house. He take care of every-ting now I working here. Hope, you and me, we talk to him tonight when we be get home. For now, we get ready for rest of day. I got more interview to do. I want hire one more office girl."

As had quickly become the family custom, Katie arrived home that night to a hearty dinner with Pete, Hope, and the children. After dinner, she played with Ruža, whom they now called by her American nickname, Rosie. Little Petey sat on his father's lap, head on Pete's chest, and eyes nearly closed. Pete scooped the child into his arms and gently carried him to the children's bedroom. Rosie followed dutifully. Within an hour both children were asleep in their beds.

This was the adults' alone time, to relax and talk, and Hope had become a member of the adult camp. Pete began the nightly conversation in their native dialect. "So how did your day go today on the hill? Did any of the applicants show promise?"

Katie responded in English, both for Hope's benefit and to practice the language. "Couple of dem look okay. I like one girl. Daughter of Serbian family. She just finish high school top of class. I goin' ask principal for recommend her. I know principal. He English man, name Mr. Woodman, but he finance house with us. What you think, Hope?"

"I'm glad you included me in the interviews. I agree that Mila Petrovich is the best candidate. She gave the best answers and didn't get flustered when you gave her the trick question."

"Man comink tomorrow for last one, look promise, too. He have business in old country and speak many language."

Katie gave thought to her next topic of conversation. "Hope, I gon' talk in our language so I be sure Pete understand."

Hope nodded.

Katie began. *"An interesting thing happened today. A lady came to the office. She is from New York, name of Lucy Burns."*

As his wife spoke Pete pulled a bag of Cutty Pipe smoking tobacco from the pocket of his ragged sweater-vest, followed by a book of Zig-Zag rolling papers. Placing a pinch of tobacco in one of the papers and using the technique learned years ago aboard the ship that brought him to America, he rolled a perfectly-shaped cigarette, licked the paper, and sealed the blunt with a twist at either end. Flicking a wooden match with his thumbnail, he lit the smoke and a sweet aroma filled the air.

"She read about me in the paper and wanted to meet me."

"Read about you in the paper?"

"Yes. Remember when Homer came to the office to talk to me about being a woman in business?"

Hope's eyes sparkled when she heard the mention of Homer's name, the only word she caught in the foreign language comments.

Pete nodded.

"Well, his story about me was printed in the paper in New York, or Boston, I'm not sure. Lucy Burns said she read about me and came here to meet me."

"She took a train all the way from New York just to meet you?"

"No, she didn't take a train. She drove her own car! She wants me to come to Washington and help women get the right to vote."

"A woman driving a car? Imagine that!" Pete took another puff, exhaled, and asked, *"Why?"*

"Why do women want to vote? Do you think ... "

Pete waved his hand to cut her off. *"No, not why do women want the vote. Why does she think you can help?"*

"She says I'm a born leader and 'unique.' Because of my being a successful businesswoman and an immigrant. She says I can help get a law passed to allow

women to vote. President Wilson is against it so women are protesting. I'll be gone a couple of weeks. Maybe less if we get the law passed sooner."

Her eyes moistened as she added, *"I made a promise to Albert as I held him in my arms that terrible morning. A promise that I would help people who are at a disadvantage in this country. This will be my first try."*

Pete shook his head. *"My beautiful, brilliant Katie. You are something special, that's for sure. The world is a better place with you as part of it. You go to Washington. We'll miss you while you're gone, but your life mission is to make this land that has been so good to us a better, stronger country. We're both American citizens. We both should be able to vote."*

Katie wasn't finished. She switched to English. "Hope and I be talk 'bout have telephone put in office. I tink I have dem put here at the house, too."

Pete's response surprised her. "I don't need that contraption in the house. Don't want it. Won't use it."

His reaction surprised Katie, but it shouldn't have. Pete's life had been traumatized, having been taken from his family at age eight and barely escaping Germany's military draft at eighteen. His unexpected journey to Mexico resulted in the death of three men. He didn't care to leave his cocoon on Arch Street. Even the short distance to Katie's business set him askance.

In America, his country of citizenship and loyalty, Pete lived in obscurity as an unknown hero and naturalized American citizen. But to himself, he was simply a shy, quiet man who wanted nothing more than to tend his farm and raise his children. He did not want to let the outside world back into his life. In Pete's mind, the telephone would be an intrusion to his solitude.

Katie continued. "Telephone is good ting have for emergency, if child hurt or you need some-ting fast."

Pete held firm. *"Have it put in if you insist, but I will not touch that thing. Too many new contraptions on this earth today. The world is moving too fast for me."*

"Okay for now. You tink 'bout it more. I need get business ready for I can go Washington."

Pete rose from the chair. *"I'm going to check on the children and take a walk."*

Katie and Hope sat in silence for a few moments, then Katie spoke. "Remember, my old man, he look tough on outside, but he no like lots of people. He like you, me, his kids, animals, and garden. He tell me sometimes he wish he be unvisible for other people."

"I understand, Mrs. Novak ..."

Katie interrupted, "When we at home, you call me Katie. Mrs. Novak only be for work."

"Okay, Katie. I can understand Mr. Novak's ..."

"Pete."

"Okay, Pete. I understand Pete's wanting to shut the world out. I feel that way sometimes, too. I can't remember anything about my life before you took me in, but I know that the people I feel closest to are you and your family."

"You part of family."

Hope wiped away a tear then continued. "I know, Mrs. ... uh, Katie. I just want you to know that I understand what Mr. ... Pete feels."

"You think I no should get phone for house?"

"Oh no, I think the phone is a good idea, but don't be upset if he doesn't use it."

"You smart girl, Hope."

"Thank you. Can I ask you something else?"

Katie nodded.

"If you see Homer in Washington will you tell him ... or ask him ... if he ever thinks of me?"

Katie grinned, "I ask him come here visit. How you like that?"

"Thanks, Mom. I mean, Katie."

The two women hugged and took their leave.

12

Off to Washington

"The probability that we may fail in the struggle ought not to deter us from the support of a cause we believe to be just." —Abraham Lincoln

CLAIRTON SAVINGS AND LOAN hummed efficiently the rest of the week. Bell Telephone Company workers installed a telephone in the business office and an extension in Katie's office. To Peter Novak's chagrin, another such device was mounted on the inside kitchen wall of the Novak home. True to his word, Pete refused to use the phone despite prodding from both his wife and adopted daughter.

When the phone installations were completed, Bell Telephone representative Buzz McGowan returned to the savings and loan for payment. "Well, Katie, I finished the job in your house but I don't think Pete liked it. He kept mumbling in Bosnian."

"Buzz, you speak same language?"

"I don't, but I've picked up a few phrases. He kept repeating, 'Ne želim tu prokletu stvar.' I can guess what that means."

Katie chuckled. "That pretty good. Take guess what you tink means in English."

"Get that damn thing out of here?"

"You pretty close. Means 'I no want damn ting.' We gon' have hire you for translate. Here is checks for you bill. Tanks for you good works."

"Any time, Katie. I appreciate you taking a chance on me to finance my house after your competition turned me down."

"No be worry," she joked, "if you miss payment I call you on telephone."

To better prepare for Katie's absence, the office needed another employee, preferably one with experience. Hope, Robert, and Katie interviewed four to five people each day. Among them, one stood out on paper. Jacob Shaheen, a middle-aged gentleman and recent immigrant.

The interviews took place in the office occupied by Katie and Robert. Hope joined the interview team as the three sat facing the applicant.

Katie opened the interview. "Good morning, Mr. Shaheen. So you interest in management position. Tell us little 'bout you-self, why you want work here, and experience before."

The applicant spoke using appropriate grammar but with a thick accent. "Good morning, Mrs. Novak, Miss Novak, and Mr. White. My name is Jacob Shaheen, but please call me by my American name, Jack. I saw your ad in the Pittsburgh Post.

"I'm originally from Europe and have been a merchant all my adult life and most of my youth. I began as a child working in a Moroccan souk in Rabat. My father backed the wrong political party and one day he just disappeared. My mother, sisters, and I escaped to Beirut where I owned several businesses, all successful. I've done everything from run errands to buy merchandise to balance the books."

Robert spoke next. "Mr. Shaheen, I'm Robert White, assistant to Mrs. Novak. I handle most of the long-term transactions. Have you any experience in the savings and loan business or calculating interest rates?"

His voice was calm. His manner easy, but, he spoke with authority. "I admit I have not worked in a bank or a lending institution, although I've had dealings with many bankers from the merchant side. My studies in night school have included the calculation of interest rates."

Hope posed a question. "What do you see as the greatest asset you bring to the Clairton Savings and Loan?"

Jack paused for a moment. "Europe, North Africa, and the Middle East have many cultures, faiths, and languages, all of which interact with one another. I chose to make my home here because I see a similar blend of people. To have order in any business and society, communication is essential. I pride myself on having the ability to speak several languages. As your business has clients of many ethnic backgrounds, my means to communicate with them and understand their needs will be an asset."

Katie interjected. "What languages you speak?"

"Of course, as you can readily see, I'm comfortable speaking in English, but I am also able to communicate in German, French, Spanish, Italian, most Balto-Slavic, and Middle Eastern languages."

Katie decided to test him. "Kako biste me pozdravili na hrvatskom?"

Without pausing, Jack answered, "If you entered our business and spoke Croatian I'd greet you as follows: 'Dobro jutro, Gospođo. Kako vam mogu pomoći?'"

Katie smiled and nodded.

Another question from Hope. "How long have you lived in the area?"

"I arrived in America six months ago. I have a cousin in Glassport who has been gracious enough to take me in and introduce me to the area. I've been living off my savings but now must find gainful employment." With a grin he added, "Travel and vacation over. Time to get to work."

Hope asked a follow-up question. "Do you plan to bring your family to settle here as well?"

"No, Miss. I have no family. Only me. My mother is gone and my sisters are married."

Robert had been making notes. "I don't want to appear to be indelicate, Mr. Shaheen, but what inspired you to leave your home and come to America?"

"I'm a businessman, Sir. Just as you are. I've spent most of my forty-two years in face-to-face contact with people. I never married or had children. I love the interaction with people and the building of success. But the past several years has become increasingly difficult in Lebanon, especially with the war. Repeated lootings and extortion by ragtag militia, increased taxes, a failing economy, the never-ending religious battles, political unrest, and assaults on innocent people. The tipping point came when I was beaten and robbed at gunpoint in my own marketplace. I became tired of paying bribes and pretending to be political when I'm not. America is the land of opportunity. I know how to work hard and serve people. That is my desire."

Jacob "Jack" Shaheen's work experience and language skills offered terrific benefits to the company. His linguistic ability allowed him to converse in the cacophony of languages heard when conducting daily business at the savings and loan, and his strong business background meant he needed minimal training. Jack Shaheen proved to be a terrific resource and a timely hire.

The other addition to the company, Natalie Anastasia-Alexandra LoPresti, interviewed as the final applicant of the week. By this time, Hope had become as comfortable in the interview process as both Katie and Robert. She opened the discussion. "Miss Lopresti, tell us a little about your background and qualifications."

"If you don't mind, I prefer to go by Natalie rather than my full name. Natalie Anastasia-Alexandra is so difficult for so many people to pronounce and spell. If I had a dollar for each letter in my name, I wouldn't have to look for work."

The panel chuckled and Hope continued. "Very well, Natalie. Go on."

"I'm first generation American, born in McKeesport but grew up in Glassport. My father is from Venice, Italy where he learned the trade of glass blowing at the Murano Island glassworks. He now works for the United States Glass Company in Glassport. My mother is from Russia. She came here for marriage, which had been arranged by her family. Two days before her arrival, an accident in the mill claimed the life of her intended husband. Instead of returning to Russia immediately, she stayed with relatives, who happened to be neighbors with my father. They met, married, and one year later I came along."

"Are you multi-lingual?"

"Yes. I speak Italian and Russian as well as English, of course. The Russian Orthodox priest taught me the Cyrillic alphabet so I can write Russian as well as read and speak it. I just graduated as salutatorian of my class in the commercial business program at Glassport High School. On my exit exam, I typed eighty-two words per minute with no errors. I also take dictation in Gregg shorthand."

Hope noticed a diamond on her finger an asked, "Are you married?"

"I'm engaged to a police sergeant, Ashton Brown. We plan to marry. She blushed and added, "but not have children for five to ten years."

Though all remaining applicants were strong, Jack Shaheen and Natalie LoPresti best fit the needs of the Clairton Savings and Loan.

Grisnik's Bakery also benefitted from Katie's candidates. Two young female applicants, both recent high school graduates were not among the Savings and Loan's selections, but both showed great promise and were referred to the bakery. A delighted Frank Grisnik hired both; Krista Starr to work the front of the store serving customers and Emily Achorn to learn the baking trade.

With the Clairton Savings and Loan company solidly staffed, Katie felt comfortable leaving for hiatus in Washington to pursue her newfound cause. The banker Robert White would oversee the operation. In addition to his expertise in banking, a spate of movement occurred that further bolstered the growing Savings and Loan's business. Many patrons followed him, departing the First Elizabeth Bank in favor of Clairton Savings and Loan.

The trek to Washington did not begin immediately upon the hiring of new employees. Instead, several weeks passed under Katie's direct supervision to assure a smooth transition and see that the new hires would work out. She stayed home two or three days each week forcing the crew to operate without her input. Once satisfied the daily routine would run smoothly in her absence, and feeling confident that Hope would serve as a contact person, Katie Novak prepared for what she correctly expected would be an exciting journey.

On this morning, though she did not have Albert's counsel, Katie selected her own travel outfit, certain it would have pleased her mentor. Deciding to make the long train ride in comfort, she chose a simple tailored navy blue dress, a pair of gloves that reached halfway up her arm, and a wide-brim straw hat encircled by a matching, neatly tied sash.

She had awakened early the morning of her departure and dressed in silence to the aroma of fresh eggs and bacon that rose from the kitchen. Pete insisted that she have a hearty breakfast for the long trip to Washington. As she descended the stairs and looked at her lair, she thought about how much her life had changed. Silently speaking, she thought, *you know Pete, It seems like ages since I arrived from Croatia. The last time I'd been on a long train ride, the itinerary took me from New York to Pittsburgh and on to Clairton. Today I thought about the young Croatian couple I met on the train. We promised to keep in touch with each other. Now I can't even remember their names.*

Upon arrival in Clairton, on the same tracks that would carry her to Washington, she remembered saving her heart for Branko Kukić, a boyfriend from Europe. She became a little melancholy as she reflected, *Ah, Branko. He disappeared just before I left for America. No telling where he might be today. Probably at war, or one of the war's many casualties.* She giggled as she tried to picture him in a military uniform. He was so undisciplined. Not the ideal soldier. Probably spent most of his time being yelled at by his superiors, or in the brig for drinking fighting and otherwise breaking the rules.

Instead of a life with Branko, the gift inside her had spoken. *You will never return to the old country but will have a good life with Peter.* Nothing short of the encouragement from her inner gift could have convinced her to face what she certainly believed would be a bleak future.

But the future did not turn bleak. Rather, her life to this point had been charmed. The building of the house, supervising workers, bearing two children, enjoying the benefits of a prosperous business. She felt certain her good life would continue. She had not heard from the gift inside her for a while, though it had helped her make most the important decisions in her life. She hoped it still lived within her and continue to guide her.

Arriving at the breakfast table she found Hope and the two little ones seated and devouring breakfast. Pete heard her footfalls and moved to the stove to bring her repast to the table.

"Here you are, my dear wife. Eggs, bacon, your favorite bread, warm pumpernickel rye from Grisniks Bakery, and hot coffee. I've packed you a basket of food so you don't starve on the train before reaching Washington. You look lovely as usual."

"Old Man, you too good to me."

The family finished breakfast. Pete put on a slicker, picked up an umbrella and bowing, he announced, *"Your carriage awaits, my lady."*

Hope and the children took turns hugging Katie, then sat on the front porch, sheltered from the rain, as they watched the couple walk toward the train station. Pete had gone to the station earlier that morning and purchased a first-class ticket with an open return. He checked her large trunk in the luggage car. That left Katie with only a grip and a cloth bag to carry aboard.

They left the house for the train amidst a light drizzle, in much the same fashion as they'd done when Katie first arrived, with Pete toting her bags. He carried an umbrella in one hand and her grip and bag in the other, just as he had when she first arrived. This time, however, the carry-on bags belonged to a successful entrepreneur rather than a teen.

She recalled that rain-soaked departure platform on which they stood where she first met Pete, but paid him little attention on what she believed to be a short visit with her parents. Instead, war and life had other plans for her.

No longer the roughshod teen who first arrived several years ago, Katie looked every bit the prosperous businesswoman, dressed to the nines but for comfort in travel. Others boarding the train noticed her very current style of clothing. Albert's legacy saw to it that her attire stood as flawless as the women she planned to meet up with at her destination.

The crisp morning air, dense with fog, obscured the two figures from their family a few minutes after stepping off the porch. A taste of soot from the mill fell on their lips. Despite the umbrella, humidity and the light sprinkle dampened their clothing.

Pete helped his wife onto the Baltimore and Ohio Railway car marked with a gold-leaf painted figure "1" indicating first-class cabins, then watched as she gracefully walked down the aisle, accompanied by a porter, to a compartment about midway the length of the car. The porter placed her grip in the overhead bin. She sat her purse and hat in the center seat and sat next to the window so she could see Pete wave to her as the train left the station.

Hordes of fellow passengers boarded that October morning; some half awake, others half asleep, nearly all commuters headed to downtown Pittsburgh for white-collar positions. Most wore suits, ties, jackets, and highly polished shoes that squeaked after unsuccessful attempts to dodge puddles. First- and second-class compartments were sparsely populated, but the masses beyond the expensive seating clung to the railcar as honeybees to a hive.

Pete and Katie, prepared for their first separation since an American adventure of Pete's, waved at one another as the giant locomotive, likely built with steel from the nearby mill, began to chug, rumble, and prepare for its morning run. Steam hissed, covering the immediate platform area. For an instant Pete became invisible, though he still held her gaze.

"All aboard," cried a conductor as he waved a lantern and looked fore and aft. Katie noticed the man's shiny black suit and brass buttons, a uniform befitting a veteran conductor. With a huff and the hiss of escaping steam, a porter shouted a repeat of the conductor's command, this time louder. "BOOOARD …"

The two-hundred-ton locomotive's steel wheels spun beneath its weight as the iron horse began to creep out of the station. Pete wiped a mixture of raindrops and tears from his eyes. Katie forced her window open as Pete ran alongside the train for the length of the platform. The heavens opened and the heavy rain soaked him through the slicker. No matter. He continued to run and wave as the train picked up speed. The white plume from the smokestack waved back.

Rotating wheels of the engine continued to churn, turning on the shiny silver rails. Clunking and screeching, reluctantly tugging behind it a coal car, three passenger cars, one for luggage, and a caboose. Slowly moving along the platform, grunting noises echoed as late arrivers raced across the scaffold to reach the moving convoy. A rough jacket-arm scraped across Pete's face as its nameless owner rushed to capture his usual seat. Pete continued to run alongside the first-class passenger car, waving and struggling to keep up with Katie for as long as possible. He called, "*You be safe, Kata,*" using her girlhood name.

Shouting back at him, Katie cried through the open window of her compartment, "You no be worry, Old Man. I take care. This be good ting for Amedigan women in Washington, just like you did good ting for this 'medigan country."

Pete could not understand her message between the noise of the locomotive's engine and discord of passengers, but he continued to run and wave until reaching the end of the platform. He watched the red lantern on the caboose disappear into the morning fog and smoke belching from the mill's smokestacks.

As the train disappeared, Pete reflected on his own departure from this platform. It was the one and only time he ventured from his home. Thanks to his professor/tutor as an indentured servant in Germany, he spoke the German language like a highly-placed diplomat instead of a peasant. That command of the language during his sailing to America found him in an accidental relationship with an aide to American President Woodrow

Wilson. That chance meeting led to a clandestine trip to Mexico to help convince the Mexican president not to join forces with Germany and go to war against the United States. Pete's action earned him the unofficial designation of "unknown hero," as well as citizenship for himself and Katie, and helped place the Clairton Savings and Loan on the preferred vendor list for government funding. Benefits of Pete's secret heroism also included scholarships to Princeton University for any of the couple's children who would choose to attend.

The train rumbled through smoke of the steel mills that lined the river as Katie contemplated on all that had happened since her arrival in Clairton. She first thought the city held little promise. Instead, its opportunity made her a wealthy woman.

Inside the comfortable compartment, Katie leaned back and stretched out across the wide seat, closing her eyes. In a matter of hours, she'd be in the nation's capital participating in dangerous but righteous work. She opened her eyes, arose, and picked up the handbag from the seat next to her. After placing her purse and umbrella on the luggage rack above her seat, she arranged herself comfortably on the cushion. A man in a suit slid open the door to her cabin and let himself in. "May I join you, Miss?"

The smell of steam, mill smoke, and cigars passed through the open door, permeating the cabin as the heavy wood and glass portal that had kept them at bay stood open. A babble of faint voices from outside the chamber floated into the cabin as well; a mishmash of discussions of baseball, business, and arrival times.

Katie shrugged as the man tossed his briefcase in the opposite overhead rack and attempted to settle into the seat across from her, riding backward.

The train's whistle, sounding much different than the mill's steam whistle, shrieked several times as the iron horse lurched, struggling to get up to speed. In doing so the fellow passenger in the first-class cabin was unceremoniously tossed across Katie's lap.

His face burned crimson as he apologized profusely and again took the seat cross from hers. Once the ride became smoother he spoke. "I'm so sorry for my clumsiness."

She showed no reaction so he continued. "Let me guess. You're not a secretary. Too well dressed. Unescorted so you're a married adult. I'm guessing you're a debutant headed for a luxury destination to meet your family for a well-deserved vacation."

The man appeared to be in his late twenties or early thirties. In another setting, he could have been one of her clients.

A demure smile crossed her face. She had encountered many men at the Savings and Loan company, but they were usually all about business. Albert saw to that, acting as a protective father. She had not been flirted with for some time.

She gazed out the open window for a moment. Having selected a seat facing the villages rather than the mills, Katie had prepared to enjoy the countryside view. Blurry landmarks close to the train rushed by as the steel engine and its retinue picked up speed. She closed the window. The faraway view revealed changing of seasons from fall to winter.

After several moments of silence the man tried again. "So, which is it? Are you a lady headed for vacation and traveling alone, a commuter, or escaping to a far-off land?

"I 'preciate you guesses, but you wrong every time. I go Washington for help women get vote."

The man pondered her comments. He studied her and tossed her words over in his mind. Something about her confidence, accented English, poise, an air of grace struck a chord. "That's it! I know who you are. You're the woman that owns the Clairton Savings and Loan."

She nodded coyly with a demure smile.

He extended his hand. "I'm James Gilchrist. I live in Clairton but work downtown and make this commute every day. I'm sorry I don't know your name, but I've heard many things about you. All good."

She grinned as she shook his hand. "I Katie Novak. Work hard every day on speak English."

"They say if you were a man you could run for president."

"Funny what you say. You tink I could be president. Ha! I be Amedigan citizen but not allowed vote 'cause I woman. That's why I go Washington. Try help womens get vote. It called suffrage."

"Well, I'll be damned." Catching the epithet that slipped out he apologized again. "Sorry. Here I sit with the smartest person in the county and the law says she can't vote because of her gender." He reached into his vest pocket, pulled out a silver container, and from it slipped a business card, which he extended in his hand.

Katie took the card that read, "James C. Gilchrist, Attorney at Law," tucked it in her sleeve, and thanked him. As they chatted, time passed so quickly it seemed like barely a heartbeat thumped before the train slowed to a stop at Pittsburgh's Union Station.

They continued to chat and wait as most coach passengers fled the train like felons at a jailbreak. Once the masses cleared the platform, James stood. "Well, Mrs. Katie Novak, I wish you the best of luck in your endeavors. I've always been a proponent of voting rights for women. When you return, please call on me to provide any assistance that I am able."

"Tank you, Sir. And if you ever in market to finance house or need loan, no forget you hometown finance in'stution." Positioning her hat, she stepped back, allowing the lawyer to demonstrate his manners.

The barrister retrieved her valise and purse from the overhead bin, handed them to her, lifted his own briefcase, then stepped aside to let the lady pass and disembark ahead of him. He could not resist the opportunity for one more chance to speak. "If you're looking for the train to Washington, D.C., it is right over there on Track Two. Good luck on your mission."

"Thank you, Mr. Attorney Gilchrist. Maybe we do business one day."

"I'll look forward to it."

Katie lumbered through the Pittsburgh train station, huge by Clairton standards, checking departure times. She had half an hour before her train left for Washington.

A small café a short distance from her track was just the place to sit, enjoy a cup of coffee, and watch people in the terminal. Most seemed to be rushing, others looked confused, and one couple appeared to be having a spat. The man walked ahead, as if trying to ignore the woman who waved her hands and shouted, although Katie was unable to hear their topic of discussion.

The huge Pittsburgh Union Station seemed a sociological phenomenon as Katie prepared to board an express train to the nation's capital. She finished her coffee, picked up her suitcase and bag, and found her cabin, anxious to get started on the events of her cause.

She dozed as the convoy sped through local stations, making a whistle stop in Cumberland, Maryland before completing the trip. She left the train at Cumberland just long enough to telegraph Lucy with her arrival time and pick up a bouquet of flowers for her new mentor.

13

Prelude to a Night of Terror

"The more you approach infinity, the deeper you penetrate terror." —Gustave Flaubert

PICKETING IN FRONT OF THE WHITE HOUSE had been taking place for weeks prior to Katie's arrival. Although no other group had ever picketed the President's residence, press and passersby paid little attention. Not a single major newspaper sent reporters to cover the protests.

One of the few reporters interested in covering the Washington D.C. activities, Homer J. Hammer had until recently been a young, struggling, freelance writer and stringer. His story about Katie changed his status. A small Boston daily tabloid newspaper, known for coverage of offbeat journalism, bought the news item and related photographs. The piece appeared below the blaring headline, *Colorful Immigrant Woman Money Genius,* complete with several photos of a smiling Katie proudly posing in front of and inside the Clairton Savings and Loan company.

The story promptly ran in several major newspapers including the *Boston Globe, New York Times,* and *Washington Post.* Homer's widely-read article served as the breakthrough he desperately sought. It led to a staff position with a byline at the Chesapeake Ledger. His duties included daily assignments, but he also had the freedom to search out items on his own, write editorial opinions, and post a weekly column.

As the train pulled into the massive Union Station, Katie spotted Lucy waiting for her, a bouquet of flowers in her hand. "Take these flowers and enjoy them while you can. Starting tomorrow things in our lives will smell more like manure than flowers."

Katie laughed, handing Lucy a bouquet. "I see we have same good manner. I bring you flower and you bring me, too."

Both adornments were promptly discarded and the two women collected Katie's trunk, placed it in the Model T, and drove to an apartment that would be the first of two homes occupied by the two women and fellow suffragettes. Their second home would be a prison cell.

At the apartment, Lucy explained her mission in further detail. "Katie, my job is to lead and monitor protests and to help each woman live up to her potential. You have many gifts and with a little help you will be able to increase your effectiveness. Are you up for constructive criticism when I deem it necessary if it improves you?"

Katie chuckled. "I do it if you not get mad when I know answer the question before you."

"Oh Katie, you are such an unpolished gem. I'm going to make you bilingual. Do you know that that means?"

"I know what means 'bilingol,' but I already know two language, Croatian and 'medigan.'"

"First, the word is 'American,' not 'medigan.' You must learn not to roll your r. It is easy, just don't allow your tongue to touch the back of your teeth. Try it."

First try. "Dddddd."

Lucy started to speak but Katie held up a hand to cut her short, then tried again. "Rrrrrrr. Amerrrrican. American."

"Perfect! Second, I will teach you proper English. You'll soon discover there are times it will be to your advantage to speak proper American English, or as you used to say, 'medigan.' You will also find situations in which speaking to a particular subset of people in American English, that use of that type of slang, or fractured English will be to your advantage."

Lucy was taken aback at the intensity she read on Katie's face as she spoke. "I ready. You say me something one time and I remember. Learn fast be easy for me."

"Let's start with the last sentence you just spoke. Proper English would be, 'You tell me something one time and I'll remember. Learning is easy for me.'"

Katie repeated the sentence perfectly. Lucy gave her another sentence, then another, and another as they drove, arrived, and walked up to her quarters. The lessons continued late into the night, Lucy describing proper tense usage and other grammatical rules. Katie repeating. As she had promised, Katie needed only one correction per try. Her learning curve was phenomenal.

"You've had a long day, Katie. Aren't you tired?"

Katie thought several seconds before answering haltingly, "No. I-do-not-get-tired, except-in-the- mornings."

"That was perfect, dear girl! You ARE a quick study."

Lucy Burns kept Katie under her wing, tutoring her several hours each day and night, offering speaking, reading, and writing lessons to make her better and stronger both as a protester and as a businesswoman. The women worked late into the night, every night, continuing to develop Katie's elocution and speaking skills. Lucy was amazed at her prodigy's ability to seize and process language and facts. Katie needed to hear something only once and it was hers. She took in each morsel of new knowledge as though it were a cat's captured mouse, wrapping her tongue around each new word, playing with it, then consuming it. Lucy had never witnessed such a gifted learner. Both women were extremely high energy and needed little sleep, thus working long hours as their sisters lay in the arms of Morpheus.

For their first several days together Katie remained in the apartment studying, reading, repeating words, and learning. Then her time finally arrived.

"Today your examinations begin," Lucy told her anxious student. "You are generally up on our objective. Let me review our technique. As we have discussed, we are passive when we march. You can answer direct questions in a calm, succinct manner, but ignore taunts and ugly language that will be directed at you. If you are singled out for particular abuse, other women will encircle you and as quietly as possible, move you from the front to the back of the protestors."

The women gathered in the large living room as Lucy went over the rest of their procedures, then reviewed the rules for the day.

"Okay, Ladies. These are your rules.

"Rule one, 'picket only at the main entrance of the White House.

"Two, do not obstruct the entrance. Do not interfere with or swarm persons as they enter or leave the premises.

"Three, do not engage in debates with individuals who shout opposing views.

"Four, do not leave the group or attempt to picket elsewhere.

"Five, do not interfere with people coming or going into the White House. Let them pass and do not attempt to engage them in arguments or intense conversation.

"Six, be enthusiastic. Chanting and yelling is okay, but do not threaten, ridicule, mock, or respond to slurs in kind.

"Seven, do not engage in physical contact with anyone or throw any-thing.

"Eight, do not behave in an intimidating manner.

"Nine, do not scatter nails, tacks, or other materials around the picket area.

"Ten, if approached by law enforcement officers, be cooperative and courteous. Refer them to me or one of the other designated leaders.

"Ladies, I want to introduce you to our newest suffragette, Katie Novak, from Pennsylvania. Today is her first day on the line so keep an eye on her. She might be as pretty as a flower, but let me assure you she is no shrinking violet.

"Katie, did you hear the rules I just cited?"

"Yes I did, Lucy."

Katie had heard and read about the general behavior required of each protester but she had not heard or read the ten rules as Lucy had just recited them.

Lucy asked, "Would you please repeat the rules just as I said them?"

Katie smiled. She knew this was her first test and she felt up to the task. The previous night her vocabulary lesson had included the term "verbatim" so she decided to show off a bit. Taking center stage, she began.

"Fellow suffragettes, as you did, I just heard Miss Lucy Burns recite what I will dub 'The Ten Commandments of Picketing.'"

Chuckles rippled through the crowd. Katie held up her hand and continued. "I will now repeat the rules verbatim."

Lucy smiled proudly knowing that her charge had just used a recently-acquired vocabulary word.

Katie continued with proper grammar, reciting the entire list of ten rules exactly word-for-word as Lucy had spoken them. Not a pause out of place, not a difference in tense or pace.

Her fellow protestors cheered and those who had not already done so introduced themselves. They then cleared an area in the center of the room and unveiled the first banner that read, 'Democracy Should Begin at Home.'

The women cheered. Two suffragettes rolled up the banner and a second one unfurled, '*Mr. President, what will you do for woman suffrage?*'

More cheers arose as the ladies refolded the slogan and the third banner displayed the strongest message, quoting the president's own words, '*The time has come to conquer or submit. For us there can be but one choice. We have made it.*'

The women hooted and cheered until Lucy quieted them.

"Today, ladies, I have asked our newest member to speak to us before our rally. You've already heard her recite the rules. Mrs. Novak, would you please address our group?"

Polite applause arose from her new peers as Katie again stepped forward and began to speak the script she'd memorized, using vastly improved English. "Fellow suffragettes, I am so excited that I become lightheaded as I read the signs we will display before the American President today. We hope to convince President Wilson to end his resistance against the proposed nineteenth amendment to the United States Constitution and encourage Congress to pass it. He has steadfastly stood and spoken out against our right to vote and we must convince him to do otherwise. The mission is to free us from the shackles of the restriction not to express ourselves in the voting booth." She paused for effect as her fellow protestors stood in stone silence, then added, "The place to accomplish that goal is here and the time is now."

The room erupted in wild cheering. Lucy shouted over the din. "Sounds like we've all become Katie's Ladies."

Cheers turned to chants: "Katie's Ladies, Katie's Ladies, Katie's Ladies…" The chants continued as the women gathered their signs and banners and marched to the White House. Katie stood as an observer.

So suffused with the excitement of the moment, she did not see Homer Hammer standing at the edge of the crowd that had gathered. As they chanted and the crowd reacted, he took copious notes, writing each statement shouted by the protestors and noting words on the signs.

Some members of the crowd watching the event were shocked to see protesters at the White House. Counter protesters jeered, laughed, and mocked the women, but their taunts did nothing to dampen their spirits.

The young man in the bowler hat with the word PRESS tucked in the hatband continued scribbling notes, writing feverishly in an effort to have enough material for a concise, accurate report. He had told the editor he had a tip that an event would happen that day.

The elderly editor had scoffed at his "tip" and suggested he go on his own time to cover his "little story."

The newly-hired staff writer continued to beg the editor to make the event an official assignment.

"Please, Boss. I know this story will explode on the national scene. I don't know when, but I just know it. I can feel it in my gut."

Finally, the bedraggled editor, worn down by the young man's enthusiasm relented. "Feel it in your gut, huh? Are you sure you don't just have a bad case of indigestion? Okay, okay! Today the White House is your beat. Go find out what mysterious happenings are going on over there. Just quit pestering me and get out of the newsroom before I pull out what little hair I have left."

Homer Hammer didn't take the time to thank his supervisor. He ran from the room and gathered his tools before the man had a chance to change his mind.

14

Homer's Breakthrough

"With sweet, reluctant, amorous delay." —Homer, The Odyssey

To DATE HOMER J. HAMMER had sold just one piece of his freelance work: the interview with Katie Novak that had taken place in her hometown. The story's success earned him a byline and a staff position with a local newspaper, the *Chesapeake Ledger*. Some fellow members of the press scoffed and wondered behind his back if he had not gotten his byline from a one-trick pony, as he'd done little to distinguish himself since.

Homer regaled in writing his first story for the Ledger, complete with byline. Pounding the keys of his shiny new Corona 3, he submitted the following to the editor, who ran it as submitted. Not a single change required.

* * *

Special to the Chesapeake Ledger
Dateline Washington, D.C.
By Homer J. Hammer
Something old has become something new in Washington. Women of the day historically have been viewed as citizens, but only in certain arenas, and that does not include the voting booth. A new era has begun as dozens of women unite in protest daily, parading in front of the White House demanding the right to vote. A highly placed anonymous source, not authorized to provide

information, told me, "The movement, called 'Women's Suffrage,' will not happen. The President is against it and there is no mood in Congress to move forward on this issue at this time. Instead of causing a ruckus in the nation's capital, these ladies should be home cooking, cleaning, and taking care of their children."

The protesting ladies, anointed by White House staffers with the moniker, "Suffragettes," march back and forth, carrying signs that reflect their demands, walking in a peaceful and orderly manner. Today ten of the group were arrested on charges of blocking the sidewalk.

The arrested "criminals" committed the indiscretion of standing silently while holding signs with messages that included, "How Long Must Women Wait for Liberty?"

I interviewed one of the movement's leaders, Miss Lucy Burns, from New York. When asked exactly what the women want to happen, she replied, "We want President Woodrow Wilson to support the Anthony amendment to the Constitution of the United States of America. That act will guarantee all women in this great country the right to vote. Our boys are returning home after fighting for liberty for Britain and European nations. Should not American women have the same right as our sisters across the ocean? We simply want that equality."

During my interview with Miss Burns, it happened that President Wilson rode through the White House gates with his wife, Edith, by his side. In typical Wilson fashion, the President tipped his hat to the protesting ladies.

* * *

The 300-word article, sent out over the wire, spread across the nation like a rushing torrent, and the number of Chesapeake Ledger's subscribers doubled. The paper quickly solidified Homer J. Hammer to its stable of staff reporters. His next article in the series, quickly approved by the editor, earned him a raise, a promotion, and a regular beat in Washington. Circulation of the newspaper increased another twenty percent. Journalism kept him busy but not too busy to think of Clairton and Hope Novak.

* * *

Special to the Chesapeake Ledger

Dateline Washington, D.C.

By Homer J. Hammer

What's in a name? A light drizzle falls on Washington, D.C., this day, but a storm of protest is in the air. Ladies from around the nation have gathered in front of the White House. Their cause is a plea for the right to vote. Calling themselves "Suffragettes," the women hold banners and placards for all who pass to see. As Russian envoys passed through the gates, the women showed a sign that read, "America is a Democracy in Name Only."

The sign and the very presence of protesters before the White House caused a reaction from the crowd gathered to witness the spectacle. Men cursed, insulted, and hurled epithets at the demonstrators. Cries rang out of "Go home to your children," and "You should be ashamed."

Dissidents stood their ground as they were being cursed at and spat upon. The counter-protesting mob gathered strength and continued to harass the women until night fell and the protesters rolled up their signs and left the area.

15

Suffragettes Numbers Swell

"The smallest number, strictly speaking, is two." —Aristotle

HOMER'S STORIES resulted in more women arriving to protest. Lucy gathered the suffragettes along with her new troops in the large living room of the apartment boarding house. Alice Paul, a college-educated Quaker from New Jersey and the head of the National Woman's Party joined the group.

"Ladies, let me introduce you to my friend and fellow warrior for women's rights, Alice Paul. We worked together to help the movement succeed in England and we'll do it again in this country."

Cheers arose from the group. Alice stepped forward. Several of her followers had joined the group, applauding and hooting. When the noise died down, Alice smiled and waved to friends, old and new.

In a commanding voice, she began. "Hello, fellow suffragettes. I'm delighted to see so many new faces. Together we will fight the fight, endure the struggle, and win the right to vote. I've been following your exploits in the newspapers. A young newsman has apparently taken up our cause. I've never met the reporter, Mr. Hammer, but am pleased to see that he follows our efforts and seems to write objectively. Newspapers around the country are also taking up our cause, reprinting Homer J Hammer's articles.

"I've just come from organizing protests in St. Louis, Philadelphia, and of course, New York, but the spotlight shines brightest here in our nation's capital."

A thrill of recognition ran through Katie's body as she heard Homer's name tied to such praise. She knew that Alice, like Lucy, must have read Homer's article that featured her struggles. She did not speak up, as the cause did not focus only on her, but all women in America who are denied the vote.

"I want to introduce some of the women who have been with us for some time. Our senior member, Madeline Douglass."

Applause filled the room as the petite, silver-haired seventy-four-year-old smiled and waved to the group.

"Catt Chapman, Elizabeth Lochlear, Alice Cosu ..." The introductions continued for several minutes. Hoots and loud applause arose with each introduction.

Alice sat and Lucy stepped forward. "Ladies, in preparation for my next introduction I want to tell you a story. As I was returning to New York from an organizational meeting in Boston last year I noticed a tabloid newspaper on the bench next to me. Normally I'd have ignored it, but below the headline blared, *'Rags to Riches Immigrant!'*

"It told of a young European girl, a child prodigy who had been expelled from school at an early age. Her crime for such a severe penalty? Too precocious for her teachers."

Katie blushed as Lucy continued. "She was tricked into coming to America, given to believe it was for a visit, but in fact, the purpose turned out to be entry into an arranged marriage."

The group gasped at the mention of the fraud perpetrated on Katie. Lucy concluded the story. "Despite the many roadblocks she faced, this woman rose above her station, became a highly successful entrepreneur, and today she is the sole owner of a very successful financial institution.

"When I finished reading her story on that commuter train, I knew I had to meet her and convince her to join our cause. She graciously agreed. Many of you heard her recite the *ten commandments of picketing*, as she calls them. We should all have the drive and focus she's shown. Allow me to introduce her to those who have not yet met her, and let's hear what she has to say. Our newest sister in suffrage and rabid activist, Katie Novak."

The room exploded in wild applause and the chant, "We're Katie's Ladies. Katie's Ladies. Katie's Ladies."

The applause quieted as Katie stepped forward. She took center stage and spoke slowly and with just the slightest of accents.

"Thank you, Miss Lucy, for the kind words and for seeking me out to join this most worthy cause. Much needs to be done to be sure for our sisters who are unable to be with us to lobby for their f-f-f-franchise." She stumbled ever so slightly at a word that had been, until Lucy's recent tutoring, completely foreign to her. Pausing, she took a deep breath, and continued.

"On a personal note, I would like to thank Lucy Burns for a gift she has given me, a gift that will help me throughout my lifetime. When I arrived in this country I spoke not one word of the language my new host country, or as I then called it, 'medigan' language. In my world of slang, 'medigan' is a shortened version of the word 'American.'

"I learned the fractured language of those around me, hard-working steelworkers, coal miners, merchants, their families and the people they served. My varied background helped me communicate as I took up entrepreneurship and inn-keeping, food service, and you don't want to know some of the other ventures."

A smattering of giggles and chuckles responded.

"For the past few weeks, Lucy instructed me in the proper use of the language. I hold two treasures close to my heart, right behind my two babies. First is the gift of elocution. Thank you, Lucy, for being so patient as my teacher. Second is my American citizenship and soon, I'll add a third, the right to take my place among all American women in the voting booth.

Again, I thank you, Lucy, and thanks to my fellow fighters for equality for your hard work, dedication, and stamina. I look forward to taking my place in the protests, standing shoulder-to-shoulder with you tomorrow and onward for as long as it takes to achieve our goal."

A shout came from the crowd. Betsy Llewlyn, a rough-hewn farm woman from Wisconsin yelled, "Hey Katie, can you give us an example of what you might have said before Lucy tutored you?"

In the blink of an eye, and without breaking stride she retorted, "You goddam betcha, sunama bitch." The crowd howled. Katie waited until the noise quieted then added, "But that is part of a language I don't think I'll use much in the future."

She took her seat to another round of thundering applause and more chants of, "Katie's Ladies, Katie's Ladies, Katie's Ladies!"

Alice Paul walked to the center of the room and held up her hand to quiet the enthusiastic group.

"Fellow suffragettes, we have work to do tonight in preparation for our protests tomorrow. Lucy tells me that several of our banners have been destroyed, damaged, or are fading. We will go out tomorrow with freshly painted messages, some of which are more pointed than the old ones. We're turning up the heat a notch. Our voice is being heard throughout the country. I've received words of encouragement, sisters, from as far away as Utah and California. And not just from our sisters. Some of our greatest supporters have been men, like the young reporter who wrote the article about Katie and now writes for the local newspaper. Every word he puts into print places us one step closer to victory. We have become part of his regular beat, and his stories have been reprinted by newspapers across the country."

Alice paused for hoots and cheers, then became somber. "We also have spies among those who would quiet us. Our intelligence tells us there may be trouble tomorrow. Hold your signs high but do not intentionally try to intimidate onlookers. Do not engage them in conversation. I'm not sure exactly who or how but I have been led to believe agitators will try to disrupt our efforts. Stay strong. Stay calm. Stay together. We'll meet here tomorrow evening to assess our progress and plan for days that follow."

Alice continued. "The first shift will stand from eight in the morning until one in the afternoon. Your relief shift will stand in your place from one o'clock until six. Katie, your introduction to picketing will take place during tomorrow's afternoon shift."

Katie nodded.

"Goodnight, ladies. Sleep well and we will see you in the morning."

Most returned to their sleeping quarters but Lucy, Katie, and a few others worked far into the night making new banners, repairing damaged ones, and building an effigy of President Wilson.

Unable to find sleep most of the night, Katie wondered what her first full shift on the line would be like. She was anxious and had hoped to be on the early shift, but she was not at her best early in the morning. Lucy knew this and that is why she wasn't part of the morning activities.

The feeling inside Katie told her that though this was the right thing to do, it would be a challenge far beyond anything she imagined, but the greater good to mankind was worth the pain. As she imagined what the following day might hold she eventually drifted into dreamland just as the morning shift prepared to leave.

16

A Night of Terror

"Terror made me cruel."—Emily Bronte

THIS DAY OF PROTEST BEGAN as had every other for the suffragette movement. Women took their places outside the White House to the cheers, jeers, catcalls, and few words of support from passersby. Nothing of significance happened that morning.

Katie, Lucy, Alice, and the rest of the afternoon shift took over at one o'clock, peacefully holding signs and banners. They increased their movement's footprint on the front lawn of the White House to the delight of Homer J. Hammer. As the scene unfolded before his eyes, he began writing vigorously.

* * *

Special to the Chesapeake Ledger
Dateline Washington, D.C.
By Homer J. Hammer
The Suffragette movement has been the bane of existence for President Wilson for some time. That trial became more pointed this afternoon when several women turned their efforts from holding signs to burning the President in effigy in front of the White House. The action prompted an even greater divide between the petticoats vs. the bluecoats.

Police and firemen who had been standing by lazily rushed to the scene of the flaming presidential effigy, wildly spewing firehoses and extinguishers, trying desperately to quell the conflagration. But the four-foot tall image of President Wilson refused to stop burning, its smoke and flames reaching toward the afternoon sky until the hanging man reduced itself to ashes.

Suffragette spokeswoman Alice Paul reported that the women planned to use the burning effigy as a kickoff event for what she described as "watchfires" to be set outside venues where the President is scheduled to speak, including the New York City Opera House.

Added Paul, "The President's words and his refusal to support our cause lights wildfires in our hearts. We plan to transcribe every word of every speech the President makes against our cause, then burn the transcriptions in public infernos. We condemn the hypocrisy of his words supporting international freedom while our own women are denied suffrage on the home front."

My interview with Alice Paul was cut short as a phalanx of police surrounded the women, beating them with truncheons, forcing them to the ground and restraining them. The women, by my estimate, fifty or so, were dragged from the gates onto the lawn, then tossed into waiting police vehicles. Their signs and banners were confiscated and destroyed.

One police sergeant, who requested anonymity, told me that the women would be held in jail overnight and then taken before a judge in the morning. The charge against them would be blocking traffic, a farce charge as the women remained off the sidewalks and streets during their demonstrations.

* * *

The following morning suffragettes, held along with vagrants, thieves, and prostitutes, were rousted after a night in cold stone cells. They were hustled to a courthouse and filed into the courtroom. The charged women were seated in the first rows of seats facing the judge. In the back of the room sat a red-haired young man holding a pad and pencil and wearing a bowler hat with paper showing the word "PRESS" tucked into the hatband. All rose as the somber-faced judge entered the courtroom.

The judge began to speak in harsh tones. "Ladies, over the past several weeks you have caused much strain on the legal system with your folderol. Yesterday you reached a new low, burning an effigy of the President of the United States. I am extremely disappointed in your displays of insolence and will not stand for further disrespect toward the President or the Constitution or the laws of this country. If you persist in your shenanigans, a fate worse than a small fine or a few days in the city jail awaits you. Heed my warning, ladies. End this foolishness. Go back to your husbands and children. Your issue will be discussed in the proper forum and in due time."

An eerie silence fell over the courtroom. Clothing rustled, but little else moved. Nobody spoke until the judge cleared his throat, and looked directly at the prisoners sitting in the front row.

"Do you have anything to say for yourselves? Are you ready to behave like decent law-abiding women?"

A barely audible susurrus of clothing could be heard as Alice Paul stood. "As long as women, wives, and mothers, have to go to jail for petty offenses to secure freedom for the women of America, then we will continue to refuse to pay our fines and would rather go to jail."

The judge, taken aback, said, "Ladies, you must be reasonable."

From the group of prisoners came another voice, "We will be 'reasonable' when we are 'reasonably' permitted to vote."

The incensed judge slammed his gavel onto the bench and shouted, "Thirty days for the disrespect shown in this courtroom. This court is adjourned."

Prisoners continued hurling cat calls and insults to the irate judge as he repeatedly slammed his gavel onto the bench, hitting it so hard the gavel splintered. He rose, red-faced, veins popping in his neck and screamed, "So that's your response to being treated in a civil manner and with dignity? You are to be confined for an indeterminate time to the Occoquan Workhouse!"

He shuddered, then hied, robes flowing, stomping out of the courtroom as police and guards whispered in awe, wondering what to do next. After several minutes of confusion, the court summoned a bailiff to the judge's chambers and gave instructions to move thirty-three of the women who refused to pay their fines. The bailiff returned to the courtroom, whispered to a police sergeant, then announced, "Ladies, you are to be transported to Occoquan."

Homer gasped when he heard those words. Having grown up in the area he was quite aware of Occoquan Workhouse, a nearby prison that had been closed, but recently reopened to house mostly violent black convicts and prostitutes. The suffragettes filed out of the courtroom. Katie and her fellow prisoners passed by the reporter as they exited the room. Reporter Homer J. Hammer caught Katie's eye, who recognized him immediately, but neither acknowledged the other. As she passed him in the tightly-packed area, Homer slipped a note into her pocket and winked.

* * *

Special to the Chesapeake Ledger
Dateline Washington, D.C.
By Homer J. Hammer
"A New Low" Suffragettes, women wanting nothing more than the right to vote, have exercised their first amendment rights, picketing and protesting the White House, a landmark event since President Woodrow Wilson took office. Protests continued through the summer months. Police Superintendent Chief Major Raymond W. Pullman announced that continued picketing would result in arrests for blocking the sidewalks and obstructing traffic, though the picketers did neither.

Initially sentences consisted of fines that the protesters refused to pay, taking instead a three-day sentence in the local jail. But protesting continued, fines went unpaid, and the jail terms increased to sixty days.

Suffragettes demand passage of a constitutional amendment giving women the right to vote. They continue protesting in front of the White House, upping the ante this afternoon by burning an effigy of President Wilson.

After a night in the local jail, the protesting women were hauled into the courtroom of Judge William McConnell. The judge scolded the women, telling them they'd reached "a new low" by burning the effigy of the President.

The falsely charged women would not be silenced in the courtroom, drowning out the judge's attempt at speaking. In frustration, the judge stomped out of the courtroom, but not before smashing his gavel on the table until it splintered. From his chambers, he announced a sentence of the entire group of thirty-three women to an undetermined stay at the recently reopened Occoquan Workhouse.

Among those sentenced were veterans Lucy Burns and Alice Paul, both of New York, who had participated in many marches. Also sentenced, Katie Novak, a businesswoman from Pennsylvania, taking part in her first demonstration.

* * *

Katie clutched the note tightly inside her pocket until she was loaded into a police vehicle for transport to the detention center, then glanced at it quickly and furtively before the police wagon door was slammed and total darkness surrounded her and the other women.

I know where they are taking you. It is hell. Be strong. Here's how you can send me notes and I'll tell your story. Once guards are asleep wrap the note around a rock and throw through a broken window on west wall. If you can't get to the window, toss it outside through bars over your cell window. I'll check after one o'clock each night.

HH

It is unknown where or how Katie found paper and pencil to write, but she tossed silent clarion calls through the walls nightly. Thus, a surreptitious pipeline of communication was set between the inner workings of the prison and the outside world. A few days later the following report appeared.

* * *

Special to the Chesapeake Ledger
Dateline Washington, D.C.
By Homer J. Hammer

Today, thirty-three women — wives, mothers, and daughters — stood peacefully outside the White House gates, expressing their dissent to not being permitted to vote. They were fined, but refused to pay, opting instead to spend a night in a jail local cell. Still, picketing continued. Judge William McConnell then took more severe measures, sentencing the women to prison.

The judge's order resulted in a wagon backed up to take the women from the courthouse to the gate of an aged, rusted, dank, dark prison, officially named "Occoquan Workhouse." Once inside, prisoners were required to surrender their clothes in exchange for filthy prison smocks. The paper-thin garments barely kept them warm in the stone cells surrounded by iron bars. Small windows in the penitentiary, caked with mud and grit, hadn't been washed for decades. Except for a few broken panes, filth on the windows denies the sun.

Some of the women in the prison are hearty, but others are frail. No thought is given to comfort and little to cleanliness. Food is rancid, causing vomiting and diarrhea. But these strong women will not be cowed, hoping their plight is shown to the world.

It is the duty of the Fourth Estate to continue reporting on the plight and conditions faced each day. We will continue to keep our readers up to date on the suffragette dilemma.

* * *

Each morning prison officials were greeted with details in the newspaper of conditions and treatment in Occoquan. Unable to trace the source of the reporting, prison officials decided to teach a lesson to their recalcitrant charges. The events were later described in Katie's next missive to Homer Hammer and written as a serial. Circulation at the Chesapeake Ledger quadrupled during the time the series ran.

Homer's series of columns continued for several weeks until a story he thought might be his grand finale appeared. This one was no single column, but a full front page article, complete with photos of Occoquan Workhouse. The thousand-word expose continued on the inside page of the Ledger.

WOMEN SUBJECTED TO UNIMAGINABLE ABUSE.

Special to the Chesapeake Ledger

Dateline Washington, D.C.

By Homer J. Hammer

What follows is a series of secret accounts of several women among thirty-three imprisoned for months. Their crime? Not fraud or embezzlement or conspiracy to overthrow the government, but a desire to allow American citizens the right to vote. The question to those providing information for this story is simple: "Tell me what you experienced and what you saw."

What follows are their responses. Though my sources of the information cannot be revealed for fear of reprisals, comments came directly from prisoners who used an ingenious method of communicating their story to me. Neither the prisoners nor their method of communication will be revealed. In the following story, they and others describe what can only be called a Night of Terror.

"Upon arrival, we were stripped of clothing and given soiled rags to wear, then herded into a cradle of filth: damp, slimy cages unfit for circus animals. The latch on the cell door clicked shut, locking us in. Welcoming us, a cacophony of decadence, rotting smells, and worse.

"My cellmate lay on the iron bunk just out of my reach in the tiny cubicle. I could hear her labored breathing, then nothing. My own breathing became labored as well and I feared I, too, would slip into full cardiac arrest, that we both would perish. Thick grey stone walls blot out everything that is not my six-by-four-foot cell.

"It must be noon outside where warm rays bathe everything they touch: flowers, green grass, children playing in the fields. Inside this crypt there is no certain way of telling the time. Miniscule cracks allow the tiniest slivers of refracted light to seep through. In the corner, there seems to be a fossilized, partly eaten scrap of food inside a congealed pool of unrecognizable muck.

"No whisper of fresh air stirs to relieve the stench of festering open sewage. No sound comes from other cells except the moaning and crying of tortured souls. The air is fetid, and sleep, if it finally arrives, comes fitfully, as rodents

choose the quiet of night to scamper up and down my body in search of food. This place is not a tool of justice but a repository for the rebellious.

"The first night we were regularly beaten, dragged, choked, pinched, kicked, and brutally tortured. Somehow, we coped with the abuse, harsh living conditions, and rancid food.

Some of our number are elderly. Others are ill. If we refuse to eat the rancid, maggot-filled food, they confine us in solitary 'punishment cells' and force-feed raw eggs through a tube shoved down our throats. The American public must learn of this barbarous treatment.

"There are two among us who so far have been strong enough to challenge the guards. Lucy Burns passively resists the goons and an immigrant woman, Katie Novak, is openly defiant of them. Guards try to beat her into submission but she refuses to cower to them. She is among the few not moaning or crying from the beatings. Though she must be in great pain from the constant thrashings, she remains quiet and resolute. One of the strongest people I've ever met. We gather strength from her resilience. I cannot see her but imagine her silhouette flat on the smooth wooden plank that is her bed, shivering beneath the threadbare covering.

"Unable to sleep from the pain, my mind drifts to a more quiet and peaceful time, remembering a clear summer day before this nightmare began.

"Though I do not resist, they torture me. I'm weak from hunger, bruised from the pummelling, and my head throbs. I fear I will not last the night.

"Three days after our arrival, under orders from the superintendent of the Occoquan Prison Workhouse, forty guards armed with nightsticks burst into the prisoners' area, rampaging from cell to cell, brutalizing we thirty-three jailed inmates.

"The other prisoners and I withdrew and huddled into the far corners of our cells. We are not men convicted of unspeakable crimes, habitual drunkards, vagrants, or child abusers. We are thirty-three women, charged and convicted, not of violent crimes, soliciting, prostitution, or drunkenness, but of the bogus charge of disorderly conduct and blocking the sidewalk while exercising our

First Amendment Constitutional rights. We peacefully protested in front of the White House.

"One of the most brutal scenes I witnessed occurred the third day of our imprisonment. A guard approached a cell and asked the occupant, 'What the hell are you doing with all these troublemakers, Granny?'

"The sneering guard who we nicknamed Pigface because of his turned-up nose, taunted the 73-year-old matron. She answered. 'My sisters I and are outspoken women who want nothing more than the right to vote in America. We want to vote for the president of the United States.'

"The guard mocked her in a squeaky voice, 'We want to vote for the president.' Ha! Women voting in national elections? Don't hold your breath, Granny. It'll never happen. Not in your lifetime.'

"The inmate retorted, 'How can you treat the sisters and wives, mothers, and grandmothers so brutally?'"

"He did not respond, only laughed mockingly and moved on to the next cell.

"A guard we called Baggypants overheard the conversation and scoffed, 'Let me show you how we treat rabble scum.' Singling out inmate Lucy Burns, he brought down his truncheon along the side of her forehead, spurting blood across the cell, then beat and chained her by hands and wrists to rusty cell bars above her head.

"Baggypants snarled a maniacal laugh, 'Hang there and shiver a while, fancy lady.'

"Blood ran down Lucy's cheek and soaked into the filthy ragged clothing as cold metal cuffs snapped into place. Baggypants then added, 'Maybe the prison experience will bring you wenches to your senses.'

"Lucy, dazed and semiconscious, refused to cry or otherwise give up or give in. Instead she drooped, hanging like a sister of Christ from the metal bars that crisscrossed the top of the cell. She was left in that state overnight, nearly naked and shivering, but her resolve only grew stronger. Her ragged clothing was later removed and replaced with a thin blanket. Her hands stayed numb for several days.

"As Lucy writhed in silent pain, two guards grabbed another inmate; I could not see who. They flung her headfirst through the partially opened door of her cell and into the dark, dank lockup. Her head smashed against the iron support post of the bed, knocking her unconscious. She bled from a gash in her forehead.

"Katie Novak had been mostly ignored in her locked cell that day until she called out, 'Why do you do this? Beat up on women who only want to vote?'

"Her answer thudded, unspoken, with another hard swat of the guard's nightstick."

* * *

Homer's story sent shock waves throughout the country as reprints landed in every major city and most small towns throughout America. Circulation at the paper continued to skyrocket and officials at the prison struggled to identify and plug the source of the leaks. They were certain the information came from inside, perhaps from a disgruntled prison guard, but were unable to trace the source of outgoing information.

Katie quietly interviewed her fellow prisoners, made notes of the conditions and clandestinely tossed them through the broken window, as Homer had directed. He wrote article after article about the plight of the incarcerated suffragettes. After the above most widely circulated story, the prison became a place of scorn. Homer became a celebrity.

* * *

Karl Blackburn, top aide to the president, clutched the newspaper tightly as he read the article. It exposed a culture much worse than he had imagined. One that never should have happened to the most dastardly criminal, let alone women whose crime was seeking voting rights. As he continued to read he began to feel sick to his stomach. Mesmerized, he could not put the paper down or stop reading.

Scanning the story as he sat at his desk in the Oval Office, President Woodrow Wilson slammed the newspaper down hard on his desk, flipped a switch, and yelled into the open intercommunication device. "Get Blackburn in here, NOW!"

Blackburn scurried into the office. "Yes, Boss."

"Have you read this morning's paper?

"Yes, Sir."

"How could this happen in America? I want this stopped immediately. Do whatever you must, but get this situation fixed!"

"Yes, Sir."

Two days after the graphic revelations appeared, Homer walked into the newspaper office to discuss his continued coverage. The editor, waving a copy of his story asked, "Hammer, are you willing to reveal the source of this information?"

"No Sir, I will not."

"Are you resolute in your position regardless of the personal consequences to you?"

"Yes, Sir. I stand firm by my story and refuse to divulge my sources or how the information is passed on to me."

The editor smiled. "Right answer. I'm glad I had the foresight to hire you and assign you to this beat, Hammer. Keep up the good work."

Homer, of course, remembered how he begged to cover the demonstrations and after being repeatedly rebuffed, how he pestered the editor until he reluctantly gave in.

Turning to leave the editor's office, Homer found his way was blocked by a tall, muscular man dressed in a seersucker suit. The man apparently overheard the conversation between Homer and his editor.

"Homer Hammer?"

"That's right."

"Come with me, please."

The man in the suit grabbed Homer's arm above the elbow and led him out of the office. The two looked a sight as they walked to a waiting car. The journalist was in a rumpled, well-worn mismatched suit, wrinkled white shirt, open at the collar, a thin tie loosely wrapped around his neck, and a well-worn derby atop his crop of red hair, with a card in the hatband that announced, Press. The other man wore a dapper, freshly-pressed suit with a slight bulge under an arm that simulated a revolver.

He dragged Homer, scurrying to keep up, toes barely scraping the ground, toward a waiting car. Homer slid into the back seat ahead of his guide, who slipped in next to him. Tires squealed as the car sped from the newspaper office toward Washington, D.C. and 1600 Pennsylvania Avenue.

Neither the driver nor the agent next to Homer spoke during the ride, despite Homer's repeated questions, "Where are you taking me? What's this all about?"

The sedan slipped through the gates onto White House property. The two men in the rear seat exited the vehicle and were escorted into the building, then to an office. Behind the desk, a balding man chewed on an unlit cigar. He rose to greet them.

First addressing Homer's companion, he said, "Thank you, Agent McVicker."

The plainclothesman left the room and the steely-eyed man extended a hand to Homer. "Homer J. Hammer?"

Homer nodded.

"I'm Karl Blackburn." He motioned for the reporter to be seated, then he also sat. "Mr. Hammer, I am interested in the material you write. You seem to have accurate sources."

"Yes, Sir."

"If I asked you to identify some of those sources, what would your answer be?"

"Respectfully, I would decline, Sir."

"And if you were threatened with loss of livelihood or jail?"

"I would again respectfully decline, Sir."

Karl offered the younger man a cigar. He declined. "Is there any way I could convince you to either reveal your sources or drop the topic of these women and their recounting of goings on in prison?"

Homer thought for several moments as Karl waited anxiously for his answer. "Yes. I would consider it if you agree to meet three conditions."

"Go on."

"First, immediately release the thirty-three women and have those who participated in brutality against them punished according to law. Second, choose one of the detainees at random and bring her in for an interview. Let her tell her own compelling story, not just what you read in my columns. Third, convince President Wilson to support passage of the Susan B. Anthony amendment, enfranchising America's women with the right to vote. Make him understand that once the amendment passes Congress, all this strife with the suffragettes disappears."

"That is a tall order, Mr. Hammer. I'm not sure granting it is within my purview. But suppose I am able to work something out. What would you do with your career? You seem to have come from nowhere. Reporting on this topic has been your entire scope of writing. Are you committed to continue your inflammatory columns and stories? Will you continue to be a muckraker with your yellow journalism?"

"Your question is a complex one, Sir. It begs the purpose of my being here today. You label me a muckraker and accuse me of yellow journalism. If you define muckraking as an attempt to raise the awareness of my readers to social issues and injustices, and highlight weaknesses in our political system, then, yes, I'm guilty as charged of exercising my right. Nay, it is my duty as a member of the fourth estate to root out tyranny and inequality. That will not change."

He continued. "I find that when light is shined on filth and decay, rats and roaches scamper to find another place to hide. The issue is not my muckraking or what my future plans might be, but the plight of thirty-three innocent victims of abuse being imprisoned on trumped-up charges. Their abusers are doing so under the color of law."

Karl Blackburn sighed. "Very well, Mr. Hammer. Thank you for the lesson in civics. I'm familiar with the law. I just want these stories to stop. It isn't good for our President or for our country."

"Is the treatment of these women good for the President and the country? Place the blame where it belongs, Sir, not on the consequences of its victims," Homer countered.

Karl was taken aback at the intensity of the young man. He responded in measured tones. "I'll do what I can do about meeting your conditions. If we need to talk again I'll send a car for you as I did this time." He began to rise from his chair.

The reporter remained seated for several seconds, then added, "I have one more request. Not a demand, but a request."

"Yes?"

"If you can arrange for me to interview several women without guards being present and assure me there will be no repercussions to the inmates, I will write one final story as a gesture of good faith that you'll move forward on the conditions I've laid out."

"You give me your word?"

"Yes."

"I can arrange for you to interview anybody of your choosing, without guards being present. But let me first see what I can do about meeting your three conditions. Give me a week and I'll contact you. But one condition I will insist is that no mention of our meetings can be reported. Otherwise, any progress I might make will be stymied."

"Done. I'll trust you for the week. If there is no movement, I'll continue to write my feature articles."

Karl buzzed the intercommunication device on his desk, spoke into it, and Agent McVicker immediately reappeared. "Take this gentleman wherever he wants to go."

Karl Blackburn, a top aide to several presidents, served as Wilson's Chief Strategist on domestic issues. He wanted to flush the miscarriage of justice through the sewer of political protocol, and give the President room to move his other agenda items forward. He was banking that one final story would accomplish this more effectively than the piecemeal drivel that had been seeping through the newspaper via Homer's columns.

Karl was not exactly sure how he would attack the tasks before him. He had not seen a roster of inmate names, so for his first order of business he dispatched an aide to the nearby courthouse for files on the thirty-three incarcerated women. The aide returned in within the hour and handed the documents to Karl.

Folders in hand, he scanned each one to determine which of the women he might interview first, and to get a sense of who these people are and what their backgrounds might reveal. As he reached the twelfth file, he looked twice at the name that stared back at him. Katheryn "Katie" Novak!

He sat, stunned. How could that be? No, that would be too much of a coincidence. The last time he saw Peter Novak's wife, Katie, he remembered her as a semi-literate housewife who had cursed him in fractured English and a foreign language. How could she …

Karl picked up the daily newspaper from his desk and began to reread the article. Feelings of nausea again swept over him as he read further and learned what had happened to Katie after she dared to speak out of turn to a sadistic guard. It sure sounded like her outspoken nature.

He read further in her file: *"Born: Sisljavic, Croatia. Austro-Hungarian Empire November 1898. Emigrated to U.S. via NY 1915. Current residence: Clairton, Pennsylvania, Employment: Clairton Savings and Loan. Naturalized citizen. Next of kin: Peter Novak. Married, two children."*

He studied the faded photo. "Well, I'll be damned! This could be the break I've been looking for." He picked up the phone on his desk. "Get me the prison."

After a few minutes a voice came on the line, "This is Assistant Warden Davis."

"Davis," he shouted, "this is Karl Blackburn at the White House. I want you to order your men to not place a finger on the women in your charge. Then I want you to send Katheryn Novak to me. I'm dispatching a car for her. It will be there in less than an hour." *Click.* Karl slammed the phone so hard it broke in two.

* * *

Prison officials cleaned Katie up as best they were able. Searching the clothing bin, they found a dress that covered as many of her bruises as possible.

The guard Pigface walked silently down the aisle of cells, dress in hand. Katie cringed as he stopped at her cell, preparing herself for another beating. He inserted the key and opened the cell door, tossing the dress at her. "Put this on. Then come with me."

Katie dressed, then silently followed the guard to an unused visitors' facility. He pointed to a lavatory door marked, "Ladies."

Handing her a hairbrush he demanded. "Go in there and clean yourself up. When you come out I want you looking presentable."

Confused but without responding or asking why, she entered the lavatory. On the sink inside the washroom she found another brush, comb, soap, towel, undergarments, and running water. She followed Pigface's orders, scrubbing up as best she could. She could not remember the last time she had taken a brush or comb to her hair. Though she was barely twenty years of age, stress and poor diet had turned her once thick, jet-black hair to a stringy salt-and-pepper color.

The refreshing routine at the sink brightened her spirits for the moment. After replacing the wrinkled dress over clean undergarments, she took a deep breath and exited the room.

Pigface had disappeared. Waiting for her outside the door was a man she had not seen before. He was not wearing a jailer's uniform but a neatly pressed seersucker suit.

"This way, Ma'am." He spoke softly, gesturing toward the huge prison entry gate with a standard size iron bar door for individual access.

She thought, *They're playing games with me. I'm not sure what they're up to but I'll continue to passively resist.*

With the man in the seersucker suit at her side, Katie, squinting, hobbled into the late morning sunlight to a waiting car. Nobody in the party, including Katie herself, spoke as the car sped along paved streets for the twenty-five-mile trip.

Her mind scattered elsewhere as they passed through the gates, not realizing she had arrived at the home of the President. Her escort in the suit gently helped her out of the car, into the building, and through the open door of an office.

As Katie was escorted into another room that served as an office, Karl rose from behind his desk and took her hand. She recoiled, not from any fear of him, but because he squeezed the same blackened and bruised hand that had been stomped by a guard the previous night.

"Mrs. Novak, I'm, uh, I-I seem to be at a loss for words. Do you remember me and the circumstances under which we first met?"

Katie gathered herself and smiled, her swollen right eye barely open. "I remember you, Blackburn. At first I hated you, thinking you were a union official who caused my Pete to be banned from the mill, but when he returned from his trip with you he told me everything. Well, he told me at least as much as he was permitted."

Something was off. Yes, she was bruised and generally looked a mess, but something else was different. Something about her language. Karl stared at her, transfixed not only at the swellings and bruises, but also by her clarity of speech. Aside from a slight accent, this young woman with barely a second-grade formal education could have easily been mistaken for a college graduate.

She read the confusion on his face and again smiled painfully. "Oh yes, my language has come a long way in a short time. You can thank my mentor, Lucy Burns, for that. We toiled late many a night to achieve this. She is a wonderful tutor and an amazing woman. But let's get down to business. Why have you me brought here?"

"Mrs. Novak, I'm so sorry for the treatment you and your fellow suffragettes have endured. I had no idea until I read about it in the paper. It is beyond the pale and will immediately stop. But I need help on another front. We need the picketing to stop. We need the "watchfires" to stop. The President is under tremendous pressure dealing with national and international issues. What can we do to help you make the protesting and hostilities toward him all go away?"

"You give me too much credit, Mr. Blackburn. I alone cannot change things among my sister suffragettes. But the answer is simple. And I think you already know it. The President has been outspoken in opposition of granting women the right to vote. He must endorse an amendment that gives women that right. Susan Anthony has already drafted such a document."

"If you know about that, Mrs. Novak, you also know it will likely not pass Congress."

Katie stiffened and retorted sharply, "I know this ..." She now glowered at him. "The amendment will die if the President persists in opposition to it, but I also know that with our victory over Germany in Europe, Mr. Wilson likely has the political capital to push it through."

Karl was dumfounded as he sat and stared at her. He was amazed at Katie's depth of knowledge and understanding of the process of political give-and-take. He reconsidered exactly what he hoped to gain when he brought her to the White House. "Mrs. Novak. Do you trust me to keep my word?"

She sat, back stiff against the uncomfortable straight chair-back and answered, "Well, you kept all your promises to Pete including fast-tracking of our citizenship, and you placed my business on the preferred list of vendors as promised, so yes, I believe you are a man of your word."

"What if I told you I will guarantee the President's support of the amendment if you will dissolve the protesting and overt opposition to his efforts, and have your reporter stop writing stories about suffrage and abuse." He did not want her to know that he'd already been in communication with Homer.

"What makes you think he's my reporter?" She wondered if she had been found out as the source of information leaking from Occoquan.

"Figure of speech."

Katie sighed deeply, her bruised lungs hurt as they pressed against her ribcage. "That's a big order. I would also need the unconditional release of all suffragettes and all charges against them dropped. And I want the sadistic guards removed and charged. I can provide you with names and descriptions of the most brutal."

"Yours is also a big order, and I'll do what you ask for, the immediate release your women, and toss in prosecution of the guards who behaved in such a sadistic manner."

Katie spoke. "Okay, let me do this. I will try to do all the things you suggest, but for a defined period of time. If the President does not support us and get the amendment passed, we revert to our tactics."

"Give me a year," he interjected.

"Two weeks," she countered.

"Six."

"Three," she said firmly, not willing to bargain further.

"Done. Give my regards to your husband. He is a fortunate man. I now see what a very special wife he married."

"Thank you."

Karl gingerly walked the staggering Katie to the door and summoned a uniformed officer. The same agent who had driven her earlier escorted Katie to the waiting car. She was deep in thought, hoping she could pull off her end of the bargain. Karl was equally hopeful that he would be able to convince President Wilson to hold up their end of the deal.

17

Getting the Vote

"Women, we might as well be dogs baying at the moon as petitioners without the right to vote." —Susan B. Anthony

THE MOMENT KATIE EXITED THE BUILDING, Karl Blackburn raced to the Oval Office and rapped on the door.

President Woodrow Wilson, looking every bit like a proper professor, waved Karl into the office. The President had earned a Ph.D. in Political Science from Johns Hopkins and had been awarded professor emeritus status by Princeton University. Despite his excursion into politics, he still considered himself more of an academic and statesman than a politician.

He held his index finger up in a "one moment" gesture as he finished reading the newspaper article before him, then removed his pince-nez eyeglasses and took a deep breath.

"Terrible, Karl. What is happening to those ladies, if it is true, doing nothing but exercising their constitutional rights. What can we do to stop this? I'm less concerned for me personally or my legacy than for our country at large. What is your take?"

"Well, I just left a meeting with one of the leaders of the movement."

The President did not seem surprised at Blackburn's efficiency. "Good work. What did you discover?"

Karl responded. "Remember the gentleman who was so pivotal in helping us with the Zimmerman Telegram affair? The one who accompanied me to Mexico?"

"Of course. We lost some good agents on that job. Your shining star was a foreign fellow, a Slav who happened to speak impeccable German. What does that gentleman have to do with our current situation?"

"Him? Nothing. But as fate would have it, his wife is one of the leaders of the protestors. She is among the women who have been brutalized at Occoquan."

"That is quite a coincidence. How did you discover that?"

"After reading the article in today's newspaper, I ordered and reviewed the records of the thirty-three women being held and stumbled across her name by chance."

President Wilson squeezed the bridge of his nose where his glasses had left identical indentations on either side. Inhaling deeply, he exhaled — more of a sigh — and spoke. "Such a miscarriage of justice. What is our best course of action to counter the damage done?"

"First, the women must be released immediately and all charges dropped. I've already begun the process. Next, they must be interviewed regarding the brutality heaped upon them, and any prison guard who participated in garish and sadistic behavior will be charged."

The President nodded. "Go on."

"Before I give you the next point, let me ask if you feel any differently about supporting the Anthony amendment."

"After reading the article in today's newspaper, and assuming it is accurate…"

Karl interjected. "It is."

"Then I've done a one hundred eighty degree turn in my position and can fully support the amendment."

"But, Sir, can you get a divided Congress to vote in favor of what will become the nineteenth amendment? They've fought tooth and nail against you on a variety of other issues."

"You just watch me."

With all the pressure from publicity generated by the brave women who picketed the White House and the atrocities by guards at Occoquan Prison out in the open, President Wilson lent his support to the proposed Susan B. Anthony suffrage amendment, the nineteenth amendment to the Constitution of the United States of America.

As agreed to by Katie, picketing of the White House was suspended for three weeks.

President Woodrow Wilson addressed the Congress of the United States in one of the most endearing and powerful speeches of the eight years of his presidency. When he finished, Parliamentary Procedure in the House of Representatives followed:

"Mr. Chairman."

"The Chair recognizes Mr. James R. Mann, Republican from the Great State of Illinois and Chairman of the Suffrage Committee."

"Mr. Chairman, I propose the House of Representatives approve resolution of the Susan Anthony Amendment granting women the right to vote as the nineteenth amendment to the Constitution of the United States of America."

"House members will now be polled. Yea if you support the amendment, nay if you do not."

The voting poll took place. To ensure passage, a two-thirds majority is required. The stentorian voices of three hundred and four congressmen voted "yea" for the amendment, with eighty-nine voicing "nay."

With the count completed, the nineteenth amendment giving women the right to vote in all U.S. presidential elections passed, with forty-two votes to spare.

Two weeks later, Wednesday, June 4, 1919, the Senate passed the Nineteenth Amendment by two votes over the two-thirds required majority, fifty-six to twenty-five. But the victory was not yet complete. Ratification by two-thirds majority of individual states is required for passage of a Constitutional Amendment.

Within six days, Illinois, Michigan, and Wisconsin each ratified the amendment. Kansas, New York, and Ohio followed a week later. The following year, by March 1920, thirty-five states had ratified the amendment, leaving only one more state to complete the required two-thirds majority.

The vote went to constituents in the Southern states. Alabama, Georgia, Louisiana, Maryland, Mississippi, South Carolina, and Virginia expressed opposition by all soundly rejecting passage of the document.

As the hot summer wound down, crisp winds of change were to blow in Tennessee. Both sides fought adamantly in hopes theirs would be the vote to tip the scale in or out of favor of passage of the amendment to make woman suffrage the law of the land.

Passions flared. Name-calling, threats, lies, and misrepresentation flew on both sides, and August 20, a vote among the Tennessee legislators came to a 48-48 tie with one vote remaining. Twenty-three-year old Representative Harry Burn would cast the deciding vote.

Burn, a Republican, opposed the amendment. Before casting his vote, he read and re-read the many letters he had received from constituents on both sides of the issue. The letter that carried the most weight in his decision came from his mother. She wrote, "Dear Harry, we raised you to be an honest boy, to fight for what is right, regardless of if it is popular or not. Your vote is important. Perhaps one of the most important you will ever cast. Do not let us down. Be a good boy and help Mrs. Burns, Mrs. Catt, and the rest of Katie's Ladies put the 'rat' in ratification."

Harry Burn strode to the floor that morning, took the podium, and with the country holding its collective breath, began his brief but historic oratory.

He spoke for nearly half an hour, waxing eloquent until one of his fellow legislators called out from the chamber, "Don't be such an old windbag, Harry. Cast your damn vote!"

The legislators began to bay at one another. Harry lifted his hand to quiet the din and loudly proclaimed, "Gentlemen, it is with mixed feelings that I cast this deciding proposal for the enfranchisement of the women of this great land. I cast my vote as… 'YEA!'"

Fellow Republicans were stunned and sat in shock as whoops and hollers rang out from supporters of the legislation. Burn's vote ratified the nineteenth amendment in favor of women's suffrage. Certification followed by the U.S. Secretary of State, and less than one week after Burn's decisive vote, August 26, 1920, the nineteenth amendment became the law of the land.

Less than ten weeks after its certification, on the second day of November that same year, more than eight million women across the United States of America voted in elections for the first time.

Of historical note, it took more than sixty years for the remaining twelve states to ratify the amendment. Mississippi was the last to do so on March 22, 1984.

The House overwhelmingly approved the amendment and it moved on to the Senate, which approved it fifty-six to twenty-five, two votes over the two-thirds majority required for passage.

18

Branko Kukić

Cowards die a thousand deaths.
A brave man only one. —Julius Caesar

AT AGE THIRTEEN, Katie fell hard for her first love, Branko Kukić. Born a coward, bully, swindler, scoundrel, and thief, he had the bad boy air that teen girls often find so irresistible. He stole money, cigarettes, and worst of all, at age twenty-four, stole the heart of an innocent teen-aged girl.

Kukić joined a politically radical group and rose in the organization to become part of a small, elite group given the mission of murdering the Archduke Franz Ferdinand, nephew of Emperor Franz Josef and heir to the Austro-Hungarian Empire.

In the middle of the night, he was awakened by a persistent rap on the flimsy wooden door of his rented apartment.

"Who is it?" Branko mumbled, still groggy.

A faceless voice from the other side of the door whispered the code words, "It is time."

He sprang from the soiled mattress to the door, opening it to a shadowy figure. "When?"

"Now. This minute. You must leave immediately. Be in Sarajevo tomorrow for final instructions."

The young Serb had been marking time in this small hamlet. He did not know until that moment where the assignment would take him or the exact nature of the endeavor. As the senior member of this cell, he had waited impatiently and now the time had come. He would not discover until the following day that his mission included his own suicide after the assassination of the Archduke.

By the time the morning sun rose, he had unceremoniously left town, the young brash girlfriend, and all memories of his life of small time crime. He had become so caught up in the romance of his task, he left without bidding his young girlfriend adieu, save for a self-aggrandizing note.

The message left behind and Branko's sudden departure left Katie with the fantasy that her lover would one day return. He promised they would be married and live happily ever after. But that fantasy would be replaced by a much different reality.

Once the assassination plan was put in place and began to unfold, Kukić and his fellow assassins secreted themselves as part of a large crowd in Sarajevo, Bosnia. A bomb hidden inside his coat and a pistol in his pocket were weapons to be used for the horrific deed. He fingered his supposed last meal, not a platter of roast pig as he's imagined, but a cyanide pill inside his vest pocket.

The euphoria of becoming a martyr quickly faded as reality smacked his face. Standing on the sidewalk where the Archduke would soon pass, the coward Branko Kukić had an epiphany that led to a change of heart. Instead of participating in the murder and his own demise, he dropped his bomb and gun into a refuse can, picked the pocket of a bystander, and disappeared.

Following Branko's defection, assassination attempts by the others were folly. The first effort failed when bombs hurled by would-be executioners missed their target. However, fate, gave the assassins a second chance when the Archduke's driver made a wrong turn. The car stalled and one of the opposition group members hurled a bomb into the vehicle. The ensuing explosion killed the political leader and his wife.

Unlike Kukič, four of the murderers followed their instructions and attempted suicide, but the cyanide pills they'd been given were old and had lost their potency. One shooter placed a pistol to his head but the gun misfired. Another attempted suicide by jumping from a bridge into a river but was fished out, beaten, and dragged into custody. All except Branko were captured, almost instantly. They were quickly, tried, convicted, and sentenced to harsh prison sentences. But the fifth planned assassin, Branko Kukić disappeared, never to be found. The mystery ersatz executioner seemed to have disappeared into thin air.

Once beyond the crowds and free of the hubbub, Branko examined the booty stolen from a tourist in the crowd. Rifling through his newfound possessions he discovered cash and the identification of a young man about his own age. Using his newfound identity, the coward fled Sarajevo and Bosnia, running and hiding from the authorities. He slept in fields, barns, and empty rail cars, until reaching Croatia's capital city of Zagreb. From there, he hopped a train to Düsseldorf, Germany. Using the stolen identification, he made his way quietly through Austria and France, then sailed to England. His history of thievery did him well as he purloined purses and wallets of several other victims along the way.

Assuming identities of his victims, he did his best to assure that all traces of Branko Kukić had been cleansed from his person. His pilfered identities helped him board a steamship from Scotland to Quebec, Canada. Blind luck smiled upon the coward Kukić, for his last theft victim had the French name, Eduoard Caron, one that would easily slip into French Canada without detection.

The Black Hand group that trained Branko and assigned him the assassination mission had inadvertently given him an unrealized benefit for his New World escape. His training included lessons in basic French language and customs. In the event he became a suspect, the plan was to pose as a French tourist.

Branko's flight from country to country intended to put as much distance as possible between himself and the Bosnian authorities. He did not realize that the most common non-native language spoken throughout Canada is French.

Despite understanding some of the language, his initial few months spent living on the streets and begging were difficult. He became disheveled, with long, unkempt hair. He covered his head with a knit woolen cap drawn low around his forehead and ears. Scruffy salt-and-pepper stubble covered his wrinkled face. Shabby patched rags clothed his body from foot to neck, leaving little of his sallow flesh exposed. Sorrowful deep-set black eyes peered stoically at people he begged from, most of whom ignored him. Whenever possible, whiskey eased his pain.

With few means, the young derelict was frequently set upon by other vagrants. One such attack in Quebec resulted in a broken nose that became bulbous and misshapen. The disfigured nose and his natural high cheekbones gave him the mien of an American Indian.

The young Slav's appearance, aged and bedraggled beyond his years, offered him no asset when he stumbled into a bar. He had begged a few coins for his pocket and needed to self-medicate his pain. Few heads turned as he staggered to a bar and demanded in French, "Whiskey."

The tavern keeper had earlier seen him begging in the street. "Be gone, ya drunken Indian." He had been refused service at the inn in the past. Owners thought him to be Cree Indian and as a policy did not serve Indians.

Branko pounded his fist on the bar and again shouted, "I want whiskey!"

The barman pulled a club from behind the counter, raised his arm and aimed the truncheon at the tramp's head, but Branko was too quick for him and wrested the weapon from grasp of the bartender.

Several patrons advanced toward him. Branko spun around, facing them, and took the first two out with the sturdy club, but others rushed him. The lone vagrant fought valiantly for several minutes until he was subdued and inelegantly tossed out the tavern door and into the muddy street.

The disheveled man, beyond humiliation, sat in the mud for several moments, feeling as depressed as he'd ever been, even wondering whether he should have left Bosnia. No matter the consequence he faced there, it could be no worse than his current lot.

The tavern doors swung open. A short, portly, balding man appeared before him, offering a half-full bottle in his extended right hand. Branko snatched the bottle and killed it with several large swallows, belched, then responded. "Merci, mon ami."

Speaking the Cree Indian language, the man said, *"Chief, we can make some money, wampum, together."*

Branko stared at him blankly.

"Wampum."

Banko shrugged his shoulders and the man tried in English. No response. Then French: *"Est-ce que tu comprends?"*

Branko nodded and the conversation continued in French. *"I thought you were a Cree Indian. Aren't you Cree?"*

He shook his head and the stranger asked, *"What is your tribe?"*

"Tribe?"

"Yes. If not Cree, what are you? Mohegan, Mohawk, Huron, Inuit?"

Caught off guard and fearing he might be exposed, Branko thought quickly and answered, *"That's my business, not yours."*

"Well, you sure look Cree to me." He extended his hand. *"Beauregard Rubidoux, but my name is so long, most just call me Beau Ru. What's yours?"*

Branko took the outstretched hand, shook it, but said nothing.

Beauregard Rubidoux spoke again. *"Okay, your name. Your business. How 'bout I just call you 'Chief.'"*

Branko shrugged and nodded.

"Like I said, Chief, we can make some money — wampum — together. You see, I'm a promoter. I watched you coldcock half a dozen men inside that bar and thought to myself, 'Beau Ru, this is your next big moneymaker.' Interested in turning your fists into gold?"

"Might be. Tell me more."

"Well, here is how it works. We travel around Canada to every city and little town. I arrive first and begin the promotion, boasting that I have an Indian who can whip any white hometown boy in the area. Then I take bets on it. We get a preacher or the local sheriff to hold the money. We put up a ring and you take on as many of the local lads as possible, one at a time, of course. Everyone you beat puts money in our pocket. I'll front the money for the first fight but after that we use the proceeds for future bets."

Thinking for only a moment, Branko asked. *"Our split?"*

The rotund man replied. *"Fifty-fifty."*

"You really think we could make money from this idea?"

"Chief, I KNOW we can. Done it before. How about it?"

Branko nodded in agreement.

Beau Ru continued. *"First thing we need to do is get you cleaned up, then we give you a name. You look Cree. How about that for your last name, Mr. Cree?"*

"Okay."

"We need a first name, too."

Branko remembered a name from the documents in the first pocket he picked. Brodie something or other. *"How about Brodie?"*

Beau Ru ran the name combination through his mind. *"Brodie Cree. Chief Brodie Cree. Sounds like a half breed. Even better. Both sides will hate you and that means more bets. Yes, Chief, 'Chief Brodie Cree' will do fine. Now let's get you a warm bath and a bed for the night. Kiss those rags you're wearing goodbye. From now on, you're going to dress in the finest white man style any Indian ever dressed. It really pisses off the Whites to see an Indian in fine clothes. And it pisses off the Indians to think a half breed might beat a full blood."*

That chance meeting with Beauregard Rubidoux ended the life as Branko Kukić, and began his existence as Brodie Cree, Canadian Indian chief, fighter and brawler. His first fight took place in Saint Adele, a small village just outside Quebec. He fought three white men and whipped them all. His payday was less than he had expected but it was a payday, his first in a long while.

Paydays became better as the abuse to his body got worse. The two men traveled from venue to venue in royal style taking bets and winning fights. Chief Brodie Cree won nearly all his events except when the wagering suggested he take a dive.

Still, the bare-knuckle fighting game exacted its price. Once post-fight numbness wore off, Brodie found himself wallowing in constant agony. To dull the pain of injuries suffered during each bout, he drank heavily. His body wracked with soreness, cramps, and spasms from repeated internal injuries. The scam finally became too much. Brodie Cree and Beauregard Rubidoux eventually parted company, both leaving the other with a handsome amount of money. Once his earnings melted away, his brief fame evaporated. He kept the moniker Brodie Cree, but returned to a life of poverty, stealing from innkeepers and travelers and begging to eke out a squalid living.

Sitting in a tavern drinking rotgut whiskey, Brodie Cree noticed a discarded newspaper on the floor. Grabbing the paper to use as insulation against the holes in his shoes, he glanced at a photo of somebody who looked vaguely familiar. Though he could not read the English words, he recognized the name Katie. He stared at the image of the powerful businesswoman, Katie Novak.

He called out, *"I'll buy a drink for the man who can read an English newspaper."*

Another bum, balding and rotund, staggered over to where he sat. *"I'll read it to you, Chief. No booze required. For old time sake."* It was Beauregard Rubidoux, who happened to be in the same bar. His once fine clothing was patched but clean. He read the newspaper story to Brodie, translating as he spoke.

Could it be? Similar first name and those features … it had to be her. He had to see her. This could be his lucky break. He sat and imagined …

Brodie Cree thanked Beau Ru, then sneaked behind the bar while the owner was distracted and stole money from the cashbox. He disappeared with the cash but this time did not spend it on booze as he had so often done. This time his ill-gotten gains went for a bath, a new set of sporty clothing, and a one-way train ticket in preparation for a surprise visit to an old flame in Washington D.C.

19

Seeing Double

"It is best to be off with the old love before you are on with the new."—Colossians 3:1

AS SHE PACKED LUGGAGE FOR THE RETURN TRIP HOME, Katie ruminated on the many changes in her life. Reflecting, she recalled the beatings by teachers and her carefree life in the river. The silent gift insider guided her through mazes of torment toward a better life. Her disillusion with life continued with expulsion from school and becoming enamored with an older, politically active boy during her teen years. Smiling, she recalled the repeated scrapes they got into together, accusations of shoplifting and worse. When Grandma could no longer handle the teen, she and Katie's mother hatched a plan, shipping the girl off to her parents in America to marry Peter Novak, ten years Katie's senior. *Funny,* she mused, *Branko was about the same age as my old man, but Pete seemed so much older. I think he was born an old man.*

Several days before her departure for America, Branko received orders to leave his location at a moment's notice. Thus, his goodbye was written in a note and secreted in a hiding place known only to her and Branko. Though she often wondered what had become of him, Branko Kukić seemed to have disappeared from the earth. She was certain he had been killed in the war.

Humming as she folded and packed her clothes, Katie remembered how she adamantly refused to marry the "old man" her parents had chosen for her, holding out instead for her fantasy man back home. At long last her internal gift spoke and assured the girl that marriage to Peter Novak would be her best choice.

Her faith in the gift allowed Katie to enter marriage with the vigor of a hyperactive teen. Dedicating herself to her new station in life, she helped build the family house, making it a home with two babies, and became a dynamo of schemes to supplement her husband's meager steel mill salary. But she kept her pride by refusing to address her husband by name or any affectionate sobriquet, referring to him instead as "Old Man."

Thinking of her most recent lost love, though platonic, Albert also occupied a large part of her heart and soul. Still amazed at the success in business and all that had happened in Washington, D.C., in such a short time, she closed and locked the bag, preparing to return the following day to Clairton and the business.

Startled by a knock at the door she called out, "Who is it?"

"'Tis me, Mum, Chloe," answered the Irish day maid.

"I'm just finishing packing, Chloe," Katie answered, "Come in."

The maid opened the door. "A visitor ta see you, Mum."

"Who is it?

"Says 'is name is Brodie Cree. He's all decked out in fancy leather clothes and got long braids like a girl. Looks like a wild Indian ta me."

Katie hadn't expected a visitor. Perhaps he represented a group that had questions about their success.

"He probably wants to speak to one of the leaders of the movement. Did he say what he wanted or ask for Lucy?"

"No, Mum, 'e asked for you by name. 'Mrs. Katie Novak,' he said."

Katie walked gently down the stairs and into the receiving area of the house and encountered a tall Indian. His full head of shoulder length salt-and-pepper hair was neatly braided from ears to waist. His face, wrinkled and weather-beaten surrounded by a large, misshapen nose suggested a harsh life. A fresh-looking but well-worn leather greatcoat surrounded his ample frame. Hand-cut fringes loosely covered artwork of Indian culture. The coat hung well below his waist, reaching the tops of his boots.

She extended her hand and using her most professional voice asked, "How may I help you, Mr. Cree?"

The 'Indian' responded in her native Croatian language, *"My Little Pumpkin. How you have grown!"*

Stunned into shock, Katie stood frozen, clutching the arm of a chair to keep her balance, unable to comprehend the scene. Several seconds, which seemed like hours, passed until she gathered her wits about her. "Branko?"

"In the flesh."

"You look so ... ah, different. I thought ... I ... "

"You thought I'd gone to the Happy Hunting Ground?" He winked and whispered, *"But I'm no longer Branko Kukić. He was killed by the political forces while trying to escape after the assassination. His body was never found. At least that's what the records show."*

She hushed him. *"Shhh. Say no more until I'm sure we're alone."*

"You're worried that somebody besides us might speak Croatian?"

"Oh, of course not, but you never know who is what around here. I learned that lesson the hard way."

She looked behind the parlor door. All her friends and housemates were out, gone to their homes or preparing to wrap things up and move on to the next protest. The landlady busied herself doing regular morning routine, straightening the sleeping rooms. Chloe had disappeared, nowhere to be seen.

"Come. Sit." She directed him to the sofa and took her seat at the high-back chair facing him. *"First, how on earth did you get here? And how did you find me?"*

Still speaking in the Serbo-Croatian language, he began. *"Oh, finding you was the easy part. You're famous. I saw your photo and write-up in the*

Canadian newspapers several times during the protests. The last name, Novak, was a bit puzzling. Katie, of course, would be a grownup name for Kata, and the pictures made it a dead giveaway. I knew I had to come to see you."

"Canadian newspapers? What does Canada have to do with anything? You look like an Indian from the Wild West."

"No, the Cree tribes are mostly in Canada and the Northwest Territories. I learned a little of their language and some of their customs. I've been living as Brodie Cree pretty much since I arrived in Canada years ago."

"Aren't you at risk telling me this?"

"You mean from the political powers in Europe? No, I'm small potatoes to them. Besides, their records show me as dead or missing. As you probably figured out, my purpose for being in Šislavić served as a cover for a sleeper cell. I didn't have much to do but try to blend in and hold meetings to stimulate opposition to the fascists who ruled us. I knew the call would come at some point, but I didn't realize that in the meantime I'd fall in love with a small-town kid."

Katie was rapt as she listened to the voice that had meant so much to her all those years ago. Were those feelings of rapture being reignited? She wondered.

"The call came with very short notice in the middle of the night and I only had time to leave you a note. You did get my note from our secret hiding place, didn't you? I felt so bad that I couldn't tell you goodbye in person, but what if I had been able? I couldn't take you with me. The mission was too dangerous."

Katie, staring with piercing eyes, nodded, but said nothing.

"I had to go to Sarajevo. Took a blood oath. But once I got there and received my orders, I realized my role in a plot to kill Archduke Ferdinand, I just couldn't do it. I ran away. I left everything behind; my name, my family, and most of all, the girl I loved."

Katie's eyes began to moisten in spite of herself. She spoke in uneven tones. *"You made me believe our future would be together. The note made me so angry, I called you everything but a dead man."* She dabbed her eyes and looked away.

He skipped over much of his life, ending with his travels to Canada. *"I decided to use my looks to my advantage and blend in. I knew enough of the French language to get by in Quebec, and of course, the whites, mostly French, could not be bothered to learn the Cree language, so I became an Indian, using the first name Brodie, since it sounds a little like Branko, and took the name of an Indian tribe, Cree, as my last name. I dress like an Indian and my background has not once been challenged."*

"What do you do for a living?"

Like all liars, Brodie was quick with an evasive answer. *"A little bit of this and a little bit of that. Whatever I need to get by."*

She sat, staring at the man who had been her first love. The man for whom she would have done anything. The man she believed would become her life partner. The man from another life.

"Oh, Branko, uh, Brodie, so much has changed. My life is more different than you know …"

"Hush, now, my Little Pumpkin. Let me take you to dinner. We can talk. You know I've always loved you."

She could smell liquor on his breath as he spoke, but paid it no mind. Could he still be her one and only true love? Might fate have brought them together to fulfill her destiny? Thoughts raced through her head until she felt the voice inside. No? Not him?

The voice must be mistaken. It had never been wrong before but this time she was certain it didn't understand the real identity of Brodie Cree. Besides, what could be the harm in dinner and an evening out with an old friend? Certainly, even the old gossipy biddies in Clairton would grant her that much. She stood. *"Wait here until I grab my shawl and handbag. Have you ever been to the nation's capital before?"*

Brodie shook his head.

"Then let me take you on the grand tour. We'll see the sights, eat the best food, drink fine wine, and have a great time. This is a celebration. We'll drink champagne!"

She hurried upstairs, unpacked an evening dress and slipped into it, picked up her handbag, and hummed a tune as she returned to the parlor.

Brodie stood. Katie took him by the arm, and the couple waltzed out the door heading to see the sights and dining at one of the finest restaurants in the nation's capital.

Brodie Cree cut a fine figure in his Native American chic attire. His broad shoulders and chiseled features screamed "Washington VIP!" Arms locked together like a couple of teens, the two long-lost friends sashayed down the boulevard.

They drank and talked, danced, reminisced, and laughed, paying little attention as the hours whizzed by. Katie declared, "Bring us your best champagne, and keep it coming."

Eventually the restaurant owner apologized that he must close the restaurant. He brought the bill to the table and handed it to Brodie.

Brodie touched his breast pocket and exclaimed, *"Oh no! It seems my pocket has been picked. Must have been those hooligans we passed earlier. My billfold and money are gone!"* He whispered, fingering the dinner check that showed a substantial figure.

She giggled, *"Don't worry, I've got it."* Katie reached into her purse, and left enough to cover the bill plus a generous tip. The danger impulse from her gift had been blocked by the champagne. She felt neither pain nor guilt. Without further words, they left the restaurant. Brodie let her pass then surreptitiously scooped up the tip money she'd left on the table, stuffing it in his own pocket.

Holding hands, the twosome went to an out-of-the way hotel, drinking and celebrating their reunion until they fell asleep shortly before sunrise.

As she lay in bed in a half-asleep state, Katie reasoned that she had always done the right thing since her arrival in America, even though her parents brought her under false pretenses. She had married Pete, built a house, and made it into a home, and bore two children. She'd affected excellent business decisions and under the able guidance of Albert, had been the power behind the dramatic growth of the business. She had overcome self-doubt, removal from school, the disappearance of her first love, the death of her dear mentor, poverty, and maltreatment.

But in the past twenty-four hours, her world had been turned wrong-side out.

Circumstances and her state of mind were not ideal to make life-changing decisions, but she was prepared to make a substantial one. She stood ready to disappear, to go to Canada with her lover and make a new life. Pete would be fine with the children. The business would continue to operate with Robert and Jack at its helm. Pete, Hope, and the children would be financially fixed, and she could spend the rest of her life with the man she truly loved.

Stretching as she woke to sunlight pouring into the room, and rubbing her eyes, Katie studied the empty spot in the bed beside her. "Branko," she called out. "Brodie?"

No answer. He must be in the bath. But looking in the direction of the bath, the open door revealed no movement. *"My love ... are you hiding from me? Come out and show your handsome self."*

She glanced the floor. Her purse lay open, contents scattered and in disarray. She snatched the handbag, only to discover all the money gone. *No, no, NO! It could not be!* But the truth refused to change. He had broken her heart again. This time he didn't even leave a note!

Slowly, reality sunk in. He had used her. The signs were all there. How could she have been so stupid and not seen them? She knew his true irresponsible self. Her inner voice had tried to warn her, but she blocked it out. She came to the realization that the tree of perfidy bears bitter fruit. Sitting on the edge of the bed, stunned, just as she had done as a girl of fifteen, she believed his lies and promises. For the first time since that day spent sitting on the railroad tracks behind her parents' boarding house, Katie had a good salubrious cry.

The first teardrop rolled down her rosy cheek. Once it broke free a gusher followed, soaking her face, neck, shoulder, and the bedclothes. All the pent-up emotion from Albert's death through the jailhouse beatings to Branko's betrayal swept the pain from her psyche, much like the overflowing Kupa river of her youth had done.

After what felt like gallons of tears, red-faced, blotchy skin, bloodshot eyes with puffy lids, Katie blew her nose into a handkerchief. She arose from the bed and stood erect. Taking in several deep breaths, the woman who resisted the worst of jail beatings without a tear calmly walked to the washbasin, dipped the edge of her hankie into the water, and wiped the sorrow from her face.

She remembered something Hope's doctor in Pittsburgh said. "Tears are known to be therapeutic. Psychologists believe that as long as one is able to release suppressed emotions through the tear ducts, psychosis is kept at bay."

After resting to quell the physical evidence of her breakdown, the grand lady dressed, gathered her purse, collected herself and the remnants of her pride. Katie quickly realized that the shame and indignity of the tryst had yet to leave her. She must face the fact that with her cash gone, she would not be able pay the hotel bill.

Approaching the gentleman at the desk, Katie forced her most convincing smile. Before she could get a word out, the man behind the desk spoke. "Madam, we are honored to have you as our guest. I understand your need for anonymity given your fame. My wife so admires you. She walked to the White House every day to watch the protests. Each day she came home and told me of your strength and spirit. She kept every newspaper article about you and the other brave women."

Katie tried to speak, "I really need to settle my bill. Once I get to a bank…"

But the man held up his hand, cutting her off.

"Please, Mrs. Novak. My wife would crown me if I allowed you to pay. She's out grocery shopping, but is due back any minute. I'll tell you what

…" He rifled through newspapers under his desk and pulled out one that included Homer J. Hammer's byline along with a photograph of Katie and Lucy Burns.

"Would you please sign a copy? We'd much rather have this than the pittance we charge for the room."

"Of course. If you insist." Katie smoothed the paper, picking up the pen from the holder on the desk. The inn proprietor removed the cap from the ink bottle. "What is your wife's name?"

"Carol. Carol Walsh."

Katie carefully touched the nib to her tongue, then dipped the fine point into a vessel of blue-black substance in a small bottle-shaped vase with a narrow cylindrical neck, tapping the excess liquid from the pen. Writing in the margin above her picture she inscribed, *Mrs. Carol Walsh, the heart is hardy but delicate. Strive for your destiny but do not let it break you. Katheryn Novak.*

Handing her a blotter, the innkeeper said, "We will treasure this forever, Madam. Thank you."

Katie left the inn and walked the several blocks, empty bag in hand, to the boardinghouse that served as her home for the past weeks. She first made a quick stop at the local bank to replenish the supply of cash in her purse.

Upon leaving the bank her pace quickened as she walked briskly, chiding herself for having been such a fool over what might have been — twice. *But,* she thought, *not my first stupid mistake. Not my last. Not fatal. My bruised heart will heal and from this point onward in my life, I swear to myself I will always listen to my gift.*

The following morning Chloe, the maid, carried Katie's luggage to curbside. A yellow hack pulled up to the sidewalk, brakes squeaking as the front wheel came to rest with a plop into a pothole puddle. Chloe, soaked to the skin by the hole's dirty water, yelled a series of epithets that burned the cabbie's ears.

"If my mistress got a splash like I just did, you'd have hell to pay."

The surly cab driver responded. "Well, she ain't here to get her pretty clothes all wet now, is she?"

Katie emerged from the front door, walking slowly, head down, but not from the previous night's escapade and betrayal. That chapter of her life was forever gone. Though she felt a bit melancholy to be leaving behind the excitement of the hearings, picketing, comradery, even time served in Occoquan, the results made it all worthwhile. Happy it was over and satisfied at what she and fellow suffragettes had accomplished, the time had come to return home to a routine. Smiling, her thoughts were filled with how much she missed her children, the business, and even Pete.

The taxi driver, hoping for a tip, doffed his hat. "I was just about to load yer trunk and bags into the taxi, Ma'am."

Chloe sizzled. Katie flush with a purse recharged by coins and banknotes, noticed the drenched apron, and handed the girl an extra gold coin. "I'll give you the driver's tip so you can launder the uniform he nearly ruined."

The maid sneered at the driver as Katie continued. "Thank you, Chloe, for all your attention while I stayed. I'm sure our group made plenty of extra work for you."

"'Twas my pleasure, Ma'am," Chloe curtsied.

As the cab started to pull away from the curb, Katie reached over the seat and placed her hand on the driver's shoulder. "Wait a minute, I hear somebody calling my name."

Homer ran up the street, yelling and waving, as the driver jerked the taxi to a halt.

"Mrs. Novak, Mrs. Novak," Homer shouted, breathing heavily as he approached the vehicle.

"I'm so glad I caught you before you returned to Clairton. I wanted to congratulate you on the wonderful and hard-fought victory. It's a landmark that will stand long after we're both gone."

Katie smiled, though her heart still ached. Despite her attempts to quell the emotional hurt, Brodie's betrayal stung far greater than any physical injuries endured during the night of terror. She managed to paste a smile on her face. "Homer, our victory would never have happened if not for your hard work, defiance of the system, and brilliant writing."

"Mrs. Novak, you are too kind. Those newspaper columns paid big dividends to me as well. I've had so many offers from other outlets. My head spins just to think about it."

"You deserve each one and more."

"Can you keep a secret?" he asked.

Smiling at the irony of the question given the previous night's events, she replied, "You have no idea."

"Well, I was just informed that I've been nominated for an award. The publisher Joseph Pulitzer made a fortune in the newspaper business. He died last year and his will stipulated that a prize be awarded in his name in several areas. My series on the suffragettes movement has been nominated and is being considered for exposing abuses in the Occoquan Prison system."

"That's wonderful, Homer, and well deserved. I wish you the best of luck. Let me know if there is anything I can do, and please visit us when you come to see your aunt."

"I wonder if I might ask you a favor."

"Of course, Homer, ask away. We're all so deeply indebted to you. If it is in my power, your wish will be granted."

Homer handed an envelope to Katie. "Would you give this letter to Hope? Don't tell her, but I started and rewrote it over a hundred times."

"I'll deliver it personally. We've been going on about the events here. Let me ask you, what are your plans for the future now that you're a revered writer?"

"I don't know about that revered part. But to answer your question, I'm not sure. *The Observer* has offered me a fulltime city editor position with a handsome salary. I've also heard from papers in Boston, New York, Washington, and even the Pittsburgh Post."

She reached out the window and squeezed his hand. "You are destined for continued success. Best of luck to you. I'm certain you'll make the right decision."

Turning back to the cabbie she said in a firm voice, "Driver, take me to the railway station."

20

The Plan

"By failing to prepare, you are preparing to fail." —Benjamin Franklin

KATIE'S TRAIN RIDE BACK TO CLAIRTON was uneventful. The impact of the historic event she, Lucy, and fellow suffragettes had achieved was maximized by the euphoria shared by all women. Just as her husband and Karl Blackburn's role had been held secret, so were the details Katie had agreed to that shaped the plea for passage by the President.

Shortly before noon the train made a brief stop in Cumberland, Maryland, en route to Pittsburgh. Katie disembarked and found a telephone. Since Pete refused to answer the phone Katie had a Bell Telephone employee install in their home, she phoned the office. After several raspy rings, a scratchy voice announced, "Hello, you have reached Clairton Savings and Loan, Hope Novak speaking. How may I help you?"

Shouting into the telephone, she responded. "Hope. This is Katie. I like the way you answered the telephone. Very professional."

"Oh, Mrs. Novak. Congratulations on achieving your mission. Will you be home soon? Everybody is anxious to have you back."

"Yes. We have much to discuss. Will you get a message to Pete? Tell him my train should arrive around two o'clock this afternoon. Do you want me to send a telegram to confirm?"

"No. I'll get the message to him as soon as our call is completed."

Katie continued to shout into the device. "Okay. See you soon."

The line disconnected. Something about the call bothered Hope. She went up the stairs to Katie's office and spoke to Robert. "That was the boss on the telephone."

"I gathered. I could hear your side of the conversation all the way up here. How did she sound?"

Hope seemed to be in a quandary. "Different."

"Different? What do you mean?"

"I mean ... it didn't sound like our Mrs. Novak."

"Well, she's more than a hundred miles away and talking onto a 'new-fangled contraption' as Mr. Novak would say. Of course she would sound different."

"No, something more than that." Hope paused, then added, "She sounded ... American."

Robert pondered the comments for a moment. "Well, we'll find out soon enough. When does she arrive?"

"Oh, that's right. I need to get a message to Mr. Novak. She'll arrive in two hours."

Hope rushed down the hill to the Novak home. She found Pete rocking back and forth on the porch swing, smoking a hand-rolled cigarette, a child on either side. "You be home early. Want me fix you for eat?"

"No, thank you. I just came to let you know Katie will arrive in a couple of hours. I'll help you get the children fed and dressed."

* * *

As the train pulled into the Clairton depot, Pete and Hope stood on the platform to greet Katie, each holding one of the children's hand.

Breaking from her father's grasp and darting toward her mother, Rosie chose to be the first to hail a dramatic greeting. "Mama, Mama. I'm so glad you're home." Holding her hands as far apart from one another as possible, she added, "I missed you so much. I don't know what I'd do if you stayed away one more day!" With arms wrapped around Katie's ample waist and hips, the little girl squeezed as tightly as she could.

"Well, I missed you, too, my little Rosebud." Reaching into her handbag she pulled out a metal replica of the White House. "Maybe this will help cure your loneliness."

The child snatched the present and returned to her father's side.

Little Petey was a bit more reserved, not quite sure who this person might be. He watched his sister take the souvenir but did not move from Hope's grasp. Katie again reached into her bag, as if searching for a prize. The item she retrieved brought a broad smile to the little one's face. Katie held out a working model of a red fire engine. The boy stepped forward and plucked the toy from his mother's grasp.

"Hope, your surprise and Pete's come next but you must both wait. Your favors are tucked away in my trunk. We'll get them later at the house. But in the interim, I do have a little something that might be of interest to you."

The unofficial adoptee found no disappointment in her stepmother's comment to wait, as she had not anticipated a gift.

"Here is a letter handed to me by a young journalist just as I prepared to leave."

Hope's eyes sparkled as she reached for the sealed letter. Clutching it to her breast, her voice cracking, she asked, "May I be excused?"

"Of course. You hurry back to the house and read it. We will gather my grip and luggage and follow with the children."

The teen moved Petey's hand to his father's, then hastened up toward the house. Pete, Katie and the children walked toward the baggage car to retrieve the trunk that had already been offloaded and sat in the afternoon sun, and waiting to be claimed. She slung her purse over her shoulder and took both of the children's hands. Pete toted the trunk and grip. As they traipsed slowly up the hill to the house, Pete spoke to Katie in Bosnian. *"While you were gone, I finished the room for Hope on the other side of children's. I figured a young lady needs her privacy."*

"That was a nice thing to do. How does she seem to be working out at the Savings and Loan?"

"Like an old hand, Robert tells me. I walked up to the business each day to check on things. Seems like you did a great job hiring." He smiled, adding, *"I'm not sure if you should be happy or sad that things went so well while you were gone."*

"Happy. And happy that we were able to get legislation passed so women can now vote."

Pete wrapped is free arm around her shoulders. *"You're quite the celebrity around town. Danica tells me that according to the Pittsburgh Post and local folks, you got the vote for women passed singlehandedly."*

"Not quite, Old Man. I had plenty of help. But a person who played a huge role was your old friend, Karl Blackburn. He sends you his best."

Surprised at the revelation he repeated her comment. *"Karl Blackburn? You saw Blackburn? How is he?"*

"The same. Still looks like a heart attack waiting to happen, and chewing on an unlit cigar. He was a big help convincing President Wilson to support the amendment. And Homer's stories really played a major role, too."

"Danica read the stories to me. We were all shocked when you and the ladies were thrown in prison. And for what? Standing in front of the White House?"

"It happened. It was hell. I try not to think about it."

They approached Pete's grapevine-covered porch, the refuge where he spent much time with his beloved children. He looked down, but before he could say a word the little ones broke free of Katie and tore into the house. *"Well, here we are."* Pete continued. *"Tell me everything about your trip."*

Katie gulped, thinking of the beatings in prison and of time spent with Brodie. *"There are things that happened you do not need to know."*

They sat on the swing and he rolled a cigarette. *"Okay, tell me the parts you choose. But first, what can I get you?"*

"A glass of your wine and a hot bath."

"Done." He dashed into the house and half-filled two Mason canning

jars with his homemade wine. Back on the porch he kissed her on the forehead.

As he handed her one of the glasses, she took a sip and said, *"The bath can wait. Let me kick off my shoes and enjoy this wine and your company for the moment."*

* * *

Upstairs in her newly-completed bedroom, Hope carefully undid the sealed envelope and read the enclosed letter:

My Dearest Hope,

Let me begin by telling you once again what a special person you are, and though I deeply admire Hope Novak, how I pine for you to discover from whence you came. I know that unlocking your past, though it might reveal pain, will satisfy you more than anybody else. To that end, I will volunteer to be your Sherlock Holmes. I have taken a leave of absence from the paper and commit to you that I will use every ounce of energy in my soul to discover your origins. No matter if they be humble or royal, you deserve to know them. Once the discoveries are made, I'll place them in your hands and surrender my heart to you.

With deep affection,

Homer J. Hammer,

Newspaper Reporter

By the time Hope read his letter, Homer had already begun his journey. Leave of absence granted, he packed his belongings into a rucksack and his portable Corona in its carrying case, and set out to explore as many villages as needed to discover Hope's beginnings.

Homer's first stop was, Harrisburg, the state capital of Pennsylvania. There he searched through documents that might be of help. He laid out a grid over a map of the southwest corner of Pennsylvania. On a sheet of paper in his notebook he listed all the cities and towns in order of their population, according to census records, then plotted a course. Next stop, Clairton to visit the Novak family and, of course, their adopted daughter.

The locomotive hissed as the powerful engine came to a screeching, hissing stop at Clairton's train station. Few passengers disembarked: a businessman wearing a suit, a family of recently-arrived immigrants, and Homer. The family was met by relatives whose spoken language Homer could not decipher, but whose body language, hugging, and crying made it evident that they were happy to greet one another.

The journalist-turned-detective and the businessman nodded to one another as both climbed aboard the trolley that would take them up St. Clair Avenue to the business district. As the two men boarded, the trolley driver welcomed them.

To the businessman: "Hello, Sir." Once he recognized Homer a broad smile crossed the face of the driver. "Well, if it isn't our town's favorite newspaper man. Coming to visit your aunt, Mr. Hammer?"

The young man blushed and answered, "Yes, I'm here for a little visit."

"Well, Margaret sure will be right happy to see you. She's doing fine. Gimpy leg is all healed up. Never know it got busted."

"That's great. I'm anxious to see her."

The bell on the trolley rang as the driver snapped the reins and called out, "Hup," to start the horse moving. "Hup, hup. Let's go, Augustus."

The streetcar began its trek up the hill. The trolley driver turned to the businessman. "Not sure if you realize it but you're riding with a celebrity. Newspaper reporter Homer J. Hammer. He put our little town on the map."

The man extended his hand to Homer. "Proud to know you. Sam Russo, hardware salesman."

Homer shook the man's hands and nodded.

Then the driver turned to Homer. "You know, the whole town, we're all damn proud of your newspaper stories. Pittsburgh Post carried every one of them. And that Mrs. Novak. What a character. Have you seen her yet?"

Homer opened his mouth, but before he could utter a response, the driver continued. "Course not. You just got off the train." Slapping his forehead with an open palm, he quickly added, "Yessiree, Bub, we're mighty proud that one of our own made the big time."

Turning to the other passenger he continued, "Where can we take you, Mr. Russo?"

"Crucible Hotel."

"Crucible it is. I'll bet you don't often get to ride with a famous person, right? And I don't mean me or my horse, Augustus."

Sam Russo spoke, nodding to Homer. "I've read your work. Fine writing. I'm surprised you're so young."

"Yup, I get that a lot. Lucky for me the byline doesn't include a photograph."

They reached the top of the hill. "Whoa, Augustus. Your stop, gentlemen. Crucible Hotel is across the street and I'm guessing that Mr. Hammer is still able to find his way to his aunt's house."

Homer thanked the driver, paid his fare and added a tip, and both men left the trolley.

"See you later, Mr. Hammer."

Homer, out of earshot, didn't respond, but strode up Miller Avenue to his aunt's house.

Margaret was pleasantly surprised when Homer rang the doorbell. "Well! How's my chief cook, dish, and bottle washer? Let me get you some of your favorite tea and scones. Will you be here long?"

Margaret went to the kitchen while Homer found his way to his room and set his rucksack and Corona in the corner, then returned to the parlor.

Sipping a cup of Oolong tea, Homer began. "No Auntie, I'm here just until I get oriented. I'm headed to every town and village in this part of the state, bound and determined to uncover Hope Novak's history."

"Well, I'm glad to have you back even if for a little while. You spoiled me. Once a person learns to enjoy the lap of luxury, it's difficult to unlearn. And on a more serious note I'll tell you, Nephew, I have missed your vibrant personality. And of course I'm so proud of the work you've been doing."

"Remember, Aunt Margaret, my road to achievement began in this house. Had you not given me the tip about Mrs. Novak, I might still be searching for my byline."

"Oh, you've got grit, boy. You'd have been successful regardless. It just happened that the stars aligned for you here first. Now tell me, are you certain that you'll still have a job when you return to the paper?"

"Yes, Auntie Margaret. I've got it in writing. A six-month paid leave-of-absence, then return as a staff writer and city editor. I'm on what is called a sabbatical leave."

"Good. I'm glad you cleared that up for me. Next, tell me exactly why you are undertaking this project. It sounds like you will be wearing out plenty of shoe leather."

"I have my reasons. This could lead to another big story for me."

"So then, might it have something to do with the fact that you're googly-eyed over that Novak girl?"

"I didn't say that."

"You didn't deny it either."

Homer grinned. "Check mate. You got me. But please keep that information to yourself. When the time comes, I want to court her properly. To do that I'd like to know for certain, if she'll have me, who it is that I must ask for her hand."

"My, my, my, you do plan well. But remember what the poet Robert Burns said about plans."

"I know. He's one of my favorite poets. *The best laid plans of mice and men often go awry.* But truth be known, I'm doing this as much for Hope as for me. She deserves to know who she is."

"You're right, dear boy. Now tell me how you plan to solve this mystery."

They moved to the dining room and Homer laid the map of Western Pennsylvania on the table. "Here we are," he said, pointing to a dot followed by the name Clairton.

"She is not from here or somebody would have recognized her, but the professor told Mrs. Novak that Hope's manner of speaking placed her somewhere south of us. I plan to move from town to town, starting with those less populated and work my way to the more populous. I have copies of the 1910 census for the area. That might help me track down names. At each stop I'll find an official and ask if her description fits anybody who disappeared over the past few years. I've learned a lot about rooting out facts and I hope my skills help me uncover her story."

"When do you plan to start?"

"Well, I'd like to spend the weekend here with you, scout around and see if I can uncover any hints from the local police. I've read the police reports of when she was first discovered, but maybe I can jog a memory or two and jar something loose. I also want to stay with you over the weekend so I can accompany you to church this Sunday. You have such a nice congregation."

"I'd like that very much," smiled Margaret.

"Monday will be my 'loose ends planning day' and I'll leave Tuesday morning."

Margaret answered, "Not until I fix you a full breakfast. Who knows when you'll get your next decent meal?"

Homer left the house that afternoon to pay a visit to the Clairton Savings and Loan. He entered the office and was met by a receptionist. "How may I help you, Sir?"

He surveyed the office staff, most of whom were unfamiliar faces. "I'd like to see …"

From the back of the office a voice cried out, "Homer! What a pleasant surprise."

He was caught off guard. Katie Novak looked just as she had during their interview, but her voice … no, it was not her voice, but her manner of speaking was different. He first noticed it when they spoke in Washington.

She recognized his confusion and added, "Aha, it is my speech that is different, right?"

He nodded dumbly.

"It is an absolute marvel what can be attained with weeks of intensive study and training, isn't it?"

"It's ... it's wonderful, marvelous, fantastic. You sound like one of those posh women who came down from New York."

"I have Lucy Burns to thank. She's an amazing tutor. Do you have time for a visit? Let me introduce you to our new staff members." Turning, she raised her voice and announced. "Everybody, this is the famous journalist, Homer J. Hammer."

Katie made introductions all around, but the one employee Homer hoped to see was not among them.

"I sent Hope to the house to help with the kids, but I just received some legal papers for Pete to sign. Do you mind taking them to him?"

His grin widened. He snatched the envelope full of blank pages that Katie held out to him, waved to the employees, and hastened down the hill.

21

Homer's Odyssey

"If thou hast any sound, or use of voice, speak to me." —William Shakespeare

WHILE CHARTING HIS ROUTE, Homer switched his original plan and decided chances would be better in places with larger populations. His first planned stop was Monessen, then Connellsville, Uniontown, then circle back to Waynesburg and Washington, Pennsylvania, filling in with smaller villages as he went. If he had no leads by his last stop, Homer would return to Clairton, rest, then make another trip. He vowed to continue his odyssey until he discovered his first love's history.

The quest began in the gritty mining towns and villages south of Clairton, using the same format at each: seeking out the local constable or other civic leader and asking a series of questions. His first stop, Monessen, tested the plan. He arrived at the office of Mayor Theron Ray Crane promptly at ten o'clock in the morning.

"Good morning, Mr. Mayor. Thank you for taking the time to see me."

"Please have a seat. How can we help you?"

"My name is Homer Hammer and I'm investigating the disappearance of a young girl from your area. She might have come from an abusive environment. Does that ring a bell in your memory? If so, can you review your records of the past few years?"

"Are you a law enforcement officer?"

Homer was coy in his response, not wanting to give too much information. "No, Sir. I'm a newspaper reporter trying to track down leads on a missing girl."

The mayor sat pensively for several minutes. "Give me a moment." Theron turned in his swivel chair, pulled out a drawer, removed several files, and pored over them. "Hmmm. m-hmmm, m-hmmmm. Nope. That wasn't it."

Waving a file in the air he continued. "Thought it might have been this one. I remember an incident. Eye-talian fella caught his wife running around on him while he was at work. Got sick on the job and came home early one day. Caught 'em in the act, if you know what I mean. Said they didn't even hear him come into the house or see him in the doorway of the bedroom. Picked up and loaded his sixteen gauge double barrel and went back to the bedroom. They was goin' at it like a house afire till they heard the chk-chk cocking of the shotgun. Blasted 'em both. Her and her paramour dead as hell. Gave 'em both barrels full on, reloaded and shot 'em once more for good measure.

"He's doing ten to twenty in the Western Penitentiary in Pittsburgh. West Penn, we call it. 'Crime pf passion,' his lawyer pled, so the jury didn't fry him. But that one happened maybe ten, fifteen years ago now. We had some domestic squabbles since then, but nothing like that one, and nothing like you describe."

The mayor thought for another moment, then with an empathetic shake of the head. "Nope, no other similar thing on record or in my memory."

"Thank you, Sir. Here is my business card in case you think of something after I leave. You can always reach me at the *Chesapeake Ledger.* I'll be back there by spring."

The mayor read his card. "Wait a minute. You're the guy who wrote about all those women getting the vote, aren't you?"

Homer nodded.

"Well, not sure what the country's coming to what with women voting and all. Next thing ya know the coloreds gonna want to have the vote. I can't see it. But I'll tell you this. The wife thinks you're the cat's meow. Read every word you wrote that she could get her hands on. Wait till I tell her who came to my office today."

The mayor rose and shook Homer's hand. "Good luck, young fella. It was a pleasure meeting you. I hope you find what you're looking for."

"Yes, 'Hope' is the key word here."

The mayor, of course, didn't get the double entendre.

Homer walked the beaten paths and back roads, continuing his search through small towns and villages: Elrama, Dunlevy, Elco, Allison, Smock, Republic, and others. No luck, no leads, but the reporter worked with vigor. He vowed not to cease his mission until he had visited every village in Western Pennsylvania and Northern West Virginia, or until he discovered what he was after. He did it for Hope.

The venture continued through late fall and into early winter. The Farmer's Almanac forecast predicted a cold one coming. Homer's money was holding out, but rather than searching during snowy weather he decided to skip the more time-consuming smaller villages for the moment and go back to his original plan: try two larger communities in the area, Connellsville and Uniontown. If nothing turned up, he would return to Clairton and stay with his aunt until spring. That would give him a chance to see Hope, bring her up to speed, and perhaps begin a courtship.

Connellsville and Uniontown, only ten miles apart, boasted larger populations than the villages he'd been visiting, and by extension, he posited, they'd have larger police forces and better record keeping than the one-horse towns he'd been calling on.

He arrived in Connellsville late that snowy morning, going directly to the police station. After listening to Homer's story, the Connellsville Chief of Police Thayne Nelson glanced at his files. "I know there's nothing in my files that could help you, but I seem to remember an incident similar to the one you describe. Happened down around Uniontown. I'll put in a call to the police chief there. Let him know you're coming. He's also the mayor."

He decided to give it one more shot in Uniontown before turning back for Clairton. The Connellsville police chief had provided reason for optimism, but cautious optimism. A light powder of snow blanketed the well-travelled road between the two cities and provided an opportunity for Homer to stand with his thumb extended. Within ten minutes a grocery delivery truck slowed to a stop. The driver shouted through the cracked passenger side window. "Headed to Uniontown then Morgantown."

Homer answered, "Uniontown for me," tossing his rucksack in the bed he climbed into the cab of the truck.

The two men enjoyed small talk as the rickety truck chugged southward.

Over the din of the engine the driver asked, "Been there before?"

"Nope, looking for information. I'm a newspaper reporter."

"Sounds interesting. Write for the *Post?*"

"Sometimes. But mostly for a small paper in Virginia, the *Chesapeake Ledger.*"

"Never heard of it. Well, here we are. Where can I drop you?"

"As close to the police station as you're going."

The truck's brakes squeeked as the driver slowed the rig. "That's easy. My first stop is Restagno's Market, half a block up the street."

"Thanks for the ride."

"Short distance but still made the time go faster."

The two men shook hands and Homer climbed down from the cab, slammed the door to make sure it latched shut, grabbed his rucksack, then waved as the grocery delivery van rumbled an additional few hundred yards to the market.

Upon reaching the police station he was directed to the courthouse and a local judge's chambers. Gold letters on the etched glass window proclaimed the occupant to be Judge Jason P. Graft.

A friendly smile greeted Homer as he entered. The judge pressed a wad of smoking tobacco into the bowl of his pipe and lit the leaves. His shock of silver hair neatly trimmed at the collar gave him the appearance of a young man, though he must have been in his sixties by Homer's guess.

"How can I help you, young man?"

Homer posed his usual question, flipped open a note pad he'd gotten from his backpack, and retrieved a pencil. After touching it to his tongue he poised the tip against a notepad, and began his spiel.

The judge sat and pondered for several moments, taking a few deep puffs of his pipe, bringing a pleasant aroma into the room.

"Hmm, I think you might mean the Elwell girl. Her father was a banker, name of Oliver Elwell. Wife's name of Martha. Don't know her maiden name 'cause they was already married when they moved down here. She come from Mingo Junction way, I believe. He came from just outside Pittsburgh. Don't remember exactly where, but he went to school in the city. Studied to be a banker. Damn fine one, too, so we all thought, but weak when it came to women. God rest his soul.

They had a little girl, cute as a button. Blonde hair and big blue eyes, deep set. Color of the sky on a cloudless day. Those eyes could pierce a guy's heart, know what I mean?"

Homer nodded as he scribbled, but didn't speak as his heart pounded and his pulse quickened. He surely knew those eyes. The mayor described them perfectly. Homer resisted the urge to prod the man for more information about the girl. Pauses in the judge's conversation rendered torture in his gullet.

Judge Graft switched topics as Homer silently writhed in agony. He knew if he wanted a good interview he must allow the man to be comfortable.

"Always thought I might try my hand at newspaper writing, but life takes funny turns."

Homer stifled his anxiety to question the mayor further at the moment. He knew he must let the man talk and release information at his own pace.

His editor's words rang in his head. "A good technique for putting a person at ease is to let them talk about themselves, thus making them more apt to give up information. You must have discipline."

He remembered that as an old interviewer's trick. His editor taught him well.

Judge Graft continued. "Got my start in this business as a prison guard down at West Penn. I was big for my age and strong, though just a kid of eighteen. Before I knew it, I worked my way up to supervisor. The warden told me about an elected position of high sheriff about to open up in this area, so I ran for it and got elected. Been the law in Uniontown ever since. Four years ago, they made me mayor, too. Guess I should be flattered. But by me doing both jobs it saves the city one salary." He chuckled and took another draw on the pipe.

"So back to the Elwell case. Oliver up and died of the Spanish flu. Young man. Healthy as a horse till he caught the flu, or I should say it caught him. But I'm sure you've seen lots of events just like that in your business."

Homer nodded and continued scribbling furiously, dying inside, and hoping more of the story would unfold more quickly.

"You'd 'a thought that being a banker and all, he'd 'a left the wife and kid with a goodly amount of money and property on his passing, but it seems he'd been embezzling from the bank and using the funds to keep his Polish mistress down in Chalk Hill. Everybody knew about his shenanigans, except poor Martha and the kid.

"Anyhow, Elwell died and left his wife in debt and destitute. The couple always were a little standoffish so nobody in town offered to help out when her old man passed. Martha, penniless and poverty-stricken, with a kid and both mouths to feed, became desperate. Had nothing. No funds, no property.

"Even when the banker was alive they didn't own their own home. Rented the place from Weiss, the grocer. He has several properties that he rents out. Miserly fella if you ask me. Terrible landlord. Don't keep up the houses.

"Elwell finally had to threaten to call in his loans if he didn't fix up the place — a banker could do that, you know, if the house don't get the repairs it needs. The threats also served to keep the landlord off his back when Elwell fell behind on his rent. But don't you know that when he died, Weiss not only threatened to put them out on the street, he tried to place a lien on Mrs. Elwell's few trinkets of jewelry to settle back rent. I told him I'd make life damn miserable for him if he didn't withdraw the complaint. He did.

"She pawned the stuff to buy food but that soon ran out. Said she had no kin to take her in. Martha was desperate. No skills, no money, a kid to support, and Weiss threatening to put her out on the street since she was still behind in the rent.

"Her only choice was to give herself to somebody who could support her. Married the first guy who came sniffing around thinking he might find a rich widow. Figured she might be well off with the deceased husband a banker and all. Clay Gibson from the sticks. Working man, so he had a few coins in his own pocket from time to time."

Homer could no longer stand the suspense and interrupted, "So she and the child became financially stable?"

"Naw. Gibson worked in the mines. A hard worker but a hard drinker and a gambler. Some days he was rich, other times he'd lose the whole wad and go on a toot. And a mean major drunk. He'd come home all liquored up and wail on the wife. Blame her for his own shortcomings. Called her a tramp and said she tricked him into marriage. Up and busted her nose and couple 'a ribs, blacked her eyes. Beat her pretty good.

"We hauled him in a few times when neighbors complained 'bout the noise, but she'd practically beat the paddy wagon down to the station. Crying, saying it was her fault, she provoked him, and begging us to turn him loose. If he raised hell with the officers, and stayed out of control we'd keep him overnight. But if he calmed down, we'd let her take him home. Never could understand women who protect guys who beat them. Never could."

208

The judge continued to describe the beatings in graphic detail. Homer shivered at the recounting of the abuse.

"What did the girl do while she witnessed her mother getting beaten up?"

"The kid tried to protect her mom. Screamed at Gibson and tried to intervene, but Clay tossed her away like a little rag doll. When she came back, he beat on her, too. Busted her arm and a couple 'a ribs.

"Sometimes after we let the wife take him home, we'd get a call from neighbors that he was at it again. One of the deputies would go down and drag him off to jail to let him sober up 'n sleep it off."

"Sounds like a real bad actor."

"Only when he got drunk. Once he sobered up he was the nicest guy you'd ever wanna meet. Gentle as a lamb. Give you the shirt off his back. After he beat up her and the kid, he'd cry and beg her ta' forgive him. Promise never to lay a finger on her or the kid again. He'd buy her stuff to make up and all would be okay until the next time he went on a bender. Then the cycle started all over again."

Homer recoiled at the thought of a child, any child, but especially Hope, being subject to such bullying and abuse. But he was still not one hundred percent ready to accept this story as Hope's.

"Where is the wife? I'd like to interview her. Maybe if he's sober I'll interview Gibson, too."

"Well, that's what I been getting 'round ta' tellin' you. When 'e got his bonus at the mine, he'd really go on a jag. Come home and beat the hell out of his wife. Last time he beat her so bad till there was no life left in her. When he realized she might be dead, he run out the house and headed for Chalk Hill."

Homer looked puzzled. "Chalk Hill?" Glancing at his notes he added, "where the ex-husband's mistress lived?"

"You got it. Whenever Clay got boozed up like that, especially if he lost his money gambling, he blamed Elwell's mistress for his woes. I know it don't make no sense, but a drunk man's head can get pretty twisted. So he'd run down to the ex-girlfriend's house and beat the hell out of her, too, but Chalk Hill's out of Uniontown's jurisdiction, so we didn't pursue it and the mistress never filed papers on him. Guess she figured nobody could do anything about it.

"Time before this last one, he got his bonus, drank some, lost the rest in an illegal card game, then went to Chalk Hill. That time he beat up Elwell's mistress pretty bad. She got herself a forty-five-caliber pistol and warned him that if he ever came around again she'd shoot his balls off. And that's exactly what she did. Then she came up here to tell somebody what happened. I interviewed her and wrote up the report myself. Let me read some of it to you."

The judge leafed through a thick file, pulled out a form, and began to read silently, refreshing his memory of the details. He set the file on the desk and recited the happenings of that night from memory.

"Gibson loses his bonus money and gets drunk. Beats his poor wife to unconsciousness. Leaves the house for Chalk Hill. Gets to pounding on the door of the occupant. Polish woman, last name of Pazinski, first name P-a-t-r-y-c-j-a, goes by Petty.

"Victim picks up her forty-five, aims toward his crotch, and 'bam- bam, bam, bam,' puts all six bullets through the door. Shoots his balls clean off and the gun's recoil bounces up and adds two in the gut, plus one to the head, according to the undertaker. Killed him stone dead. She was never charged. Self defense."

Homer sat pensively. *Could this be Hope's story?*

"What happened to …" glancing again at his notes, "Martha and the girl. What was her name?"

"Martha Elwell, er, Gibson, after the marriage, died from injuries inflicted on her person by Clay Gibson. Buried in a pauper's grave.

"The daughter, Adeline, they called her Addie. Smart as a whip. Sharp as a tack. Top of her class in school. Sang like a lark, that girl. Teachers loved her. Never caused a problem. Pretty little girl, too. Like I said earlier, perfect long blonde hair, color of flax. Eyes as blue as a clear summer sky. Kind eyes, though sad as somebody who has seen the ugliest part of humankind, but is ready to forgive. Shame her mother got caught up by a toper. No doubt the kid would've gone to college."

"What happened to her?" Homer asked as he held his breath, "Did she perish also?"

"Nope. 'Least we don't think so. She just up and disappeared. Couple 'a hobos claim they might 'a seen 'er down on the tracks. Described her eyes. That's why I thought it might be her. She didn't have no money. If she hopped a train, who knows? Could be anywhere. Wherever she is, it's got to be better than her life here. If the authorities got her, she's probably been sent to a convent or an orphanage."

Homer breathed a sigh of relief and gathered himself for a summary. Reviewing his notes, he began, "Okay, Judge, let me sum this up to see if I've got all the facts straight. Husband, Oliver Elwell, a banker. Dies of the flu, leaving wife Martha and child Adeline destitute. Martha remarries, an abusive drunk, Clay Gibson, who kills her and in turn is shot to death by the first husband, Oliver's, mistress. Daughter disappears. Is that about it?"

"You got it, Sonny. I hope you find what you're looking for."

"Thank you, Judge. I think I might have done so."

Homer left the judge's chambers with mixed emotions. On one hand, he wanted to find Hope's story, but on the other, he had no idea it would be so painful. He had written about pain and struggles before, but this time it was personal. This was one story that would not be printed.

23

Facing the Pain

"All's well that ends well." —William Shakespeare

HOMER PHONED THE CLAIRTON SAVINGS AND LOAN, and without identifying himself to the secretary, asked to speak to Mrs. Novak.

"This is Katie Novak. How can I help you?"

"Mrs. Novak, it's Homer. Please don't say anything to reveal it is me on the line."

Katie said nothing in response, but held the receiver to her ear for a moment, then said, "Just a moment, Sir. I will close my office door for privacy. Then we will discuss your situation."

She turned to her manager and asked, "Can you give me a moment, Robert?"

As he stepped out and closed the door Katie returned her attention to the phone. "What is it, Homer. Are you in trouble?"

"Oh no. Nothing like that. Everything is copacetic," he shouted into the phone. "I just wanted to share with you what I discovered and plan how we should handle the information with you-know-who. Can you meet me at my aunt's house at noon?"

"I could, but I don't think I know your aunt or where she lives."

"Oh, that's easy. Margaret Hammer. Her place is right around the corner from you at 313 Miller Avenue. I'm there now."

"Fine. I'll just tell the office staff I have an early lunch meeting with a client."

She glanced at the clock on the sidewalk below her office as its big gong rang ten o'clock. "See you in a couple of hours."

She waved Robert back into the office but made no mention of the phone call, nor did Robert ask.

Katie wished she had arranged to go immediately. The suspense on what the meeting held in store weighed heavily on her. Thoughts of his discovery ran wild as she tried to imagine why he wanted to speak to her before sharing the information with Hope.

The next two hours dragged as slow as tar running uphill. Hands on the big clock outside seemed frozen in time. Unable to keep her mind on anything else, she mentally paced, waiting for the elusive noon hour to arrive. When the clock bonged eleven-thirty, she could wait no longer. Rising from her chair, she left the office, stopping first at Robert's desk. "I'll be away from the office for a few hours. Think you can handle things until I return?"

"Well. Let's see. The bucket of sand is in the corner in case of fire. Police are a block away. Doctor's office is up the street. I think we can cover any emergencies until you return."

She loved Robert's sense of humor. He brought more to the office than efficiency and knowledge. His all-business persona edged itself in a gift package of an upbeat outlook.

Katie traipsed up and down the city's two main streets until she could stand the wait no longer. Fifteen minutes before the noon hour, as the City Hall carillon pealed, she pressed the doorbell button at 313 Miller Avenue.

Homer answered, and with a broad smile, invited her into the house. A statuesque middle-aged woman stood behind him. "Let me introduce two of the most important women in my life. Mrs. Katheryn "Katie" Novak, this is my dear, sweet aunt Margaret Hammer, now standing on two strong legs. Mrs. Hammer, may I present the most astute businesswoman in Pennsylvania, and the toughest suffragette ever."

The two women smiled at one another. Each held out her hand.

"Please, call me Katie."

"And I'm Meg. Welcome to my home."

The trio walked into the well-appointed living room. Homer excused himself and went to the kitchen, returning several minutes later carrying a silver tray that held tea service and an array of crustless sandwiches, scones, and sweets.

"Thank you, Homer." Then, turning to Katie, "Such a resourceful boy. I don't know how I'd have survived without his company during my convalescence."

The two women sat as Homer poured tea into each cup. Remembering her first lesson from Lucy Burns, Katie took her tea as elegantly as any debutant.

She sipped, then spoke. "We both owe him a debt of gratitude. His story about me led to changes in my life and ultimately benefitted our sisters throughout the country."

"Indeed. Congratulations on the accomplishments of you and your fellow suffragettes. Your efforts to have the nineteenth amendment passed were Herculean. I read every word of your exploits in the Post and so wished to be there."

"There is much more to be done. Not all in Washington. So many humanitarian causes. Children in need, poverty, veterans with disabilities, lack of safety regulations in mines and mills, so many more. My own father was incapacitated in a coal mine disaster. If you have an inkling to become an activist, I can certainly provide you with direction."

"I'd like that, Katie. I believe we're going to become great friends."

Katie agreed, then set her cup on the silver tray. "Very well, Homer. I'm most interested in what you discovered and curious why you wished to meet away from the office."

Homer took center stage. "I wanted to share what I found and ask you for direction." Reading from his notes taken at the Judge Graft interview, Homer retraced the story.

"So, her name is Adeline or Addie, Elwell or Gibson, depending if she took her stepfather's last name."

"Are you certain this is the family?"

"Yes, it all fits. Especially telling are the mended broken bones revealed by your Pittsburgh doctor's X-ray machine. I interviewed two of her teachers at school and both descriptions fit her to a tee."

He pulled a photo from his briefcase and handed it to the two women. Both studied it for several moments.

"Her second-grade teacher gave me this class photograph that includes Addie Elwell. As you can see, there is little question that the girl in the top row is our Hope."

Katie nodded. "Look at that forehead and hair. Yes, you found her all right."

Homer retrieved another document from the valise. "Here is a copy of her birth certificate."

Both women examined the document closely.

Homer asked the next question. "What do you think we should do? How to approach it? Auntie, feel free to contribute. We can use as many good ideas as we can come up with."

As Katie mulled over Hope's story in her mind, Margaret spoke. "You took her to a doctor and a language professor. Is that right?"

Katie nodded.

"Before sharing the information with Hope, why not make another appointment with the two of them and review your findings together? As professionals, they might have a better sense of how to bring back her memory, and if it comes back, certainly they can provide therapy to help her move forward with her life."

"I like the idea, Meg. I'll call the doctor from my office. His contact information is still on my desk. But I think we owe it to Hope to share the information with her first."

All three agreed on that point. Katie suggested Homer come to their house for dinner and afterward, share his findings with Hope.

* * *

Dr. Fritz Gleirscher and Dr. Robert Vitori greeted the troupe as they entered the office. "So nice to see you again, Mrs. Novak, Miss Novak," turning his attention to Homer added, "and you are?"

"Homer J. Hammer, Sir."

The doctor thought for a moment. "Ah, not the famous journalist?"

Homer blushed. "In the flesh."

"I read every word you wrote in the Pittsburgh Daily Post during the Women's Suffrage movement but didn't realize you were from these parts."

"No, Sir, I'm from Alexandria, Virginia. I write for the Chesapeake Observer. What you read in the Daily Post were reprints of stories I wrote for the Observer."

"Well, that is amazing. And might I ask what your interest is in Miss Novak's medical condition? Do you plan to write a story about my diagnosis of her?"

"Oh, no, Sir, I'm a friend of the Novak family, and am here at their request as an advocate for Miss Novak. I've done considerable investigative research to uncover her history. We'd like to show you what I found and ask your thoughts of the possibility of her memory returning."

The doctor directed his next comment to Katie. "Mrs. Novak, as Hope's guardian, are you comfortable with the young man being present during our review and analysis?"

"Oh yes. As Homer told you, he is a family friend, and has grown particularly close to Hope."

Homer blushed again.

"And you Miss Hope?"

The girl nodded.

"Very well, let's move into the conference room next to the office. Elsa, would you bring an extra chair for Mr. Hammer?"

The secretary ushered the group into a conference room as Homer carried a chair from the front office into the room, relieving the secretary, Elsa, of the task.

The seating arrangement for the small group allowed for a comfortable, nonthreatening discussion. A hand-carved oak table, large enough to accommodate up to a dozen people, took up the center of the conference room.

During the introductions, Dr. Vitori, a linguist from the University of Pittsburgh, remained silent, then directed a question to Katie. "Mrs. Novak, would you mind repeating the comment you just made?"

"I mentioned that Mr. Hammer has been a close family friend for some time. Do you have a problem with that, or with him being present today?"

Dr. Vitori listened closely, then said in amazement, "If I had not seen you with my own eyes I'd swear you're a doppelganger for the real Mrs. Novak."

"A what?"

"A double. Your manner of speech. When we last saw you, I heard you speaking a street level version of English ..."

Katie smiled. "Oh, thank you for noticing. Part of the time I spent in Washington, D.C. was devoted to cleaning up my language. I have Miss Lucy Burns to thank. We spent many a night burning the midnight oil over proper language, diction, tense ..."

"Never in my career have I seen such a vast improvement in elocution and vocabulary. I now wish we had tested you as well as Miss Hope."

She teased the linguist. "If you prefer I am still able to converse in my other tongue. 'No you be vorry 'bout me. Ve be here for Hope.'"

The others chuckled, but Dr. Vitori shook his head. "Amazing. Simply amazing. You're multi-lingual in a nontraditional sense. Let's discuss your transition later. For now, I agree, we need to address the issue at hand."

After a pause, Hope, Katie, and the two doctors took their seats. Homer remained standing and proceeded to share the information he had uncovered about the Elwell/Gibson connection to Hope, ending with the sharing of the photo and birth certificate of Adeline Elwell.

The group sat and digested Homer's discoveries.

Hope, who had remained quiet through the introductions and Homer's presentation, broke the silence. "I listened closely to what Homer has uncovered and it seems like somebody else's story."

Dr. Gleirscher took the floor. "Does the name Adeline Elwell mean anything to you, Miss Novak?"

"Other than what I just learned from Homer, no."

"What about Addie Elwell?"

"No."

"Adeline Gibson or Addie Gibson?"

"Uh-uh."

Oliver or Martha Elwell?

"Nope."

"Clay Gibson? Landlord Weiss?"

"Nothing."

He showed her photographs that Homer had taken of the Elwell and Gibson houses.

Hope shook her head.

"It would appear to me that all memories of the time in her life prior to her coming to you have vanished. When I say 'vanished,' I actually mean 'suppressed' somewhere deep in her subconscious mind. Theoretically, the memories, or parts of memories may return, but my best guess is that they will not.

"My diagnosis is that Miss Hope Novak suffers from transient global or anterograde permanent amnesia. Defined in layman's terms, that is a sudden episode of memory loss in which recall of events simply vanishes and the subject cannot remember who she is, where she is, or how she got there. It is a post traumatic state that can be caused by acute brain trauma, such as a physical blow to the head, or witnessing one or more traumatic events. We've seen similar symptoms in soldiers returning from the war in Europe. Other similar cases have been documented during and after the Civil War.

"In theory, the cause could also be a tumor on the brain but that is not evident in this case. The condition does not prevent the brain from creating new memories, so it is entirely possible, even likely that Hope will live a full and normal life."

He continued. "The mind is an interesting part of our psyche. It does not always act in a predictable manner. What we have here is a mind that has had at least two major emotional shocks combined with a body that endured an unknown amount of physical trauma. It has buried those events deep within itself. The horrid memories will likely never return in total, but from time to time when the subject is relaxed ... Excuse me, when Miss Novak is relaxed, parts of the most shocking aspects could reappear. They might manifest themselves as nightmares or dreams, or not at all. Psychology is still an inexact science."

Dr. Gleirscher leaned back in his chair and lit his pipe. The sweet smell of cherry tobacco filled the room. "Are there any questions?"

Hope spoke first. "Thank you, Doctor Gleirscher, for your analysis. And thank you, Dr. Vitori, for identifying the locale of my birth, which allowed Homer to track down my origins. It is really an odd feeling. What Homer disclosed from his findings seems like a story that somebody else has written. I try to remember it, even bits and pieces, but none of it feels like me."

"That is perfectly understandable, Miss Novak. Don't try to force it. Instead, focus on the other part of my original diagnosis. You are highly intelligent and have a kind soul. I would like to see you every six months to examine and monitor you. With your permission, Dr. Vitori and I plan to co-author a professional paper about this case. We will, of course, respect your privacy and refer you as 'the subject.' What are your thoughts? We would need the permission from you as well as your guardian, Mrs. Novak."

Both women looked at each other, nodding in assent.

"Do you have any other questions before we conclude?"

Katie posed the question the group had all pondered. "Given the findings of Mr. Hammer, what is to be done about her identity? What is her legal status?"

"That, Mrs. Novak, is a legal question, hence, one I am unable to answer. You must seek the advice of an attorney for the answer."

They stood and all shook hands with one another.

Dr. Vitori made the final comment. "Mrs. Novak, I would like to interview you separately as a linguistic case study."

"Get in touch with me, Doctor. I'm always interested in expanding scientific study."

By the time the group left the doctor's office, afternoon began slipping into dusk. They walked briskly but in silence to Pittsburgh's train station, catching the last commuter train back to Clairton.

Katie pretended not to notice Hope and Homer holding hands and gazing into one another's eyes.

Author's Note

KATIE'S LADIES IS A WORK OF FICTION. Names, characters, businesses, places, events, locales, and incidents are either the products of the author's imagination or used in a fictitious manner. Any resemblance to actual persons, living or dead, or actual events is purely coincidental.

The struggle for women's suffrage and maltreatment of women, especially immigrants, was very real. For the story, timelines of historic events have been condensed, though otherwise accurately represented. Some accounts were taken directly from historical records

References

Day, Dorothy. *The Long Loneliness*, Harper Brothers, New York, 1952

Editors of Encyclopedia Britannica. "National American Woman Suffrage Association (NAWSA)." Encyclopedia Britannica. 7/14/2016. https://www.britannica.com/topic/National-American-Woman-Suffrage-Association

Lavender, William, and Mary Lavender. "Suffragists storm over Washington: wartime Washington dealt brutally with imprisoned suffragists who dared picket the White House for the right to vote in 1917." American History, vol. 38, no. 4, 2003, p. 30+.

Leaming, Barbara. *Katherine Hepburn* (New York: Crown Publishers, 1995), 182.

Lunardini, Christine. "From Equal Suffrage to Equal Rights: Alice Paul and the National Woman's Party, 1910-1928 (American Social Experience, 2000)

"Miss Alice Paul on Hunger Strike; Suffragist Leader Adopts This Means of Protesting Against Washington Prison Fare." New York Times, November, 7, 1917.

McArdle, Terrence. "Night of Terror," *Washington Post,* November 10, 2017.

Milliken, Nancy. "The Night of Terror," November 15, 1917, Women's Right to Vote, University of California, San Francisco

Reiter, Anna. "Fearless Radicalism: Alice Paul and Her Fight for Women's Suffrage," Armstrong Undergraduate Journal of History, 3, no. 3 (November 2013).

Stevens, Doris. *Jailed for Freedom,* Boni and Liveright. 1920.

"Three United States Feminists – A Personal Tribute, Jewish Affairs. 53-1 (Johannesburg, South Africa, 1998) 37

Trecker, Janice Law. "The Suffrage Prisoners." *The American Scholar.* Vol. 41, No. 3 (Summer, 1972). Ph6i Beta Kappa Society.

Also by Andrew R. Nixon

50 Shades of Grades

Three Lives of Peter Novak

Filthy Lucre, a short story in *It's All in the Story, California, An Anthology of Short Fiction.* Edited by D. P. Lyle"

Filthy Lucre, a short story in *One Million Project Fiction Anthology,* compiled by Jason Greenfield

AVAILABLE NOW ON AMAZON AND BARNES & NOBLE

Visit Andy at: http://andynixonwordsmith.com/

CPSIA information can be obtained
at www.ICGtesting.com
Printed in the USA
FSHW021521250119
55233FS